Praise for *Hurry Home*

NATIONAL BESTSELLER

"*Hurry Home* makes for a perfect summer read."

Vancouver Sun

"A must-read page-turner."

Samantha M. Bailey, #1 bestselling author of *Woman on the Edge*

"A taut, beautifully written story of sisters, motherhood, and the kind of secrets that turn a person into a monster. I devoured it."

Robyn Harding, #1 bestselling author of *The Swap*

"A brilliant cat-and-mouse game."

Winnipeg Free Press

"Gorgeously written with hairpin twists and turns, Roz Nay's elevated second outing proves that she just gets better with each book."

Chevy Stevens, *New York Times* bestselling author of
Never Let You Go

"Roz Nay expertly creates real and deeply flawed characters who pull you in and hold you close, only to make you question and shift your allegiances as the story unfolds. This tale about two sisters who love—and love to hate—is as dark as it is twisty, emotional, and suspenseful."

Hannah Mary McKinnon, bestselling author of *Sister Dear*

"A powder keg of a story!"

Hank Phillippi Ryan, bestselling author of *The Murder List*

Praise for *Our Little Secret*

NATIONAL BESTSELLER
Winner of the Douglas Kennedy Prize for Best Foreign Thriller
Finalist for the Kobo Emerging Writer Prize
Finalist for the Arthur Ellis Best First Crime Novel Award

"Roz Nay's addictive debut proves the dark secrets of the past cannot be forgotten."

Us Weekly

"One of the best grip-lit titles of the year . . . Nay draws the reader in with compelling characters, deliciously dark themes, clever turns of phrase, and heightened levels of suspense."

Toronto Star

"A cracking read . . . Builds to a deliciously dark conclusion."

Ruth Ware, #1 *New York Times* bestselling author of
The Woman in Cabin 10 and *One by One*

"A memorably twisted love story."

Entertainment Weekly

"Lures readers down a dark and tangled path that explores the aftereffects of lost first loves . . . A gripping addition to the psych thriller world."

Mary Kubica, *New York Times* bestselling author of *The Good Girl*

"A guaranteed good read . . . You're likely to read it in one breathless sitting."

The Globe and Mail

"A sneaky-smart, charismatic debut."

Booklist (Starred Review)

"The breadcrumbs Nay expertly leaves behind reveal a dark truth you won't see coming. Ruth Ware fans will love this compulsive, impossible-to-put-down novel."

Karma Brown, #1 bestselling author of *Recipe for a Perfect Wife*

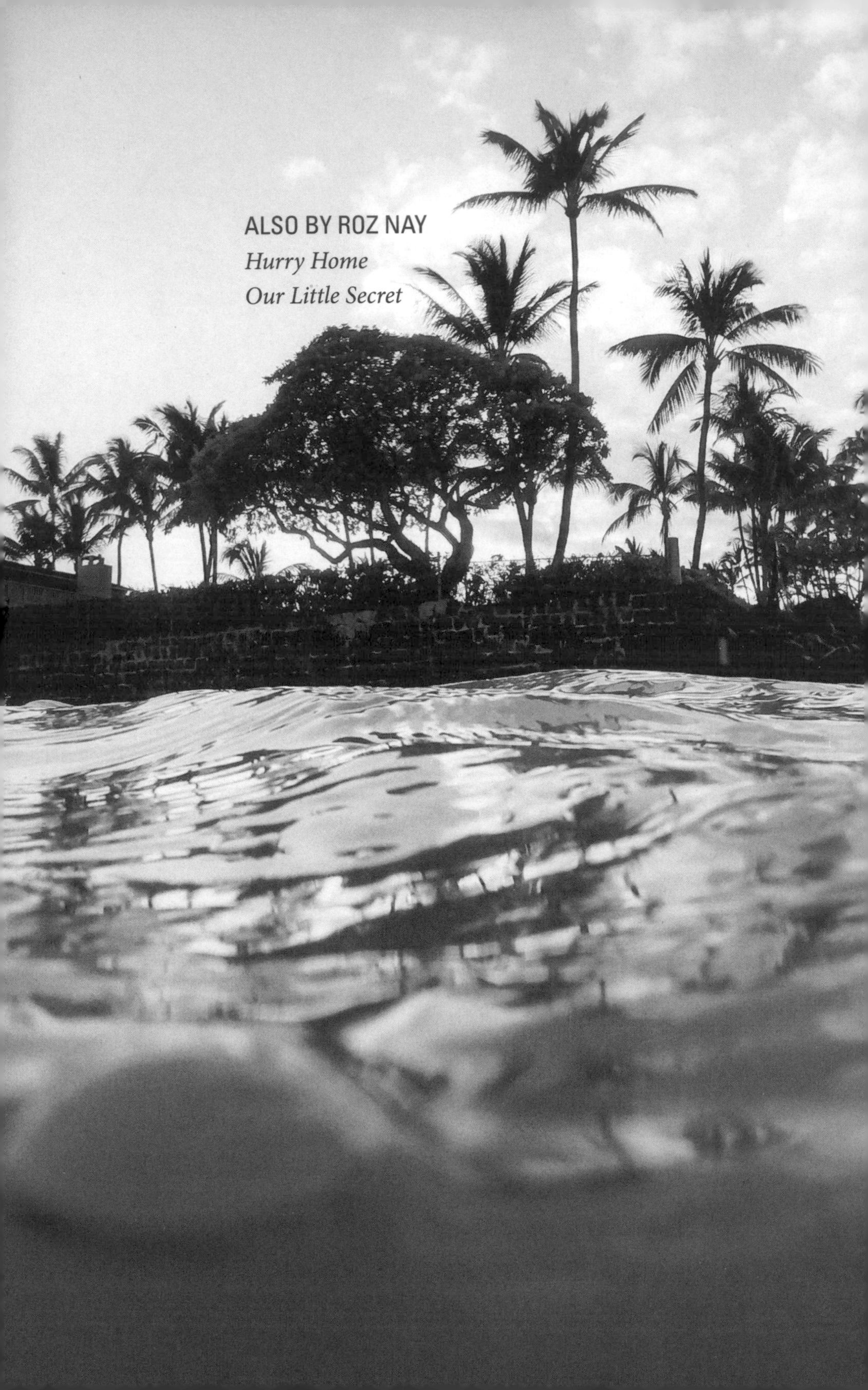

ALSO BY ROZ NAY

Hurry Home

Our Little Secret

THE

HUNTED

Roz Nay

Published by Simon & Schuster

New York   London   Toronto   Sydney   New Delhi

Simon & Schuster Canada
A Division of Simon & Schuster, Inc.
166 King Street East, Suite 300
Toronto, Ontario M5A 1J3

This Simon & Schuster Canada edition July 2021

SIMON & SCHUSTER CANADA and colophon are trademarks of Simon & Schuster, Inc.

For information about special discounts for bulk purchases, please contact Simon & Schuster Special Sales at 1-800-268-3216 or CustomerService@simonandschuster.ca.

Manufactured in the United States of America

10   9   8   7   6   5   4   3   2   1

Library and Archives Canada Cataloguing in Publication
Title: The hunted / Roz Nay.
Names: Nay, Roz, author.
Description: Simon & Schuster Canada edition.
Identifiers: Canadiana (print) 20200384961 | Canadiana (ebook) 20200384988 | ISBN 9781501184840 (softcover) | ISBN 9781501184857 (ebook)
Classification: LCC PS8627.A98 H86 2021 | DDC C813/.6—dc23

ISBN 978-1-5011-8484-0
ISBN 978-1-5011-8485-7 (ebook)

For Mum, who once took a banana boat to Libya.
And for Dad, who has always loved home.

THE
HUNTED

A hand over my mouth wakes me, the skin of it tinny with metal and salt. I gasp awake and squirm. Beside me, Jacob's face looms, his eyes ghostly wide. He's bunched my mosquito net around his shoulders, as if emerging from a cobweb.

"Stevie," he whispers, his voice hoarse. "It's not safe here. You're not safe." Still he presses his briny hand across my mouth. I push at his wrist and sit up.

"What's happened?" I whisper. "What are you *doing*?"

He's panting, and I notice his hair is slicked against his forehead and his shorts are soaking wet. Behind him, bush babies screech lunatic catcalls into the trees. For more than two weeks we've been on this dive camp and I still haven't gotten used to their screams.

"We have to get out of here." Jacob pulls on a shirt, puts a shaky finger to his lips. "Right now. Don't make any noise."

It must be close to midnight: the hut is quiet—the cluster of volunteers all asleep—some of us on the cement floor, others on ramshackle beds bought from the local village. Jacob stands and stuffs items into my backpack. A book, my journal, my bikini top. His pack lies bulging on the floor. What's the matter with him? He's never this urgent, this intense. He's the placid boy, a chameleon in any room.

"Jacob, stop! Don't put that in there." I struggle out of my sleeping bag and grab Tamsin's T-shirt from his hand. I glance at her bed across the aisle from me, but I can't quite make out her shape.

Jacob snaps my backpack closed and pushes it into my chest, knocking me back a step. Down the row of sleeping bodies someone shifts and cries out—a Larium dream, the nightly anti-malarial horror for anyone taking those pills. Jacob swallows, his chin strangely pocked with sand. A straight line of blood glistens by his earlobe as if he's wrenched it free of a fishhook, but when I reach up toward his neck, he flinches away.

"Come *on*," he says, and I stumble out of the hut after him into heavy blackness, my brain foggy and clogged.

The generator has long since shut down for the night. Above us the stars blaze unchallenged. Jacob hurries past the smoking fire pit, the earth oven, and the long table under the riveted shelter where we eat. Inside Duran's office, a streak of light is shining. He must be awake, catching up on paperwork with his headlamp on. If something is unsafe, shouldn't we be telling him? Instead, Jacob goes straight to the rear of Duran's Jeep and throws his backpack in, gesturing for me to hand over mine.

"You're borrowing Duran's car? Jacob, tell me what's wrong." I cling to my pack, the air around me thick with spices and heat. In our seven years together, I've never seen him this fitful or angular. Whatever's happened, it's somehow changed the shape of how he moves.

"There's been—" he begins, his throat sounding gummy and tight, but then he stops and ducks down, squinting at the knotted path that leads down to the beach. I follow his gaze but it's impossible to tell what's moving toward us and what isn't. When he speaks again, his voice is so quiet, it's terrifying.

"He's coming for you. Get in."

He tosses my bag in the Jeep, then throws himself into the driver's seat and scrambles around for the key. It drops from the sun visor into his lap and he fumbles it into the ignition. I'm trying to open the passenger door, but the lock is jammed, and I tug at it once, twice, while Jacob fires up the engine, the roar of it startling enough that the young camp dog, Crusoe, sits up on Duran's office steps, his ribs glinting sharp under his skin.

"Wait!" I shout, because suddenly I think he might leave without me. I've never thought that before. I step on the Jeep's runner and pull myself over the top of the door, slithering in, scraping my ribs and hips as Jacob reverses in a spray of grit, his knuckles white against the steering wheel. Behind us, the entrance to the sleeping hut yawns dark and wide. Tamsin's T-shirt is still in my hand.

"Who's coming for me?" I yell against the judder of the engine as I struggle to lock in my seat belt, but Jacob just clenches his teeth and grinds the Jeep into first gear. I let go of the belt strap, feel it snaking away from me. "Is it Leo?"

Jacob turns then, his eyes heavy and full of fear. To the right of him in the shadows, wetsuits sway like bodies on hooks.

1

STEVIE

Stepping off the plane in September, Africa explodes onto us like shouting, like light. After seventeen hours of travel and three stops in places I've barely heard of, I feel like I've entirely switched planets. But we're not at our final destination yet. Tanzania is still a long bus and train ride away.

It was the cheapest route we could find to go from Maine to Kenya. Each time we landed, all the overhead compartments flew open and everyone's bags fell out. And the weather got hotter and hotter at each stopover. In Abu Dhabi, we were herded out of the plane and given mint tea and dates to eat by cafeteria staff, although for us it was three in the morning. And in Aden, Yemen, I was slapped on the knees in the passport lineup by an old lady in a burka because I was wearing shorts.

"That was an oversight," Jacob said. "Are you okay, Stevie? All this planning we've done, and we forgot to research the dress code for Middle Eastern transit lounges."

"It's fine," I replied, although my legs felt shaky. I couldn't believe I'd just offended the woman so badly.

"We'll get the hang of it," Jacob said. "It's all part of the adventure."

Getting slapped by old ladies isn't my kind of adventure, but I didn't say anything as we joined hands and walked across the hot runway asphalt to the plane that would take us to Nairobi.

Jacob's taken a job as a diver off the coast of Tanzania. He'd been offered the post a year ago but had turned it down because back then we were safely settled into our routine in craggy, stormy Anchorite Bay. That was before everything changed and the ground got ripped out from under us.

Six weeks ago, I was running my grandmother's stony old pub, Jacob and I were living in the one-bedroom apartment above it, and Jacob was working with his dad as a commercial diver. They own a hull cleaning company together: Jones Boys' Boats. They scrub barnacles, mostly, and on an exciting day, mollusks. It wasn't a glamorous life, but it was one we knew inside and out.

Then, my grandmother Nattie died, and everything went with her. She'd always promised me her share of the pub, as well as the apartment, but she spoke of it so often and so matter-of-factly that she never did write it down. When she died intestate, as the lawyer kept calling it, it meant that on top of the tailspin of loss, suddenly I had no job and no apartment. To be honest, I'm not sure I've processed it all. I've been trying, but the more things I dig through, the more memories I seem to unlock. Jacob said a change of scene would be good for us, so rather than fight it out with Nattie's business partners in a small-town scrum, or pick like buzzards through the belongings she'd left behind, he got back in touch with the Tanzanian dive company. The job is for three months. *We need a break, Stevie. Think sunshine, warm water, and coconuts. We'll go and shake off all the darkness, exhale for a minute, come back new.* It sounded so great when he said it.

Once we're through Kenyan immigration and the border guard has licked a stamp and stuck it to a page in our passports, Jacob turns to me.

"Let's get a cab," he says, tucking all our documentation into a tightly zipped side pocket of his backpack. "We'll head straight to the hostel. Take a shower. Settle in."

"Okay," I say, looking around at the hubbub of the Arrivals hall.

Already it's clear that at twenty-four, we're older than the average backpacker, and yet everyone else is moving through the airport as if they have a map of the layout in their heads. Jacob and I haven't traveled beyond the States—not because we didn't want to explore, just that we never had the money—and yet here we are in Africa. It's not a dipping-your-toe-in kind of decision. It's not like we tried a road trip to Canada first. No, we went straight to level ten on the traveling scale and in moments of total privacy, I'm aware of a shrill hum of panic in my head.

But Jacob and I deserve an interlude, an opportunity to calm down. I mean, if we grow apart, what else do I have? And change is like a holiday, Nattie used to say, though she was always hell-bent on keeping me still, slowing me down, settling me. *Anchorite Bay and Jacob Jones. What more do you need, child? Why go haring off elsewhere?* She spent a lifetime trying to erase the genetic blueprint of my mother in me—a woman who'd excelled at being spontaneous—although that's not what Nattie had called it. So if I had a roil in my blood as a teenager, an early rumble in the deepest parts of me, that life was bigger than the town in which I lived, I've buried it. I've buried a lot of things.

But we're here, and we're together, and Jacob's pumped. In the lineup for cabs outside the airport he pushes a dark strand of hair away from his brow. He has a beautiful face, oak-brown eyes, with just enough tragedy behind them. In high school, he'd have gotten a million dates if he'd gone to a few more parties.

"If anyone offers," he whispers, breath warm against my ear, "let's *not* share a ride into the city. I saw a movie about that once and they track where you go and then come back later to get you."

"Who does?" I ask.

"I don't know." He shrugs. "Bad guys."

I look around at the throng of other Westerners waiting alongside us. Beaded necklaces. Velcro-strapped sandals. Happy tattoos. "Jacob, there aren't any bad guys here. You watch too many scary movies."

Even so, I make sure the cab door is shut before I tell the driver the name of our hostel.

We take off into the city, braking sharply for lights, cutting corners inches away from neighboring vehicles. The cab driver has CDs hanging from the roof of his car as decoration, and as he changes lanes, they swing and bang against the side of his head. On his radio is sunny guitar music, and the city is all car horns, women carrying wood on their heads down the sides of the road, and men in nylon pants selling corn and boiled eggs.

When we get to the hostel, we exit the car and the cab driver presses the tinny buzzer at the entrance for us. Jacob pays him from a security pouch he has strapped around his middle, counting out bills against his thigh before handing them over. Beside us, there's a click of a lock releasing, and we push open the metal-barred door and step into a damp stairwell.

"Okay, then," Jacob says, shouldering his pack. He googled the hostel, but neither of us really knows what to expect. We'd have booked a hotel, but until Jacob's job starts in four days' time, we're on a tight budget.

"Here we are," I say, my smile a little watery as my mind flashes Nattie's face, the reliable fury of the Anchorite Bay sea, the smell of coffee in our kitchen above the pub. We've literally been jettisoned.

But I need to be brave, so I take a breath and we climb the stairs, passing a couple of sunburned boys in Ralph Lauren shirts who for some reason step to the side for me, nudging each other, pushing out their chests. Jacob gives them a knowing nod.

"Is it me," he says once we're beyond them, "or do all the teenagers look rich?"

I murmur agreement because he's right: everyone in the main area of the hostel seems fresh out of Western private schools. They wear the collars of their polo shirts up, woven bracelets on their wrists, Keds. They also sound alarmingly confident about every aspect of being in a developing country. Behind the reception desk, a boy who looks twelve is cataloging his African expertise.

"Oh, God, yeah, in *Zim*," he says in an Australian accent, tossing an unfamiliar fruit from hand to hand, "you'll be lucky if the buses even show up. There's no schedule. D-I-A, boys, D-I-A. You could spend your whole gap year waiting." All the other twelve-year-olds laugh. "Hel-lo," he says, suddenly noticing me. "You're very blond and blue-eyed. I'm Elijah. What's *your* name?"

"What's D-I-A?" Jacob cuts in, holding out his hand for a room key.

"D-I-A? Dis Is Africa! Haven't you heard that saying yet? Wow, you really are newbies."

"We just got here," I say, glancing at Jacob, whose lips look dry. "One thing at a time. Do you need us to sign in?"

"Right here." Elijah points at a ledger in front of him. "Hold on a sec, I'll fetch you a pen." He sets down the strange oval fruit and begins to search in various desk drawers. "And I'll need to give you both security bracelets to prove you're staying here. There's been a recent . . . upswing in safety checks."

"Why?" I ask.

"No reason."

To my right, a guy passes me a Sharpie. He holds on to it for half a second longer than he needs to, it feels like, so that I almost have to tug it from his grip, but I take it, muttering a vague thank-you, signing the guest book. Nattie would be shaking her head. *Six weeks I've been gone and you're standing where?!* Maybe we should just load up our credit card and check into a brand-name hotel. But when I look over at Jacob, he's taking the key from the desk.

We bump our way back through the main area, past abandoned stacks of Uno cards and a globe. In the corner by the bookshelf, a girl is reading a well-thumbed copy of *The Beach*. I've read that book—my grandmother passed her adoration of British writers on to me—and I still love the last sentence. I want to tell the girl so, but worry I'll ruin the ending. As we walk by, she stares hard at the page and doesn't look up.

Our room, when we find it, is a square box with four beds in it, all tucked in and unused. There are bars on the outside of the window, but I push one of the panes open as far as it will go. Hot air seeps in, sour and dusty.

"What do you think that reception guy meant about added security?" I ask Jacob.

"Probably nothing." He sets down his pack against the wall, nudging it with his knee until it promises to stay upright. "I don't think that guy knows a lot about a lot."

"But do you think something bad happened in this hostel?"

"No, or I'd have read about it online." He moves behind me at the window, wrapping his arms around me. "I wouldn't worry about it. And besides, we're only staying two nights before we head south."

"Right," I say. "What's the worst that could happen?" *Do not think about death, Stevie. Do not think about it.*

Together, we crane forward to look out onto the street. Below us is a medley of busy people, some pulling wooden carts, others flapping leaflets at passing backpackers. Dogs run in the street.

"It's so different," I say, keeping my voice level. "It's going to be good for us."

"Wait 'til we get to Rafiki Island. It'll be heaven there."

The job Jacob has set up is through GoEco, a dive operation for ecotourists who want to help protect the reef from dynamite fishing. It's on an island ten miles south of Zanzibar. His old friend, Mike Duran, is running the camp. They trained together when they took their commercial diving course. Duran is older, midthirties, and ex-military, apparently. Jacob says he's no-nonsense, but I've never met the guy. The way Jacob describes him, he sounds like he's more function than feelings, which is fine with me. I don't want any more people asking if I'm doing okay. It sets me off more than anything else. Several times lately I've cried in the Anchorite Bay grocery store because someone in the lineup has smiled tragically at me. That was another reason Rafiki Island sounded good: no one would know my history there. The dive camp looked like a total paradise in the photos Duran had sent, too: off the beaten track with miles of empty white sand and a wooden boat bobbing alone in a shiny bay. *Don't think, just keep moving*, I told myself again and again the past month. This island will be gentle. In Swahili, *Rafiki* means "friend."

"GoEco is a well-known outfit," Jacob told me as we sat in bed together in his parents' spare room. "The camp will be a ready-made community. It's paid work. And I can't do this anymore."

Had he meant his parents' house, the daily barnacle scrubbing, or the people and things we'd lost? It was a miserable sum of parts, and I was barely coping myself—lapsing into silences that stretched into days, crying at night in the bathtub. Even Jacob couldn't reach me. So go to Africa? Sure. Anything.

From somewhere nearby comes a wailing, Islamic cry over a crackly loudspeaker. I lean back against Jacob's chest. He's so tall and lean, built for running, swimming, climbing—nothing that ever won him a team.

"That's a call to prayer," he says, kissing me on top of the head. "We must be near a mosque."

"Everything's brand new," I say, trying to hide any doubts.

"Good." He kisses me again and then moves away toward one of the beds, sitting down on the thin mattress to the creak of old springs. "We've made a good move, Stevie. We're grand-slamming." He bounces a few times on the rickety bed, his eyebrows comical. "But just so you know, a ton of hostels have bed bugs. I read it on Tripadvisor. So, we should roll out our sleeping bags just in case."

Don't think, Stevie, just keep moving. It's all part of the adventure.

t's close to 3 a.m. when I wake up. I drank so much water on the plane to avoid dehydration that my bladder is like a space hopper and I can no longer lie on it. Jacob is sleeping restlessly in his bed: all night I've heard him tossing and turning on the rusty springs. I get up and open the door to our room a little, wondering if anyone else is still up. But the whole main area of the hostel is silent. The only light is an amber glow from a bug zapper that seems to be switched on in the communal kitchen.

The bathroom is at the end of a cracked-cement corridor and I tiptoe that way, my eyes just able to make out the shapes of the sagging armchairs as I pass by them. Should I be wearing shoes? I steady myself with a hand on the wall as I go, but then recoil as something skitters under my fingers.

The bathroom has a light switch at the entrance, and I swipe at it with relief. There's a flash of movement near the enamel of the sinks, which I think might be cockroaches, but I try not to dwell on it, and instead pick my way across the cold tiles to one of the two stalls on the far side of the room. Someone's left a wet bath towel on the floor.

I choose the stall to the left because it's the only one with a toilet seat—a fact that, once I've sat down, makes me wonder if it would have been smarter just to hover. Above my head are thick cobwebs in funnels. I try not to imagine spiders dropping.

I'm done and just standing up when I hear the footsteps outside in the corridor. They're coming closer, slowing now as they hit the clip of the bathroom tiling. Whoever it is takes two or three more steps and then stops. I can see the slivered crescent of a dark shoe under the gap in my stall door.

"Hello?" I say, my finger reaching out for the lock in front of me, holding it there in place.

But there's silence on the other side of the door. A steady, deliberate silence.

It's the sound of someone trying not to make a sound.

I stand with my ears fizzing, my eyes fixating on the shoe and then the edge of the stall above me, half expecting someone to come barreling over the top.

Then I hear movement again, a few scuffed steps, and all the lights in the bathroom turn off.

I'm plunged into darkness, the only sound now the intermittent drip of the tap and the awful certainty that whoever's in the room is making their way back toward me. Did the wood of the stall door just press inward? Is the lock moving? I stand, one hand clamped over my mouth, the other on the lock, while only inches away from my head, there's a low catch of sound, soft and velvety. Somebody inside the bathroom is laughing.

2

LEO

I first saw Stevie when I handed her a Sharpie in the reception area. She was busy. There was a lot going on. It was quite understandable that she might not look at my face. Still, I sat and watched hers with fascination, at the fleet of differing thoughts that seemed to cross it, many of them weathered gray and ragged like clouds. *Wow*, I thought. *How familiar you are. How recognizably sad. What's going on with you?* Damage is a scent, I've found, and hers was unavoidable. I found myself utterly mesmerized by it.

She was so striking, all angles and eyes, with that white-blond hair wildly unkempt after what must have been hours on the plane. And the ice-pale blue of her eyes—not unlike my mother's, I suppose— with that same stirring blend of warmth and wasteland. But what I liked most in those first moments was the smallness of this girl, the precision of her movements. Like a bird, maybe. Or a little snowy

mouse. A magician's mouse, more eyes than body, secretive and prac-
ticed and watchful. *That's it*, I thought. *She's the one. It's not even a
decision that's mine.* The man she was with looked strong, but not in
a gym-membership way. Handsome, but not in a way he knew about.
They seemed new. Vulnerable. I have to admit, I felt an almost imme-
diate fondness for them both.

Stevie Erickson and Jacob Jones, all the way from the U.S. of A.,
their names in block capitals on their baggage tags, resplendent with
home addresses. And not married, evidently, judging by the ringless
fourth fingers. For close to a minute, my Stevie pondered the charac-
teristics of a fruit Elijah was holding behind the reception desk, as if
she'd never seen a pawpaw before. She had such a depth of curiosity
that I couldn't help but laugh, and she turned then, alert, sharp, all
but sniffing the air with her whiskers. *That's right—be interested*, I
wanted to call out. *Carpe diem. While you still can.* Every moment's a
gift, after all, and my mother always taught me it's rude to send them
back unopened.

The whole time I was studying her, Stevie didn't spot me. It's a skill
I've honed: six-foot-four and yet I blend well. I disappeared into the
back corridor of the hostel, continuing to watch from a safer vantage
point. Of course, it wasn't long before Tamsin found me. She arrived
next to me in a tank top with her flawless dark skin, her long hair tied
up in a knot on the top of her head.

"What are you doing, Leo?" She was nibbling cashew nuts from
a rolled-up cone of newspaper she'd bought earlier through the bus
window.

"Nothing," I replied. *Go away.*

But it was too late: her green eyes had tracked my gaze.

"Who are they?" she asked.

"I've no idea," I said. "They just got here."

"They're sweet-looking. They seem really together." She leaned toward me, kissed me flatly on the cheek. "You should say hi. They look cool. Maybe we'll be friends."

"I doubt it," I said, my eyes still on Stevie. Because I knew, I already knew. It was only a matter of time before we were an awful lot more than that.

3

STEVIE

Seconds pass in the dark while I try not to hyperventilate. But this is my greatest fear: being trapped somewhere horrible and alone, unable to see, the presence of others at the edges of my fingertips.

"Hey!" I shout into the darkness. "I'm in here! Hey! Somebody turn on the light!" My shoulder braces against the door, but I can't tell what's moving below me or above. Rapid, shrill breaths escape my chest. Soon enough I'm kicking at the wood of my stall, my terror turning to fury now.

I don't know how long I've been screaming when the lights snap back on. There's a pause where I freeze.

"Hello?" a female voice says, tremulous, American, young. "Are you okay in there?"

Warily I unlock the stall and step out, my knees shaky, my vision puffy with tears. In front of me is a girl of about eighteen, skinny-limbed in a pink T-shirt, her eyes as big as mine feel. She's the girl who was reading *The Beach* on the couch.

"Someone was in here," I gasp, scanning every corner of the empty bathroom. "They were laughing at me. Did you see them?"

She pulls at the hem of her shirt. I sound crazy. But then she takes a small step toward me.

"Was it a man?" she whispers. "What did he look like?"

"No, I don't know. I didn't see—"

"You can't trust anyone," she says. "I don't sleep in dorms anymore. Jesus, who would?! I'm only staying in this hostel at all because Elijah promised me he hands out security bracelets." She glances furtively at each of my wrists.

"I don't . . . We didn't get them." I take a shaky step toward the sink and splash cold water on my face. In the warp of the cheap mirror, I look haunted.

"Africa's not safe for girls like us." Behind me, she wraps her arms around her ribs, the bones in her elbows knobby. "You're pretty. You stand out. My friend did, too, she's blond and she's . . . she was the one he went for."

"Who?" I turn, one hand on the sink, the other on my throat. "What are you talking about?"

"The attack at the hostel across town. You don't know about it?"

I shake my head. Everything's rattling inside it.

"My friend was taking a shower in the girls' washroom, but none of the locks work here. All the rules are different." She takes two more steps toward me, all of her body urgent. "She was shampooing her hair and her eyes were closed. When she opened them, a man was—"

"What are you doing?" Jacob stands in the doorway of the bathroom in his boxer shorts, hair sticking up on his head.

The girl flinches, grips my wrist.

"What's wrong?" He rubs his eyes. "I woke up and you weren't in bed."

"Are you her boyfriend?" the girl asks, protective. "She was yelling so loud, I heard her from my room."

"Yelling?" Jacob bends to look in my face. "Stevie, what happened?"

"I don't know," I say, as he pulls me into a hug. "I was in here alone and all the lights went off."

"These hostels aren't safe," the girl says, arms hanging limp by her sides now. "Nowhere is. I'm actually flying home today, two months early. You two should be careful." She meets my eyes. *Especially you*, she's saying.

"Thanks," I say.

"I'll leave you to it," she says. "Good luck."

Both Jacob and I watch her go.

"Good *luck*?" Jacob says, drawing back to take another look at me. "What was her deal? She made it sound like we're running a gauntlet."

"She's had a scare," I say, trying hard to get over my own. "Her friend was attacked across town."

"Jesus." Jacob shakes his head. "Okay, well, that's terrible. But it wasn't . . . I mean, the attack wasn't here, though?"

"No." I swallow. My throat is raw from screaming. "A different hostel."

"Stevie, I know this place isn't the Ritz or anything, but it's not unsafe. You're okay. The janitor guy probably turned out the lights on you. He must have thought no one was in here."

I stare up at him. "Janitor guy?"

"I passed him in the corridor. White guy in his twenties. I didn't really get a good look at him, but it's five in the morning and he was dressed, wearing clothes and shoes. I figured he must be working the night shift." He bites his lip, thinking. "You know what? Let's get back to our room. In the morning, we can ask at reception about the janitor. Tell them what happened, if you like."

"Yeah, I'd like that." Tomorrow, I'll talk him into moving hostels. There's no way I'm staying another night in this one.

"In the meantime, let's cuddle up together in the same bed, sleep a bit more until it's light out."

I nod, moving with him out of the bathroom through the main area, my eyes alert to shadows or movement. There's nothing, no one. At least, no one that we can see. Inside our room Jacob locks the door and checks it twice, so perhaps he's thinking like me. Whether there's a janitor or not, someone enjoyed scaring me in that stall. And there's a very good chance they're still in the building.

4

LEO

Poor Stevie. She's had quite the night. The lights going off in the bath-room. The talk of an attack in the shower. All that you're-not-safe business. But the American girl who warned her was right: the little white mouse is very far from safe. And mop-haired Jacob who's ap-pointed himself her protector isn't doing a good enough job.

I sit with my head resting against the flimsy wall of our room, listening to the sounds of the two of them settling back into their beds next door. Isn't it interesting that we were given neighboring rooms in the hostel? My mum always talked about happy accidents. It's almost as if the universe *wants* us to connect. Late into the night, while Tamsin listlessly flapped pages of a magazine, I could hear one or the other of them tossing and turning on their mattresses. It was only natural that I'd wake at the same time Stevie did. Of course I knew she was making her way to the bathroom.

Across from me under a white muslin sheet, Tamsin shifts and turns over. She looks peaceful: smooth lines, calm face, not a care to be had awake or asleep. She's biracial—British and Nigerian—and seems entirely at home on this continent. But it's more than that: I envy the way she moves through the world in general, how she takes from it what she needs like a daily vitamin, and never gets thrown off course. For the three months that we've traveled together through Africa, she's let the culture shock wash over her wherever we go. All the men holding hands in the street because they're friends, the women singing in harmony as they carry home wood and water, the children kicking balls made of litter and rubber bands. *It's a continent of togetherness, Leo*, she says again and again, shoulders high, hands clasped, as if urging me out to play.

But I can't. I won't. She knows I've surrendered the life I had in England—swapped my suits for beach shorts, my Audi for buses with chickens on my lap, my keynote speeches for reggae—but she doesn't understand the depth of the exile I'm in. It's hard to adapt when I can still feel the blood inside me burn, when I'm still pulsing all of this venom.

When I was younger, before all the trouble, I was still prone to long stretches of isolation. Boredom, I suppose—especially in the summer—but my mum and I shared the lethargy, as if it were a room we entered daily together. Alone by the koi pond, we'd sit beside the rosebushes, the scent of them heady and lavish between us. *My handsome hero*, she would say, smoothing my hair flat at the nape of my neck. *Beautiful boy. One day you'll find a girl you adore even more than me. Can you imagine that?* I could never tell if she was encouraging it or dreading it.

Quietly, quietly, I reach for my cell phone, open up Instagram, type Stevie's full name into the search engine. I wonder what she's doing next door. She won't be asleep, not after what we've just been through together. Both of us are far too worked up. Outside the barred windows of our rooms, the first tentative streaks of pink are starting to light the sky. Has she noticed? Is she looking at it, too? It's going to be a scorching-hot day, Stevie, but there's such tenderness in the way that it builds. I turn onto my side, my back to Tamsin, cradling my phone like a baby's head. Seconds pass, the screen settles, and there she is. Stevie Erickson. There are several, but this one is mine. @StevieE. Two hundred followers on Instagram, one hundred posts—a demure online presence—and her account entirely public. It's an invitation, yet again, to enter her world, to follow her, to watch.

And there's so much to be gleaned from how people advertise their lives. There are so many indicators in hashtags. Stevie likes storms, ravens, and stone walls. Front covers of books from the library, all of them British, which is a very good sign for me. She drinks coffee and photographs it before she sips. She likes her grandmother's hands. Hashtag TrueFamily, hashtag Nattie, hashtag MyRock. For a few weeks this June, she was fixating on Grandma, actually—posting photos of old knuckles, thick ankles, laced-up shoes—and then it all stops. Throughout July, she offered nothing at all. And then, quite suddenly in August, a change of direction. I peer at the screen, frowning, the quality of this image grainy. Stevie's posted a photo of a photo— an old one, from high school, I'd guess, judging by the purity of the two girls' skin, the crop of the T-shirts, the youth in the haircuts and eye makeup. It's Stevie and a dark-haired girl, beautiful, fun. Standing next to her, Stevie looks like an Arctic elf. Hashtag MissYou, hashtag Cassia, hashtag AlwaysTogether.

Cassia. My head tilts and I scroll back through the mosaic of photos, noting with interest how there are no other mentions of this girl at all and how, equally relevant, very few pictures of Jacob show up on Stevie's feed. Whenever he features, he's lean, athletic, with an innocence to his expression in every shot, as if he never knows the camera is there. She doesn't tag him in anything, and all the hashtags sound different. They're work-related. Stoic. Dull.

I scroll back to the latest photo. Posted two days ago, September 25, after another month of radio silence. It's an image of a beach. Hashtag RafikiIsland. Hashtag HereComesParadise. Hashtag GoEco-Tanzania. I turn the cell over for a second, thinking, and my eyes adjust to the sight of my reflection in the shiny phone case—dark blue eyes, tanned face, incisors—when I hear the voice behind me.

"Morning." Tamsin leans up on one elbow, the British clip of her voice making me jump. "How long have you been awake?"

I click the cell dead.

"Are you checking email? I thought there wasn't much Wi-Fi."

"It's patchy," I say, turning. "Hi."

She yawns, stretching all of her joints in turn. "I didn't sleep very well. God, the beds make a right racket. It's like a murder of crows in here."

I smile. *Crows. Ravens. Cassia. Grandma.*

"Have we got any plans today?" Tamsin throws back her sheet, exposing white lace underwear and a tiny camisole. She kneels up on the mattress, her stomach a series of skin lines and no fat.

"I've got a few things I wanted to do," I say.

"Are you okay? You seem . . . far away."

"I didn't sleep well either." I watch her, wondering when it was exactly that my feelings for her changed.

"Well, this hostel isn't anything spesh. Why did we pick this one? It's so dry in here." Stretching across to her backpack, she pulls out a little pot of face cream, opens the lid. "Do moisturizers go off in hot weather? Like mayonnaise does?"

"I've no idea—"

She dabs a little onto her nose and then crawls across onto my bed. "Let's kiss, and you can tell me if it smells rank."

I lean into her, press my lips against hers. She smells good, feels good, if only I could concentrate. We kiss two times, three, all of them pecks more than passion, as if we're both checking items on a list.

28

"Your moisturizer's fine." I stand up, pull on shorts. "I was going to go out and get us some breakfast. I'm starving."

"Oh, okay. But when you get back, maybe we can go over the plan. Sort out our next move?" She smiles, waiting.

"Yup," I say, pausing at the door. My next move might be very different from hers.

"Maybe we should head south toward Tanzania," she says. "I was reading about this dive camp that's running down there. GoEco or something, it's called, on Rafiki Island. It looked lush in the pictures."

I sway, one hand on the door handle. *Reading about it where?* It feels like more than a happy accident.

"Leo, are you sure you're okay?" Her face is open, eyebrows high.

"I'm fine. Let's chat when I get back. See you in a bit." I yank open the door and step out, pulling it shut behind me. In the corridor I stand, blood thudding in my ears. This can't keep on happening. Whether Tamsin overheard anything, was peeking at hashtags over my shoulder, or whether she read about the dive camp in a random magazine, the universe is propelling me onward. And it shouldn't. Because the truth is, I'm not a handsome hero at all. I rest my forehead against the wall next to Stevie's room. She's lying on a bed in there, a few short steps away. I take another breath, clench my eyes shut. *Do not go to Rafiki Island, Leo. You know where this path ends.*

In England, before I came here, I saw a psychiatrist. I'll say it. I'm not ashamed. I'd lost my grip on things and needed a little professional help. There was a lot to talk about—I was a celebrity by then, a tabloid dream, the rich boy with the film-star good looks who'd done all those horrible things to his father. My therapist sat so close to me in our sessions that I could smell the perfume on her skin. *You need to find that voice in your head,* she said in the third week, crossing one stockinged leg over the other. *Find that voice, Leo, and listen to it.* But which voice did she mean? Surely not the one that said sleep with her because when I listened to that one and we fucked on her sofa, I never went back again.

There are too many signposts in my head, too many directions I can go. My fingertips trace the veined laminate near the door handle of Stevie's room. Desire is so complicated. Last night, when I lay in my bed, I closed my eyes and thought of ways to get rid of Tamsin. It was almost therapeutic to think about, the giddy secrecy of a well-exercised plan. It was a fantasy I hugged to myself in the shadows. It's only a flicker for now, but I know what I do with those. There's never a voice that says stop. Not in time. No, when flickers dance, I follow them, a moth in the gathering darkness. I follow them all the way to the end, and then I snuff them out.

5

STEVIE

It's a long time before I fall back asleep. Even with Jacob's arms around me in the skinny bed, I don't feel safe. Something's not right in this hostel. For an hour, I watch the door, willing it not to open.

But it doesn't, and there's quiet all around, and at about 6 a.m., I let the pink hopes of dawn blush their way down the wall and drift me into a wary sleep. I don't dream, thankfully. I sink too heavily, and when I wake late, the air in the room is stifling and there's a sheen of sweat under my legs and Jacob's as they press together.

"Hello, beautiful," he says, and I move my head to rest on his chest. "Look where we are."

For a second, it doesn't feel overwhelming. It doesn't feel like anything. I smile and wrap my arms tighter around him.

"That was a really weird night," he says. "How about we get out of here and don't stay another?"

I sit up, rubbing my eyes, loving him for knowing what I want but haven't said. "And go where? Straight to Rafiki?" At least it'd be organized there. At least it'd be defined.

"My job starts in three days. We were due to get a train south to Mombasa tomorrow, but how about we do that tonight instead? There's that beach resort we read about. Diani Beach. We can stay in a hut, take it easy, go swimming."

"Yes," I say. "Please."

"We're good at oceans. The overnight train leaves at ten p.m. So we can spend the day looking around, eating nice food, taking photos. Then we get out of the city."

"And leave this weird hostel behind," I add.

"Totally. You're right. It is weird. But Rafiki won't be."

Outside the window I can hear the street bustling. It must be middle of the morning by now. I wonder for a second whether the girl in the bathroom has flown back to America yet.

"Do you want to head out of here soon?" Jacob asks. "We haven't eaten in ages."

I don't feel hungry, and yet I must be. "I need to shower," I say doubtfully. "Get cleaned up."

"Okay." He squeezes me once on the knee. "Everything's okay, Stevie. We just had a shaky start."

The shower is cold, but efficient. All the stalls are full of girls. I check their feet under the curtains before I go into my one. At no point in the application of soap or shampoo do I ever close my eyes. It feels good to be clean, though, and as Jacob and I leave the hostel, the fresh air is restorative, even though the day is already hot and loud. Within a few steps, locals jostle us, trying to sell safari trips, while little kids in bright white vests tug at the pockets of our shorts.

At first, it's cute, but after a few minutes, Jacob pushes past a guy blocking his path with a tray of sunglasses. "I don't *want* any. Stevie, let's cross the street."

He motions to a gap and heads into the road, rusty cars zooming by him, their motors buzzing as if the exhausts have holes in them. Mopeds honk, none of them signaling or using anything for brakes. But I'm not as quick as Jacob: I cross the street twenty feet farther up, and it's as I reach the curb that I see the body. There's a man lying rigid in the gutter, his pants held up by string. His toes look like he's been dead for a decade. Am I meant to just step over him and carry on? I literally don't know if he's alive or not. I should bend to help him, but I'm paralyzed in the traffic, unable to move, unable even to swallow. In a flood, my head swims with memories, and I'm lost to everything around me except this.

In the summer before eleventh grade, I was in a car crash with my best friend, Cassia Duchene. We were driving around with two boys who'd just graduated. The night was warm, like the air around me now, the midnight sky dusty and silvered as we drove up to the clifftops above Anchorite Bay. We had summer music cranked, and rabbits darted into the glare of the headlights, Josh Hollander swerving to clip them as they scampered.

"You got that one!" Cody Oakes hissed out a burp in the passenger seat, holding up his hand for a high five. "I totally heard the snap of tendons." He was eighteen, star of the high school soccer team, and was set for a scholarship at Duke in the fall.

"Neanderthal," Cassia murmured. She was the one every boy wanted to be with back then, the one every girl wanted to be. She had long dark eyelashes, flawless skin, and wore enviable sneakers. In sixth grade she'd picked me for her BFF—even though her selection was most likely based on placement of lockers—and we were quickly inseparable. She told me we were peas in a pod, and made me a friendship bracelet she wove herself, that I wore every single day until the threads wore out. When we weren't at school, we had sleepovers together watching *Gossip Girl*, and she'd always fall asleep faster than me. I'd lie awake, the television still on, snaps of differing light catching Cassia at the cheekbone.

The evening of the accident, she was sitting beside me in the back seat, her forehead on the window, fingertips near her chin. We were sixteen years old and shouldn't even have been in the car. The road outside wound up and up, patchy grass on each side and trees arching away from the roadside, dreading the next blast of winter.

"The trees are cool," Cassia said to me. "They're hunched like trouble's coming."

That was the thing about Cassia: she saw things as I did. Cody ignored her and turned up the song on the radio. I remember not knowing the lyrics as the boys shouted them. It was Cassia and me against them.

When the car went off the road it rolled, and a series of moments dangled in front of me as if on a string. I had no frame of reference for being upside down, for the objects passing by me in slow motion. A CD case, a lighter, a hat. I was the only one wearing a seat belt and it cut into my shoulder blade like wire. We crashed into something that caved in the whole left side of the car. A head hit the window with the strangest, dullest thud. Again we tumbled, and I remember Cassia's hand and arm pressing against the front of my chest, as if she were cartwheeling above me.

When the car finally settled, I was pinned beneath her, her hair fanning the lower part of my chin. It was just me and Cassia. The whole front windshield was gone. There was the sky, the stars. It was so quiet. For a long time, there was only the plinking of the engine as it cooled. A delicate noise, fairy-light, like the plucking of tiny strings. Cassia breathed above me for a while before she stopped. She sounded like a toy running out. And then there was only blackness, and dead weight, and the hideous warmth of something leaking.

"Stevie!"

In a rush of yelling, I'm snapped back into this street, this chaos, this dead body. Jacob is running toward me.

"What are you *doing*?"

A car blares past me, almost knocking me with a side mirror. Jacob catches my T-shirt and yanks me onto the sidewalk, but my limbs are stiff like a mannequin's. All I can do is point at the body on the ground, and Jacob follows the track of my arm.

"Jesus," he says, and crouches by the side of the curb. "Hey, man!" He shakes at the man's rancid shirt, jiggling his shoulder. "Dude, wake up."

The body shifts. A foot moves.

"You gotta get out of the road," Jacob says, and the man on the ground opens his eyes, his eyeballs watery and jellied. He leans up on leathered elbows, and a beer bottle rolls out from under his ribs. Jacob hauls him into a sitting position on the sidewalk, stands over him, his hands on his hips. The crotch of the man's pants darkens. He's peeing in them. People on the street pass by without even a cursory glance.

Jacob turns to me, eyes wild. "I don't know. Should we call someone? You think he's okay here?"

Still I can't form a sentence. It's all too much. This place is too much for me. I thought a distraction would help, the change of location, but it's brought all the buried things up. I can't move and not think, it's impossible.

"Stevie—" Jacob draws me to the sidewalk, into the shade of an empty shop front. "That guy wasn't dead. He's drunk. Just sleeping it off. Look at him—he's wandering off now. He's fine."

"I know," I whisper. "It caught me off guard, is all."

Jacob looks up and down the street. "Look, let's just get ourselves some food and find somewhere mellow for a few hours."

"Okay." I nod, trying to reset. "That's a good idea."

Farther down the street are vendors with glass carts in front of them. Jacob squints uncertainly. "Come on," he says. "Let's go and see what they're selling."

We hold hands as we walk, but I can't seem to lift my feet properly. The fronts of my Birkenstocks scuff the sidewalk. The carts, when we reach them, contain buns—pale dough, the tops covered with a lumpy icing across which a thick blanket of flies and wasps crawl. There isn't a bun in the tray that isn't moving.

"Oh, God." Jacob rubs one eye with the heel of his palm.

"This one's okay." I spot the last guy in the row, whose buns are entirely bug-free. "We could buy these ones." I'm not the least bit hungry, but I'm trying for Jacob's sake. The vendor rubs his hands together, waiting for us to place an order.

"I wouldn't," says a voice behind us.

Both Jacob and I turn. A man in his late twenties stands with both hands in the pockets of his beach shorts. He's wearing a linen shirt, unbuttoned to his toned mid-chest, and a battered straw hat pushed far back on his forehead.

"Hold on a mo'. Give it a minute." He has a muddled accent—slightly British, but trying not to be?—and a dimple when he smiles. Square jaw, bright blue eyes, blond hair cut close to his tanned neck.

Neither Jacob nor I know quite how to respond. Perhaps we've never been in the presence of such good looks before. Or his confidence throws us. He seems totally at home, as if he's lived on these streets for years. We turn back to the vendor. Jacob's money wavers. And it's then, in that very second, that the vendor bends down and fetches a rusted, soiled can of Raid from where he's stashed it at his feet. He opens the glass panel and sprays every bun on his tray with a long, unabashed waft of bug-killing chemical. Only when the entire container is thick with fumigation does he stop spraying. Then he smudges off any dead flies with his index finger, closes the glass panel, and puts the Raid can down. The fog inside the cabinet clears. The buns are moist. Immaculate. Ready.

"Having a rethink?" The man behind us edges closer to peer over our shoulders. "If you're hungry, the café on that corner does great chapattis and chai."

He nods toward a little doorway to our right. But when we look back to thank him or ask him his name, he's moved off. He's just a white shirt, weaving through the throng, casual and unassuming, as if he has moments like this all day long, and none of them are ever calculated.

6

LEO

After breakfast, Jacob and Stevie go to the lobby of the Hilton Nairobi, find the bar, and take a seat near the guy playing a delicate version of "The Girl from Ipanema" on the piano. I join them, since I don't feel like going back to Tamsin just yet, and they don't notice me, even though I emerged for that moment of our meeting just now—the excitement of which is still visible in the tremor of my fingers. It's important to withdraw again. It's all in the timing.

They sit opposite each other, not in neighboring chairs. Jacob looks at the drinks menu, but Stevie's lost in thought. She has her hands in her lap—small hands, delicate—and is picking at the skin of her thumb.

Stepping over that body an hour ago has triggered her. The signs are visible in every aspect of her mannerism. Why isn't Jacob paying closer attention? The dead grandmother, the arguably dead best

39

friend (hashtag AlwaysTogether), the almost-corpse that was inches away from her shoe. It's textbook triggering, and that's not even including the incident last night in the ladies' bathroom. Come on, Jacob. Get it together. You're leaving the door wide open.

I move to a table on the other side of a white architectural plinth that the hotel designers must have thought looked European when they mulled over the decor. There are several in the bar area, each one adorned with green foliage and palm fronds. I hate hotels like this. They remind me of my father, who'd choose them systematically if we ever went on holiday beyond the self-proclaimed greatness of Britain. Chain hotels that still cling to the vestiges of a so-called colonial grandeur, replicating countries the guests have left, rather than the ones they've actually flown to. All around me waiters stand at attention in identically starched uniforms. Even the positioning of their arms is the same. It's all so impeccably military-precise. It's exactly the world of Dad.

When I was a teenager he always threw parties at home when he could, the front lawns twinkling with tea lights and elegant laughter, catering staff in buttoned waistcoats moving among the guests, pouring champagne from bottles folded tightly in white napkins. I can't remember what the parties were ever for. My father didn't tend to need a reason beyond that of his own existence to gather sycophantic people around him.

"Are you mingling?" my mother would ask me, touching me briefly on the elbow as she passed by. She always wore her blond hair up at parties, pinned to look effortlessly bejeweled. Clavicles ran hard under her skin like girders. "Your shirt is hanging out at the back, darling. Do sort it."

Thinking back, it might have been how she showed me affection—the little details of what she noticed about me—even if what she saw was a deficit. "Get in the game, darling, be a contender," she'd whisper in my ear. "You're the best one here."

But what was I meant to contend? If there was a competition in play, how could I possibly win it? Every circle she stood in at those parties was made up of eminent men, none of whom glanced away from her once when she introduced me.

"Have you met my son?" Her cool fingertips brushed my cheek. "Isn't he just a doll? It won't be long before he's breaking hearts left and right."

"I'd argue he gets it from you." The man leering at my mother from across the circle had a nose like a stubbed big toe. He wore a cummerbund that was equally purple.

"Brigadier! Goodness me." Mum considered him, rolling the single pearl of her necklace between forefinger and thumb. "You're incorrigible."

My father's friends, meanwhile, were always about conformity—their maleness adamant, their athleticism elite and superior. "This is my son, Leopold." My father would present me with a manly jostle. "He's growing up tough, aren't you, boy? A science man. And not too shabby on the rugger pitch."

I don't even play rugby, I used to think. *I wonder who he's mixing me up with.* His friends all had the same cropped haircuts and the same broadness at the chest that spoke of days spent carrying heavy equipment in war zones. Even now, as a grown man of twenty-eight, I can't stand any kind of uniform. Perhaps we're all of us triggered in our own way.

I pull at the collar of my shirt. It's too hot in this posh hotel, despite all the mahogany ceiling fans and the quiet elegance. To the right of me, just to the other side of the wide sail of a palm frond, I can still see Stevie. If I stood up suddenly, she'd look straight at me. She sits forward now and then, moving in and out of view, as if swaying on a boat in the breeze.

Jacob pushes the drinks list toward her. "Is it too early for alcohol?"

"No," Stevie says, smiling. "It might still be nighttime in Maine."

Her smile is sad, though. Bereft. I want to lean across and warn her. *You start drinking, Stevie, you might as well invite the wolf in.*

When I was fifteen I stole a bottle of champagne at one of my father's parties. I was under-attended. I was angry. I slipped the bottle from the regimented rows of them standing shoulder to frosted shoulder on the table and carried it by the neck to my father's study.

I didn't even like champagne. Didn't like my clothes, didn't like my manners, didn't like my house when my father was in it. All summer long, I'd spent days alone within the walled grounds, watching my parents fake their companionship. Dad was stationed overseas for nine months every year. My mother, when she wasn't concentrating on me, seemed to spend the time attending aqua aerobics and shopping. But every year, when my father's allotted break loomed and the three members of my family were required to live together at home, none of us had any real knowledge of the soundtrack of each other's lives—at least, not how they blended together. Sometimes Dad's break would fall during term time. It was better that way. Weekdays were an armistice.

But that summer we were all stuck in the house. I should have remained invisible at the party. I shouldn't have drunk all the champagne in the bottle. But I understood so much less then about rage. I didn't mean to pick up the cigar lighter from my father's desk or hold it to the dusty pages of his prized Churchill biographies as they lined his bookshelves in chronological order. I had no concept of how quickly they'd catch fire.

The entire row was ablaze when my father walked into the study. I leaned against the windowsill and laughed as Dad jumped and flapped at the flames, knocking books to the ground and stamping at the blackness of them. How proud I was of my rebellion, how many things I thought it would change. But my father kept it simple. *So be it*, he said, when the fire was out. *What a great disappointment you are.*

A month later he sent me away. And when I came back I was so much worse.

A waiter arrives at the side of my table, forcing me to lean back in my chair and keep my voice low. I order a coffee, black, no sugar. The waiter nods like I've selected the finest of wines and moves to the neighboring table. Jacob orders a beer—no glass—and Stevie opts for a Coke. *Good girl, well played. Let's maintain some semblance of defense.* They sit in silence once the waiter has gone, until Jacob clears his throat.

"Shall we just stay here for the afternoon?" he says. "It's not really . . . our kind of bar, I know. Not like our one at home!" *That's a fail, Jacob. Have you not seen her Instagram feed? All the details of her home life, all the comfort she had there.* "But we can relax here for a bit. Then, later, go pack up our stuff and head to the train station."

I sit up. *What train station?* But Stevie's face doesn't move. For a second, she looks very like my mother used to at family dinners. Taciturn. A world going on inside.

Jacob sighs. "You're still thinking about the guy in the street, aren't you?"

Stevie crosses her arms at her chest. She looks harrowed, like she hasn't slept in weeks. I'd put money on the fact she's having nightmares. "It's not just that guy. It's everything. All of it."

Another heavy sigh from Jacob, who shifts and his chair scrapes. "Nattie, you mean? I know, but being out here is supposed to make us feel better about—"

"Not just Nattie," she says.

There's a pause. "The inheritance. I know, but we need to look again at the things Nattie actually signed. If there's a document anywhere that looks legal, we might still have a case." I see his hand reaching for hers.

"It's Nattie, it's the bar, and it's something else. I've been thinking a lot about Cassia." Stevie might as well have hit him. I hear an audible shunt of breath.

"Thinking about her how?" His fingers retreat.

43

"It's just . . . I can't seem to process one death without being haunted by another. It's like a paper chain in my head. And then with that guy in the street . . . and the creepy bathroom last night . . ."

Behind us, the jazz pianist finishes a riff. Everyone claps gently but them.

"Haunted?" Jacob echoes.

"I'm having those dreams again—of Cassia, of the crash, of falling—"

There it is, I think. I can spot neural pathways at fifty paces. And yet they've banned me from work in the UK.

"That car crash was eight years ago."

"I know." She's crying now, great tears that seem too big for her face.

"Oh God, don't cry. I hate it when you cry." He gets up and takes the seat beside her. "It's just I thought . . . I thought we were past all that."

"I want to go home," she says.

"No, but, this adventure we're on is going to—"

"I don't like it here," she says. "I don't want an adventure."

"But you . . . I thought you . . ." He shakes his head, his jaw set. *Say it, Jacob. Do it.* "You hated being at home, too."

"Wow," she says. "I'm struggling. I'm sorry if I'm being inconvenient."

"No, I'm just . . . I'm working really hard here, Stevie, trying to make things better for you. For us." He picks at the label on his beer bottle. Rips off a tiny strip of paper, scrunches it into a ball. "Can we not just put all of this down to adjusting? We've landed in a new country. We don't know what's going on. Give it a few days!" *For fuck's sake*, he doesn't add. "Once we get to the dive camp, everything will settle down."

Will it? I think. But I stand now, throw money on the table, over-tipping because it seems fitting. I head for the exit, back into the heat and clamor of the street, smiling to myself. I was right about Stevie: she's far too interesting to let go. And she blushed when she met me earlier by the food vendors. I am a contender. Jacob will talk her back into Africa, sell her the notion of escaping the city tonight, and they'll head for their precious dive camp. I cross the street, pushing past a guy trying to sell me a fake Rolex. I have to get back to the hostel and pack, discussing one plan with Tamsin while implementing another. Everyone has a paper chain in their head, Stevie. I'm silently threading mine into yours.

7

STEVIE

"You want to play Uno in the main area before we go?" Jacob suggests. "There are quite a few people out there."

It's close to 9 p.m. and I'm writing in my journal on the hostel bed. "I'm okay," I say, looking up. "But you go ahead. I think I'll just stay here for a bit."

I've agreed to give Africa more of a try. I've agreed to settle in. But I'm not settling into this hostel.

"Oh, I can do that, too," he says, uncertainly. "I just thought you might want to socialize."

"I'm good."

"What if I just grabbed a pack of cards, and you and I played in here?" His foot is tapping.

"Okay." I put the journal away. "Let's do that."

Jacob hurries out to fetch the Uno. It wasn't an easy conversation in the Hilton. I felt disloyal telling him about Cassia, about the ways in which she's come back. But for weeks now, I've been hiding the dreams. Jacob sleeps entwined with me—it's a wonder he doesn't feel the jarring inside me through my skin.

If I'd told him outright as soon as the nightmares returned, he still wouldn't have wanted to hear Cassia's name. He never liked her. At school, she was inaccessible: all the boys had the hots for her but not many of them dared talk to her, and certainly not Jacob, who was known vaguely as a long-distance track athlete, a figure in the background, the kind of person who teachers relied on to know all the answers in class. Cassia and I were none of those things. We moved around the school inside a force field of cool hoodies, city haircuts, and quick comebacks. We ditched school, ditched homework, ditched giving a shit. Wove swear words into assignments if we ever handed them in. Swapped names if we had a sub. Heckled guest speakers in sex ed. We were a handful.

Mr. Jeffers, the humanities teacher, would keep us after class most weeks. He always left the classroom door open.

"Is everything all right at home?" he'd ask us, his tie busy with Buzz Lightyear shouting something.

"Why?" Cassia would reply. "Isn't everything all right at yours?"

Was it anger that drew Cassia and me together? There was so much crackling under our skin that never did find its way out. Through tenth grade, we busied ourselves with outward appearances to deflect from anything deeper. Took selfies all day and were never ourselves in them. Dated boys who were popular and vacuous. God forbid anyone might ask us a hard question. Cassia died before we could really grow up together, but even with her gone, Jacob's uneasy when he hears her name. Just like me, he can't quite label the nature of our connection.

He comes back into our room holding the Uno cards and sits across from me on the bed, then begins to shuffle them. He hasn't asked anything more about the dreams or why I might suddenly be having them, and he won't. He knows not to press me.

I chose him in eleventh grade because he was quiet. He was the only one not throwing relentless questions at me after the accident, when I finally made it back to school. I missed the whole of September, but every kid in my grade was crawling all over me at the first opportunity, vying for a reenactment of the wreckage the minute I'd recovered. I went from the hospital to the police station, to home and to class, and all the interviews were the same. *What happened? What did you do? Did you actually see her die?* There was only one place I could go for sanctuary. And here he is, calm as ever, doling out cards on the blanket. If he was sneakier, he could have easily read my journal, but he has too much integrity for that. There are things on those pages I *know* he hasn't read. It would change his understanding of everything.

"Have you ever slept on a train before?" he asks, organizing his hand of cards. "I haven't."

I shake my head no. What he's really asking is, *Can you please get excited?* And I want that, too. I'm trying. Mostly, I don't want to be that girl anymore who's seeking shelter. I'm not her, or if I am, I want to find it in myself.

When Jacob and I took art class together in eleventh grade, I arrived guarded and frail, a small creature emerging from the safety of a burrow. Each week I moved from desk to desk, wordlessly, finding my way to him across the room. Everything I drew was charcoal—intense, bitter sweeps ridge-thick on the paper. Everything he drew was the sea. He was interesting to me in a way I wasn't used to. By April, he always fetched me a pencil when he got his own, setting it softly on my desk where I'd let it roll before I picked it up. My paintings began to change: color crept into them. And then one day in May, Jacob waited for me by the door after class. He was letting the wash of students go by him, his eyes only on me. I remember fumbling as I packed up my papers.

"You should let me paint you," he said when we were level in the doorway.

"All you paint is stormy seas." I glanced up at him from under blunt bangs.

"Exactly." His eyes didn't falter.

Across from me on the blanket, Jacob's right knee is jiggling. "It's your turn," he says.

"Oh, sorry." How long has he been waiting? I put a card of the same shape onto the pile. He picks it up, gives it back to me.

"It has to be green," he says. "Do you need to go over the rules?"

"No, I've got it." I slam down a pick-up-4 card. I've always played Uno mercilessly. This time, though, it feels less funny.

I remember that first day I walked home with him, down the grassy track to the harbor and along past the peeling painted shop fronts and rutted crab traps near the wharf, boat masts clacking in the wind. There was an ease to simply being with him. We didn't speak much, but somehow we were comfortable just to be in step. I watched his hand swinging, liking the curve of his fingers when they were relaxed. If I timed it right, our arms would bump and connect. I didn't dare risk it.

"I wasn't sure you'd come," he said when we were beyond the town, heading uphill toward his parents' farmhouse. His hair was buffeted by the wind, his thin T-shirt pasted against his ribs.

"I'm walking up a hill," I said. "I haven't said yes to anything else yet."

At the top of the bluffs, we'd reached an old brown gate with a chain hooking it closed around the post of a stone wall.

"How come you don't speak more at school?" I pulled the chain upward, letting the gate swing open and wedge into the turf. "Today's the first time you ever talked to me."

"What did you want me to say?"

I hesitated. "I just don't know much about you."

"Nobody does," he said. "Not even me."

It was the truest thing I'd heard in a really long time. "I read this book once," I said, watching him carefully. "One of those Narnia books. Have you read them?"

"Sure."

"The one with the wardrobe they step through into the world beyond?"

"I've read it. And I saw the movie."

"I think people are like that," I said quietly. "Like the wardrobe. You have to push through to what's behind."

He lugged the gate shut. "I think it's hard to know anyone. But it's still worth trying."

He walked backward for a few strides up the hill, his hands hooked under his backpack. When we were level again, he took my hand and held it. The skin of his right arm was still covered in art class chalk. Later that night I found the blue smudge of it on my wrist. I didn't rub it off.

Jacob clears his throat, puts down a pick-up-4 card on top of mine. Doesn't make eye contact.

"Pick up *eight*?" I say, incredulous. That's new. Normally he plays like he's fine if I win.

He glances at his watch. "You know, we don't really have time for this after all. We should get going. We don't want to miss our train."

"Okay. Let's go, then."

We pack up in strange silence. Is he mad at me? Perhaps he has every right to be, and yet, I think both of us are trying our best. He doesn't wait for me at the top of the hostel stairs, doesn't hold my hand once we're on the street together. He told me earlier we needed to adjust, but this new territory we're in is starting to feel more than geographical.

We walk with purpose toward the train station, the streets and roads much quieter at this time of night. People huddle in shop fronts.

There's the odd food vendor, the odd honky car. Once we get to the ticket office we buy one-way tickets, book a private sleeping compartment, and climb aboard. The platform is busy, families coming and going, but nobody seems to get on. A station master sweeps the platform, whistling.

"Here we are." Jacob shoulders his way into our sleeping cabin, which is oak-paneled with two bunks. "All the corridors look the same. We'll have to remember we're in the seventh carriage."

He's right: everything inside the train is beige and polished, and all eight carriages are identical. We take off with a jolt, the steam engine working up to a steady huffing, lanterns lighting up over the top of each cabin door. For the first half hour of the journey, we get used to the lilt of the movement, leaning out of our window as we pull into the first shack of a station in the darkness. There's a woman waiting on her own in a patch of dirt by the tracks. At her feet is a heavy sack of grain.

"Look at that," I say. "How long do you think she's been waiting? It's pitch-black and there's nobody around for miles."

"Should I go help her on with her stuff?" Jacob asks.

But the woman's making no effort to board. This isn't the train she wants. We pull away again, leaving her alone in the dark.

At around ten thirty, Jacob and I eat dinner in the old diner car, a left turn out of our room into the eighth carriage. We're the only travelers in there. White-gloved waiters bring us dessert, pouring custard from a silver chalice. It's so colonial, it's uncomfortable.

"What's everyone else doing?" I ask. "Did we accidentally book first class?"

"I don't know—I don't think so. Maybe everyone else ate earlier."

"Or it's a ghost train." I widen my eyes. "Rattling along with only us on it."

At last, he smiles. "*That's* why the grain lady didn't want on," he says. "We're riding on a Ship of the Damned."

We sit in a more comfortable silence.

"Stevie," he says, as he reaches for the saltshaker, rotates it on the table. "I'm not decreeing that Africa has to be it for us."

My eyebrows shoot up. What does he mean *it*?

"This company I'm working for—GoEco—they have dive camps all over the world." He lines up the pepper next to the salt. "What I'm saying is, if this job goes well, it could open up all kinds of opportunities for us."

"Oh, right," I say, but already my heart is skittering. *So we're even more not going to go home?*

"Why do you think we stayed in Anchorite Bay after high school?" he asks, as if hearing my panic. "Nobody else we graduated with did. They all took off for the city."

"I don't know," I say. "Because we both wanted to?"

"Huh," he says, which clearly means *nope*. "Well, I'm just putting it out there. If you're looking for something to cling to right now, you could cling to GoEco. It could be something really solid."

Cling to? I think. *Is that what I'm doing?*

Jacob throws down his linen napkin. "It's late," he says. "Let's get back to our cabin."

But as we bump our way back along the skinny corridor again, I can't shake the image of myself through his eyes. I'm swept by loneliness on this train full of ghosts, the two of us the only noticeable passengers. We reach the next carriage without passing a soul.

And yet as we near the door to our room, the one next door closes with a click.

"What do you know," Jacob says, turning. "We have neighbors after all."

When we get inside our cabin, the sheets of the bunk beds have been turned down, and a little lamp with a mustard shade has been switched on by the mirror. Dust motes spangle in the light.

"Weird," Jacob says. "We really must be in first class. All we're missing is chocolates on the pillows."

"I don't think first class means they go through your stuff." My backpack has fallen over, our Larium malaria tablets scattered in foil casings across the gritty floor. I put the pills back in a side pocket, set the backpack straight again.

"They haven't gone *through* anything, Stevie. It's all part of the old-world charm. You know—steam train, silver service, beds turned down for the night." He tips an imaginary cap. "The staff is probably next door doing the same thing for them."

I exhale, let my shoulders drop a few inches. The door's locked now. Everything's good. Jacob's right and I'm overreacting. The janitor turned out the lights, the guy in the street was a drunkard, room service turned down our sheets. But since when do trains have room service?

To my left, Jacob unbuttons his shirt, begins to step out of his shorts. I walk toward him, take him by the hand, lead him to the bottom bunk. Things need to simplify. I want to be close to him right now. We squash together in the single bed as the train rumbles down the ancient track, both of us naked in the shadowy lamplight, cocooned in our private chamber. *It's not even about sex*, I think as I keep my eyes shut, *it's about forging a familiar connection*. My hands trace the long lines of Jacob's muscle, the smooth curve of his pectorals, his triceps, his abs. The lower I go, the more he breathes out in a gasp, and I know this. It's a rhythm I've learned by heart.

"I love you," Jacob whispers, and I grip him closer like I believe him. He loves me, his little rat from a sinking ship, clinging to driftwood in the swell of a greasy sea. After he falls asleep, just like he does at home, I watch him for a while, leaning up on one elbow in the bunk. I don't want to sleep yet. One of us is slipping away from the other, but I can't tell which of us it is.

I reach up to grab my pillow from the top bunk, and there's noise outside in the corridor, a bark of laughter from farther down the train, the click of another door shutting. Where were all these passengers earlier?

As a child, before my grandmother took me in, I used to lie awake at night wondering whose voices were in the apartment. My father's I never knew, but my mother's I recognized. She was rarely alone in the living room. I was five, and the sound of men was deep. Monster-deep. Now, lying within reach of a hundred strangers, I'm not at ease under the sheets. Because I don't know who's beyond the door. I don't know who might try the handle. And I'm not certain I can control who's coming in.

Outside the train window, strange shapes fizz by—bushes that lean weirdly against a flat backdrop of black. I lie alongside Jacob, my head on my pillow, watching the shapes as if they're characters on a screen, unable to shake the feeling that I'm in a plotline I haven't chosen, surrounded by a cast I can't quite see.

8

LEO

We get onto the train ahead of them because I know exactly where they're going. Hashtag DianiBeach, hashtag OvernightTrain, hashtag Adventure. For all that Stevie's worried about, her Instagram story's on point. As always, it's about the magazine cover of one's life.

Tamsin's brought food with her: chicken, rice, and plantain she got from the café I sent Jacob and Stevie to earlier. *The food on the train will be British*, she said. *We might as well eat like locals*. It's all part of a great assimilation. When we started traveling together in Zimbabwe three months ago, both of us were shocked by the poverty we saw, by the beggars with limbs so deformed it seemed impossible that they were even still alive. There was so much dirt and sickness and noise. But as we've wended our way through Mozambique and Malawi, we've got used to it all. It feels dangerously close to not caring. Perhaps it's simply that I've abandoned my genetic, almost chromosomal wiring toward luxury. I'm nothing if not adaptable.

Once we've settled into our cabin—again, next door, although this time I had more of a say in its engineering—we leave Stevie and Jacob alone in their room and head down to the bar car, which is at the other end, nearest the engine. It's rare that Westerners eat in the restaurant, but they gather in a throng at the front of the train to drink dawas—a popular cocktail among travelers of vodka, muddled limes, and Kenyan honey. It's a well-kept secret, the bar car, not documented in any of the travel guides or websites, passed by word-of-mouth among backpackers. Clearly nobody's told Jacob. Fifteen or so people are pressed into a hot space that's twenty feet by ten. It's like clubbing in London on a Thursday.

"Well," says Tamsin, pressing her way back to me at the bar. "I've officially surrendered the last of my hygiene levels. My mother would be horrified. That toilet was just a hole in the floor. I could see the tracks through it."

I lift my drink to my lips, smiling. Tamsin's closer to her mum than her dad, and she's posh like me—grew up within the British class system, appears to understand it. Her mum was by all accounts a Nigerian princess before Tamsin's father got a hold of her. God knows where they met, although from what I can tell, Tamsin's dad is all about importing and exporting.

"Was there any—" I begin, but she holds up a flat palm.

"I carry hand sanitizer, Leo. Let's never speak of it again." She slides onto a chrome barstool, takes a huge swig of her drink. To the right of her on the counter is a decorative bowl full of pawpaws. I take one, fetch the sharpened knife I keep in my pocket, begin to slice into it.

"Are you allowed to eat those?" Tamsin asks.

"Nobody seems to be stopping me." I pass her a piece of the fruit. It's Stevie's fruit, of course, and always will be. But it's nice to pay her a little tribute, now that she's captive on the train. Neither she nor Jacob will get off it—not, at least, until I do. There's something very relaxing about that.

"Do you think they'll have a pub at the dive camp?" Tamsin asks, chewing. "On the website, it looked like a proper-organized operation."

"I think it's more about the ecosystem than the alcohol," I say.

"Lame." She takes another sip. "I called that Mike Duran guy. Duran, as he's called. He sounded . . . manly."

"Did he?"

"He booked us in but wants to see our dive tickets when we get there."

"That's fine," I say. Tamsin and I got our Open Water dive certificates at Lake Malawi. At the time, I didn't know they'd come in so handy.

"I wonder if Duran's name is any kind of throwback to the eighties," she says. "Maybe he's *hungry like the wolf*. Hey, speaking of which, look what I got today." She reaches into her back pocket and pulls out her phone, brandishing it three inches from my face as if it's filth she's just smeared from the table.

"What's that?" I ask, frowning.

"An email. From my dad. Saying he's getting married again." She puts the phone facedown next to her drink, picks that up instead. "Again and again and again."

In the time we've spent together, she's spoken a lot of her father. How he derailed her mother, stole from her every ounce of her African heritage, forced her to work even when they had the money, and then left her high and dry to remarry when the offer of a younger model became available. All of this I have gleaned without ever, ever offering any comment on the behavior of my own father. Including the fact or nature of his death.

"This is Wife Number Four. I don't know who he thinks he is," Tamsin says. "Henry the Eighth or something."

"At least he's not killing them," I say, and she looks at me. "Is he?"

"No, of course he's not killing them, Leo," she says. "Because who does that?"

"Nobody." I pick up my drink.

"But he's a predator. And yet he sits up there on his bloody high horse, lording it over the rest of us. Unbelievable. Anyway, I emailed him back, told him to stick his marriage up his arsenal. Thanked him for all the life lessons." She pauses. "What happened to Henry the Eighth in the end?"

"He died of natural causes."

"Damn," she says. "He was fat, though, wasn't he? Like, actually obese."

"I don't know." I'm starting to feel scattered again. Her outrage is hard to track.

"He looked it in all the tapestries." She sighs, glancing around the crowded space, then gestures with her head at a young couple—teenagers—standing together arm in arm in the corner. "What do you think their story is?" It's a favorite game of hers, this guessing of strangers' lives. She's done it in every country we've traveled, giving people she doesn't know names, home nations, jobs, pets. "Oskar and Freya," she says, as she twirls her cocktail spear, "recent graduates of Media Studies and Anthropology at the University of Copenhagen, owners of an old cat they rescued in their second year."

"What have they done with the cat?" My question is limp: I'm not interested in watching couples other than the one I've already found.

"Left it with her mum. The cat's called whatever the Danish word is for biscuit. It'll die, though, while they're over here." She drains her glass. "They always do."

I feel suddenly tired as the couple move toward us at the bar, putting down two empty beer bottles.

"Hi," Tamsin says to them.

"Ha-llo," the boy replies, with the unmistakable lilt of Scandinavia. But he doesn't hover. The two of them move off and out of the bar car. I exhale audibly.

"Have you had enough? Shall we go?" Tamsin asks, standing.

"What, follow them?"

She stares at me. "No, Leo, go to our cabin. What is the matter with you?"

"Nothing." I stand up, too. "We've been in here for an hour. I'm starting to feel a bit tipsy."

"Well, you've been chugging your drinks. Three dawas and you're anyone's," she laughs, and she leads us out of the bar car and up the rattling corridors to our cabin. Several times we stumble into the wall. It's either the drink or the speed at which the old train is traveling.

Our room, when we get into it, is murky and dimly lit. It's past eleven and outside the train window everything is black. We might as well be inside a tunnel. I move toward the sink to turn the light on overhead and bump into a backpack that topples over. Behind me, Tamsin snorts. But the bag isn't mine. Nor is it Tamsin's.

"Which room are we in?" I ask.

"Shit!" She peers at the back of the closed door. "Our one, aren't we?"

I turn on a light near the mirror. "Tamsin, this isn't our room! We're in the one next door."

But she's interested now. She's not hurrying. She's paying attention. Leaning down, she flips over the baggage labels on the backpacks.

"Oooh, Jacob and Stevie, from . . . Anchorite Bay, Maine! Where the fuck in the world is that?" She straightens as I grip her by both arms and turn her toward the door. "He's a farmer, she's a cocktail waitress. They have a pet donkey they keep in a field."

I try to steer her forward, but she swerves left.

"Let's just pull down their sheets," she says. "Make it look like we were chambermaids."

"Let's go, Tamsin—" I push her another step, but my foot connects with something and I punt a leather-bound book across the floor. It thuds against the base of the bed. Tamsin crouches to pick it up.

"Oh my God, Leo, look!" In her hands is a journal, a skull and crossbones on the front. Tamsin fans the pages, most of which are full of handwriting. "Stevie is a pirate! No, she's a spy . . . an international secret-keeper . . ."

"Put it on the bed," I say, but Tamsin freezes suddenly, listening.

"Someone's coming," she says, her face alight with mischief. "Quick!" She jams the book into my midriff, and I hold it there, scrambling with Tamsin to get out of the room. We make it next door just in time, shutting our door a second before Stevie and Jacob reach theirs.

"Holy shit, that could have got really awkward," Tamsin says. "What would we have done if they'd come back?"

"Nothing," I say. "Explained." But I don't like that we went in there. I don't like that we went in there together.

"Are you cross with me? Christ, Leo, it was an honest mistake. This train would be right trippy if we were *sober*. Everything's cloned." She kicks off her flip-flops, pulls off her shirt, walks toward me.

"What am I going to do with this?" I hold up the journal. "Stevie will know it's gone."

"*Stevie?*" She eyes me, naughtiness creeping back in. "Are we on a first-name basis now? Good old Stevie from the spy network of Maine?"

"Tamsin—"

"Oh, for God's sake, relax." She pushes me back until I'm sitting on the velvet couch by the window. "We'll catch her in the morning, say we found her diary lying in the corridor or something. Tell her it fell out of her bag." She climbs on top of me, her thighs on each side of my lap, pressing the diary onto the seat beside me.

If people photoshopped themselves, they'd want to look like

Tamsin. Her body is so fit against mine, I can't help but get hard, especially now that I'm drunk and she's blurring into all this talk of Stevie.

"That's better," she says, nuzzling near my ear. "You worry too much. Good-looking boys are usually so dangerous. You're such a sensitive soul."

I don't answer. It's best that she doesn't know. When I kiss her, her tongue is cold and smooth and tastes of citrus and vodka. She pulls at my belt buckle, tugs at my shirt, and we slide into each other, muscle against muscle, my breath against her lips until everything's white noise in my head and it's all I can do to keep one hand on the soft brushed leather of Stevie's journal.

Afterward, Tamsin gets off me, steps to the sink, runs water over her hands. She trickles drops of it across her throat and down her back.

"I'm so hot all the time," she says, as I button my shorts on the couch. "It's totally your fault."

"Is it?" I ask.

She smiles, grabbing a toothbrush, plying it luxuriously with toothpaste. "I'm getting into the top bunk. Is that okay? It's too hot to cuddle."

"That's fine." My fingertips caress the cover of the diary. "We'll be in Mombasa in about six hours. Both of us should get some sleep. When we arrive in the morning, we can catch a cab out to Diani Beach. Like I said, it's the best place to stay."

"Do you know what I like about you, Leo?" She spits toothpaste into the sink. "You always have a plan of attack."

For the next little while as Tamsin sleeps, I sit by the lamplight, reading Stevie's secrets on the page, listening to the sound of the functional sex she's having next door with Jacob, the boyfriend who she's not sure she'll marry and doesn't know if she can. He can't possibly have read these pages. I go back to the beginning with Cassia—her closest tie, revered to the level of a lost first love—and the questions

Stevie has about the accident that crawl in her head like beetles. *Did I do that? Did I mean that? Would I do it any differently if it happened again?* On the train rattles into the darkness while I move closer to the light, reading about her mother, the abandonment, all the betrayal and anger and pain. I sway in my seat with my heart on fire, the whole of me a siren of absolute parity, to the point where I might have written each perfect sentence myself. By midnight, I'm all but ghosting my arm through the wood paneling behind me, interlacing my fingers with Stevie's, kissing her gently on the neck.

9

STEVIE

Mombasa arrives bright and early, another riot of sound. Jacob and I pack up our things hurriedly and jump from the train. People press around us as we battle for a taxi and we get in without really knowing how much we're paying or where exactly the driver is taking us. The road beyond the city quickly turns into a rutted dirt track. There are no houses, no signs.

"I guess we just go with the flow," Jacob says, trying to pretend he's not offering me an instructional leaflet. I move to lower the window and get some air, but the manual handle has been snapped off.

An hour later, the taxi pulls through two crooked gates and stops outside of a beach hut. A sign on the paneling reads, *Diani Beach. Hamna Tabu.*

"It means no stress, man." The driver climbs out of the car. "Leave your troubles in the water."

Okay, I think. *Except what if your troubles won't leave?*

"Right on," Jacob says, picking up his pack and mine.

We pay the driver whatever he asks for and Jacob heads into the reception building while I wait on the wooden steps outside. It's close to midday and travelers in sarongs wander the shoreline, picking up shells, trailing toes in the broken waves. There's no inkling of stress or hurry. It's like a whole new world. A group of four girls younger than me are practicing yoga in a wide gap between palm trees. Everyone has tattoos, swirly, patterned ones that draw attention to the depths of their tans. I look at my arms, the paleness of them, the plainness. In the distance, someone is playing a guitar.

Jacob emerges and tries to close the reception door, which doesn't fit its jamb. "Okay, all set. We're Bungalow 8. Down the path, he said, on the left."

"Do you know how to play the guitar?" I ask him, thinking maybe we should have learned. "Weren't you in band in high school?"

"I know how to dive," Jacob says. "That's way cooler."

I watch him as he leads us down the beach path, noticing how his confidence grows the more mine fades. It's almost a teeter-totter balance.

We walk past tumbledown bungalows that lean and look paper-thin, the paint of them all faded blue. Flip-flops are scattered over every front doormat and a few of the bungalows have makeshift hammocks strung into the rafters of their verandahs.

"The guy on reception says to be careful of the monkeys." Jacob looks back at me. "I guess he just means don't feed them. Here— number eight. This is us." He prods into the lock with the key, which seems ridiculously small. "I don't know. It's the one he gave me." He tries again, moving the key around in the gap like a spoon in a pudding bowl. But then something connects—there's a click—and Jacob tries the door handle. We step into a tiny low-ceilinged room with a bed, a mosquito net, a chair that's lost most of its wicker, and a bathroom behind a waist-high wall of woven palm leaves.

"Okay, maybe crouch low when you're peeing." Jacob goes to

the window and opens the wooden shutters, sticking his forefinger through a large rip in the screen.

I put down my backpack and stretch. After last night's conversation at dinner, it feels crucial to hide any misgivings. I don't want to be the clingy one, the resident desperation. "Shall we go for a swim?"

"Yes," he says, glancing around again. "Yes, good idea."

As soon as we step into the Indian Ocean, all my shaky confidence—the grime and worry of the city, the creepy first hostel, the strangely deserted train, and aloofness of the travelers here—washes away. The water is so much brighter than in Maine, a tropical, easy blue that slips around our skin like silk. We grin at each other as we tread water.

"Two nights here," Jacob says, "and then Rafiki Island. You'll never want to go home again."

But even if I hear him, I'm not looking at Jacob anymore. I'm squinting back at the shoreline, at the base of the tree where we've stashed our things.

"Who's that?" I ask. We bob in the water, pressing salt from our eyes. A man is kneeling with his back to us, his hands hidden from view. "Is that our stuff? What's he doing?"

Jacob starts to swim in. He's swift in the water, definite, and by the time I catch up he's already on shore under the palm tree.

"What's happening?" I pant.

"It's all good," Jacob says, shaking his head so that drops of water fly everywhere. "It's fine. This is Leo."

The man standing next to Jacob is the same guy who saved us from the flies on the buns the day before. This time he's in a tank top that shows his arm muscles, and he's wearing some kind of carving on a dark string around his neck. His tan is deep and smooth.

"Hi," he says, reaching out his hand. His fingers are warm against mine. "Are you following me?"

"No, I—" I swipe strands of wet hair from my forehead, suddenly self-conscious.

He smiles, his teeth straight and white. "I'm joking. I think we're following each other. It's the beauty of the tourist trail."

"It's lucky Leo was here," Jacob says, tipping his head toward him. "He says a monkey took the key from our pack. He watched him run up a tree with it. We'll have to go get another from reception."

"Oh, no, I don't think Wilson will have a spare," Leo says. "Wilson. The owner. The guy in reception." He still seems to be looking at me. I feel myself blushing and try hard not to.

"What do we do, then?" Jacob asks, glancing up into the palms overhead.

"Well, if you and . . ." He waits for me to insert my name.

"Stevie," I mumble. I don't know why I'm so flustered.

"If you and *Stevie*," he pauses, almost relishing the sound of it, "come with me, I'll show you what I'd do."

He leads us up through the sand to our bungalow. Jacob must have told him what number we were in. We all stand on the porch, water dripping from Jacob's shorts into a puddle by our feet. "So, in a nutshell, I'd do *this*." Leo pushes his fist through the already torn mosquito screen and then rips out the shreds of netting. "There. Bob's your uncle. Problem solved."

"Holy cow." Jacob rubs the top of his head. "Okay, then. But how can we fit through there? That gap is tiny."

"She can fit." Leo looks right at me. "She's perfect."

Again I blush. Jesus. I have to get a grip. "I'll climb through. Then we can lock the door and shutters from the inside. It's probably our best bet." *None of the locks work here*, the girl in the bathroom echoes in my head. *All the rules are different.*

Leo smiles. "Go on, then, Daisy Duke." He stands with his arms crossed against the groove of his pectoral muscles, waiting for me to squeeze through the gap. Jacob lines the window ledge with his towel. It's a tight space and fairly inelegant but I make it, unlocking the door and readjusting my bikini before letting the boys in.

"Good enough." Leo gives us a double thumbs-up. "And honestly, you probably don't even need to worry about anything here. It's pretty laid-back, all in all."

"Have you stayed here already?" Jacob asks him.

"Not really, but everywhere's the same." Leo claps his hands together. "Right, then. Crisis averted. I'll see you around."

"Well, wait up," Jacob says. "What are you doing now? We should go grab a beer." He glances at me and I shrug, hoping he means all three of us.

"I'm tied up for the afternoon," Leo says, as if there's a business meeting he needs to attend in the palm trees. "But how about dinner at six? There's a hut behind reception. Wilson doubles as the chef." He's so fluent with Diani Beach lifestyle that clearly he's been on the tourist trail for a while. He leaves our bungalow and jogs down the verandah steps, hands in his pockets, whistling.

"He's confident, isn't he?" Jacob sounds more impressed than competitive.

"Totally," I say. "Charismatic." *Careful. Don't sound too excited.* "Are we really going to meet him for dinner?"

"Why not?" We stand in wet swimwear in our room, our day pack bedraggled. "Let's have some fun out here, Stevie. We deserve that."

I nod, because it's true: nothing's been fun lately, and Leo kind of feels like a gift. Here he is in Diani Beach, calm, relaxed, and welcoming like a ready-made tour guide. It's almost as if he's been waiting for us all along.

We meet up for dinner at six o'clock that night. There aren't many other Diani Beach backpackers eating in the hut. Perhaps they've already been and gone or are waiting until much later. It does seem early, but everything gets dark so fast in Africa. Even as we walk along the path to the restaurant, Jacob and I are stumbling on tree roots, peering hard at our feet in the gathering gloom. By nine, it will be deep-oil black. There aren't many lamps around the place. Diani Beach isn't big on electric light bulbs.

We find the restaurant hut, which has a grass roof and mud walls. There's a small window cut out of each side, but neither of them has glass or a screen in them. Two rough tables fill the hut, large enough that the waiter has to press against the dirt of the walls to deliver food items. There are benches on each side of the tables, scratchy against my sarong when I sit down. The only light is a small candle in the center of each table, emitting light that barely spreads beyond the diameter of a coin.

"Here you are!" Leo stands when he sees us, smoothing down a Tusker lager T-shirt that doesn't suit him. I've only just met him, but I can already tell he's more dapper than that. "How was your journey out of the window? I assume you chose to leave your door locked, and climbed through?"

"It was okay," I say. "I think I have it figured out."

"I bet you do." The light throws shadows against his face, but it seems as if he's really grinning. "And how are you, Jacob? Settling in?"

"Yeah," Jacob says. "This place was a good choice."

"The last place wasn't?" Leo signals to someone in the kitchen and a young African guy brings out two beers in dark brown bottles, the tops of each twisted around with paper towel. "Cheers, Apologize." Leo waits for the boy to leave. "His name is actually Apologize. Isn't that the greatest?" He slides a bottle of beer to each of us. "What happened in the last place?"

"We had a bit of trouble in the city," Jacob says, glancing at me. "But we're good now. You can't ask for much more than this."

"You certainly can't," Leo says.

"Do you travel a lot?" I ask him. "You seem very . . . at home. And thanks for saving us from the Raid bun yesterday."

"Yes!" Jacob says. "We never got a chance to thank you."

Leo nods, laces his hands in front of his beer bottle. "I've been here a few months already. You pick up a few tricks."

"We're from small-town USA," Jacob says. "But we're branching out."

Leo curves his mouth like he might be impressed.

"Where are you from, Leo?" I ask. "And what do you do?"

One question at a time, Stevie, I think. *Slow it down.*

"I'm a doctor." Leo smiles. "Or I was. A neurologist in England. But I'm taking a break. Rather like you, Jacob. I'm branching out."

"Neurology is all about brains, right?" I ask.

"It's about everything, really. All the systems and pathways. I'm a specialist in what's going on in your body."

"In *my* body?" I really ought to break eye contact.

Leo laughs. "In everyone's."

"Did you have to study for years and years to be that?" My tone is too awestruck. I need to address it.

"I suppose I did. I began at eighteen. So, ten years and counting."

"Ten years of studying and residencies? Hard to take a break when you're that far in, I guess," Jacob says. "But you know what they say? Man was born with feet, not roots."

I shift on the bench next to him. Who has ever said that before? Certainly not Jacob.

"Well, my girlfriend and I—" Leo begins.

"You have a girlfriend?" I ask and immediately regret it.

"Wow." Leo sits back, eyebrows raised jovially. "Am I that hideous?"

"No," I mumble. "Not at all." Looking the way he does, it's perfectly believable he'd have hundreds, but he's been so attentive to me. Is he like this with everyone?

"Will your girlfriend be joining us for dinner?" Jacob asks.

"I'm not sure what her plans are. Let's go ahead and order; she can always catch up." Leo holds up two fingers and a thumb to Apologize, who disappears through a makeshift door. "There's only one thing on the menu, guys. Apparently it's Wilson's stew."

The food arrives on tin plates at the same moment the candle on our table sputters out. There isn't a replacement. We're given heavy forks and more beer bottles. I can't see what's on my plate, other than the general lumpiness of it. There's no color, no recognizable texture. The steam that rises to meet my face smells heavily of cardamom. When I chew a chunk of meat, it's gamey and dense in a way I've never tasted before. Under the table, stray cats rub against my shins, making me jump.

"What meat is this?" I ask Leo.

"I wouldn't ask if I were you." He swills down his mouthful with beer. "When I was in Harare, I ate soup with chicken claws hooked over the rim of the bowl."

"No way," Jacob says, hanging on to Leo's every adventure.

Leo pauses. "Stevie, were *you* born with feet and not roots?" The smile he shoots me feels conspiratorial, like Jacob's quote is now a joke between us. I'm not sure how I feel about it.

"No," I say. Even if I was, Nattie made sure I replaced them.

"But you're happy to be here?" he asks. "Not second-guessing it at all?"

My stomach is starting to feel queasy. Apart from the strange food, it's the heat in the hut, the closeness of it, the enveloping darkness. I take a breath.

"Are you okay?" Jacob steadies me with his arm. "She gets . . . it's a claustrophobia thing."

"That's no good. How debilitating. Do you need some fresh air?" Leo half stands. "We can head outside if you'd prefer."

"You know what?" I say, my vision blotting. "I think I just want to go back to the room. No, it's good—I'm not very hungry. It's been a long day. I'm worn out, is all."

"Of course. Let's get you home to bed." Leo climbs over the bench as if he'll be the one to escort me.

"It's okay," I say. "You finish your meal, Leo." I head toward the door of the hut, turning to find that Jacob is still sitting at the table. "Oh, are you staying, too?"

"Only if you're okay getting back," he says.

"Oh, yeah. No. Totally." It's the first time he's ever not chosen me. It's such a tiny thing—not walking me fifty feet down a beach path—and of course I can make it on my own. But the whole thing feels odd. Even Leo looks apologetic.

I walk out of the hut on my own and stumble back to Bungalow 8, squeezing myself through the window frame. I lie wide-eyed under the mosquito net, wondering when Jacob will get in. Of course he can stay up later than me. It's good he's making friends. And Leo's magnetic: it's natural Jacob would want to sit longer with him. I want to, too, and maybe that's the clincher. I'm jealous. But of Jacob or Leo? For hours, I toss and turn, feeling weirdly unsettled. Outside, strange animals screech in the trees.

Jacob doesn't get in until 1 a.m. and he's drunk. I hear him and Leo sniggering outside the bungalow, pressing their faces low to the window as if they're at a bank teller asking for foreign currency.

"Stevie!" Jacob hisses. "The door's locked. You gotta open it. Stevie!"

"Okay," I say. "I'm coming. Hold on."

When I open the door, Leo is leaning against the frame. "Hi," he says. "You look nice."

My T-shirt feels suddenly too short, but I say nothing and help Jacob to the bathroom. Both boys are snorting with laughter.

"Stop hitting on her." Jacob burps, giggling. I hear him sigh and crash into the sink.

"I can't help it!" Leo says. "She's outstanding. She's model material."

"Okay, *thank you.*" I steer Leo out of the door and lock it behind him.

"I'm not joking." His face appears in the window gap. "Are you a little bit Icelandic? My mother's Scandinavian. You're all hot and cold at the same time."

Behind me in the bathroom, Jacob can't figure out how to turn off the tap. He grinds the faucet one way and then the other, still sniggering. "Dude, you think your *mom* is hot?"

There's a second at the window where Leo's eyes seem to reach for mine. The pause is full of something big, something yearnful and raw, but he blinks it away. "No. I'm saying Stevie is. She's the best one here."

"Where's your girlfriend?" I ask, even though I find I'm smiling. "Go home." I swing closed the thick wooden shutters, blocking out his face. Then I hook the latch shut.

By the time I get back to the bed, Jacob is already flapping his way under the mosquito net from the opposite side, almost pulling the whole thing down. He pats my thigh twice. "Great guy. Totally the greatest. Best night ever, swear."

"Good, Jacob. I'm glad." I'm not glad. I'm irritated, but he doesn't notice.

He sighs happily again and turns over, thumping his pillow a few times to try and make it plumper. A minute later he's asleep, the beer he's drunk coming out in steady, uncharacteristic snores.

I sleep fitfully all night, alert to Jacob's clumsiness and troubled by horrible dreams. In all of them I'm pinned in blackness with cold fingertips pressing me. At one point, I jump awake, certain that someone is watching me through the mosquito net. Someone shiny-toothed and close, sitting on the broken wicker chair. But in my blur of jet lag, Larium trippiness, and deep sleep, I lose the image until morning when I wake to find the chair pushed up close to my side of the bed. So close that whoever's been in it could have touched me. And when I sit up, the door to the bungalow is open. Wide, wide open.

10

LEO

I can't say I slept very well. There was too much to think about, too much to do. Yesterday was momentous: finally speaking to Stevie, finally managing to converge after two whole days of wanting to. When I dropped Jacob home at Bungalow 8, Stevie flirted with me through the gap of her window. Before she closed the shutters, we had a moment. I know how to spot those because I've been taught, but this one—gosh, it felt like a mutual dropping of masks, just for a second, and only for each other. So, could I really walk away and not come back? It's undeniable, the connection we have. It's surface and it's soul. The trick is keeping it hidden from the others.

After I left her, I wandered the beach for a while, sat with my back against a tree, listening to the waves and the occasional wash of palm leaves overhead. It was like a lullaby—extremely soothing—and in the end, I must have fallen asleep because it's around 6 a.m. now and I just woke up under the same tree, with a crab tickling under my chin. I sit up, caked in sand, dusty inside my mouth, disoriented.

But there's nothing that will set a man straighter than an early-morning swim in the ocean. I've learned this since I've been over here, and it's made me wish my life had always been more coastal. I could have used the clarity. I strip down to my underwear and wade out into the warm sea.

Fish dart around my ankles like little beads of glass, moving at the same speed as my thoughts. I remember everything about last night. I wasn't drunk. I'm not hungover. I had one drink for Jacob's every three. There was a drive in him—interestingly—an almost manic need to get down to the nitty-gritty. At first, I'd been irritated when Stevie left us: she was, after all, the main attraction. But I realized very quickly that Jacob had a lot to tell me. Nice guy, completely transparent. And for every question he asked, he handed me another piece of the puzzle.

"Have you slept with a lot of women?" he blurted, three beers in. It took me off guard, to be honest. Men don't tend to ask those kinds of things, especially not so soon within a burgeoning friendship. Jacob's tally of conquests, I thought, must either have been high, and he wanted to prove it to me, or low, and he wanted to work on it. My money was on the latter.

"No, not a lot," I said.

"But more than one, though." He stared into the opaque brown of his beer bottle.

"Yes, of course." There was a pause. "Are you tiring of Stevie, Jacob? Branching out in more ways than one?" I kept my tone level, even though I felt outraged. Protective. Excited.

"No." His eyes widened. "No, I mean, it's not about that. But I do wonder sometimes what it'd be like. With other women. We're young men, you and I, right? And Stevie's my only . . . well, you know, and at high school I didn't have a ton of luck."

I crossed both arms at my chest. I didn't know. And talking about school was pointless. But Jacob sat across from me, rotating his beer bottle by inches, hoping I'd bond with him. What could I share with him of my school years? I didn't have reams of love stories to describe. My path was more one of rebellion. I could have told him that it had been a mistake to send me away to military college. That my father hadn't been thinking clearly. At Whitechapel, the expensive day school to which I had been deployed at the age of seven, there was only ever one other rebel per class. Two, at a push. And the scale of their uprising was tepid: a thumbtack on a teacher's stool here, a forged letter getting you out of games there. It was never really enough for me to work with.

But at Ridings, the military academy in well-behaved Kent where I was dispatched after the fire at fifteen, the rooms were filled with disenfranchised teenagers. Here were all the rich kids who'd disappointed their parents, the problem children, young heirs to fortunes and dynasties who really ought to know better. The teachers might have been strict, and the days overly scheduled, but nobody—least of all my father—had quite taken into account the complex, intelligent, elite layers of defiance within the caliber of peer I would find there. A collective sense of go-fuck-yourself fueled the entire student body. In terms of insurgence, it was a huge leap in possibility.

"Luck?" I tilted my bottle toward Jacob's, creating the tiniest of clinks. "I think you make your own luck."

"You look like a guy who's made plenty," he said.

Do I? I withdrew my bottle. *Appearances can be deceptive.*

"So Stevie's the only girl you've been with?" I asked, nodding slowly.

"I kissed one other girl in my life. She was a French exchange student in our art class in eleventh grade. Stevie doesn't know anything happened with her."

"You were going out with Stevie at the time?"

"No." He bit his lip. "We weren't dating yet but we both knew we were kind of heading that way. You know? It's a commitment but it isn't."

"I understand." I smiled. "The anticipation stage. All the circling."

"Right," Jacob said. "And I knew I liked Stevie, but I was asked to show this French exchange girl where the art supply cupboard was and while we were in there, she kissed me. Man, I can't lie. It was superhot."

"And you never told Stevie."

He shook his head. "The French student went home. It was only a kiss. A week later, Stevie and I started dating."

"What are you doing over here, Jacob?" My voice sounded a little jaded.

"I've taken this job," he went on, "as a diver. It's not like I'm sure about it, but I'm trying to—"

"You're *working* as a diver?" This was new. "What will Stevie be doing?"

He blinked at me, already a little bleary. "Not much," he said. "Volunteering?"

"Oh, right. Okay, then. She'll have lots of free time." *Idle hands, Jacob, are the devil's workshop. Didn't your parents teach you anything?*

"Stevie can dive. I taught her when we were just getting together. It was kind of romantic."

Was it really, though? I think.

"But she needs a vacation. I told Duran she can help out, and I'm sure she'll keep busy one way or another."

I nodded reassuringly. *Oh, I'm certain she will.*

I dive into the ocean, the water around my skin smooth and perfect as I swim twenty strokes one way, twenty strokes back, enjoying the healthiness of muscles in motion. Treading water, I notice a couple of young girls walking along the beach, bending every now and again to look at shells. They've woken up early to watch the sunrise.

Next, it'll be yoga and a fruit-based breakfast. I know the rhythms of backpacking life so well. It's a language I've learned in three months. My mother would be impressed at my versatility. Look at me: I can say anything now and people believe it.

"Do you like being out here?" Jacob asked me last night. "How long of a sabbatical did you get off work?"

"I'm thinking of changing my career," I said.

"Oh, wow. I've heard travel does that." He signaled to Apologize for another beer. "Gives you crazy perspective on your life at home."

"Crazy," I echoed.

"And why did you—"

"Not all who wander are lost, Jacob," I cut in. He raised his empty beer bottle to that little backpacker bumper sticker. *Amen to that, brother.* Except we are lost. All of us.

"Leo!" Tamsin stepped suddenly into the eating hut in a sarong and tiny T-shirt. Both Jacob and I jumped. "I thought we were eating together! I was waiting for bloody eons in that hammock. Did you go out the back way or something?"

"Sorry," I said. "Crossed wires."

Across the table, I could see Jacob taking in Tamsin's long, elegant arms; the tightness of her hips and belly; the overall sleekness of eyelashes, hair, cheekbones.

"Tamsin, this is my new friend, Jacob."

Tamsin slid onto the bench beside me. "Jacob?" Her green eyes widened.

"Yup. That's me." He coughed out a bubble in his throat, leaned forward to shake her hand.

"Are you a farmer?" she asked him, her palm against his.

He frowned then, momentarily, but didn't withdraw his fingers. *Here we go, Jacob,* I thought, watching him shake his head. *Buckle up. This is where it all starts to go faster.*

11

STEVIE

Jacob's hungover when I wake him. I kneel beside him on the bed, pressing every syllable of my sentence into the sheet with a clenched fist.

"Someone. Was. In. Our. Room."

"Stevie. Come on." He rubs his eyes, which have been shut throughout. "I was in our room. You were in our room. Leo dropped me back here last night. Is that what you mean?" He scans the floor by the bed. "Do you have a water bottle? My tongue is like glue."

"You're not listening to me," I say.

"Maybe we didn't lock the door! Leo said there wasn't much need." He sits up, blinks a few times.

"You didn't lock the door, Jacob. I did."

"Okay, then. So it *was* locked." He waits for a few seconds. "I don't really get . . . Okay, look, I'm sorry the night kind of took off on me.

Is that what this is about? I'm sorry, but Leo's a great guy. He's really easy to talk to. It's a shame you couldn't have stuck around for longer."

"I locked the door. I one hundred percent know I did."

He massages his temple. "The door. Okay, so you're saying . . . What are you saying, exactly? That someone used a key to get in?"

"They must have. I latched the shutters and they're still closed. And there's no sign of forced entry."

He burps a little and grimaces. "So a monkey came in, then? What, Stevie? It's no more ridiculous than what you're saying. Our key is up in a tree, remember?"

"Wow, Jacob, you're so naive. Why is there a chair right next to my side of the bed? Did a monkey move that, too?"

"*I* probably did it. I don't know! I'm jet-lagged and I was hammered and I'm very sorry about that. I can't say for sure what I did in the night. I might have opened the door to get fresh air and banged into the chair on the way back to bed." He looks like he wants to lie flat again.

"What if there wasn't a monkey?" I bite at the skin of my thumbnail. "What if someone took the key from our bag when we were swimming? We just assumed the monkey thing was real because Leo suggested it. But did you *see* what happened?"

"No. I . . . But who would do that?"

"I don't know. All kinds of people."

"Wait, are you saying *Leo* took the key?"

"No, not Leo. It can't have been him. But someone was in here—"

"So, you're saying they broke in to—do what, though? Stare at you through the mosquito net?" He makes it sound like it's unheard of, like it would be such a waste of time. "Stevie, that's a crazy leap. Think about it rationally. Most people, if they break into a place, are looking for stuff to steal. Right? We're not missing money. Our passports are right there on the table. Your journal's there. My wallet. It doesn't make any sense."

"Not everyone's a burglar," I say quietly. "Sometimes they're just creeps."

Jacob puts his hand over mine. "Do you feel different? Are you hurt? I'm sorry. I should have asked you that right away—"

"No, I'm not—"

"—because if you are, let's go right now. Let's pack up and get back to the city and properly deal with this."

"I don't feel different." My head is low. "I'm just super freaked out."

"Okay." He strokes my fingers with his thumb. "Do you want to leave?"

"I don't know. I don't know what I want. Or where I want to be."

He puts his arms around me, pulling me into his chest. "This might all be part of the same thing."

"What thing?"

"We're in mourning. We're out of our element. We're all churned up. You said it yourself yesterday. You're haunted. You're having bad dreams." I nod miserably. "When you had those before, you got up in the night and crashed about a lot. You know you did that. If it wasn't me bumping furniture, it might have been you."

I take a deep breath in and out. "It probably wasn't anything."

"Most likely not."

"It's just a flimsy door. The wind blew it."

"Right. Not that we need anything sturdier. There's nobody here preying on us, Stevie. Nobody at all."

"Okay. No, I know. And I wasn't talking about Leo. He's a stand-up guy. A neurologist."

"Exactly. Well respected. He's just here on vacation, taking a break. I don't know if he likes his career."

"Right," I say, even though something's still tapping in my head.

"And you get a sense of people, don't you?" Jacob pulls back to look in my face. "You can tell if they're weird or not."

I hesitate. In my experience, people stash thoughts more than they show them. For example, my initial reaction to Leo. Or the moment we shared last night as we stood by the window—that look between us that had held something so deeply private. I definitely don't want to showcase any of that.

"You know, it could also be the malaria meds we're on," I say. "The Larium. Are you having weird dreams?"

"That's true! I'm not having any, but Leo's girlfriend said she's been getting side effects. She's . . . umm . . . hot all the time." He stops talking suddenly, as if he's lost his point.

"You met Leo's girlfriend?"

He snaps back into focus. "She joined us for drinks. But she left early. Her name is Tamsin." *He's avoiding eye contact. Why?* "I'm just saying, don't write off this whole adventure because—"

"What's she like?" I get up quietly and walk to the bathroom, where I run the water, splashing some on my face.

"Nice," he says. "Seems nice. She's British like him."

In the doorway, I hold both palms to my cheeks, cooling off. "Are we meeting up with them today?"

"Probably. I mean, if you want to." Is he blushing? He's busying himself with his watch strap.

"And we'll stay one more night and head to Rafiki Island tomorrow morning?"

"Yup. That's the plan."

"Jacob, did you tell anyone in the hut last night where we're heading next?"

As closed as the subject of the door and the chair is now, there's a sliver of doubt that remains in me. It's the same uneasiness I had as a kid, after my mom used to carry me to bed from the couch at two or three in the morning. I'd be drowsy, breathing in the smokiness of her hair, watching the lilt of my red sneaker as she carried me, my arms around her neck. In the morning, though, my feet were bare. My clothes weren't on me. When had that happened? Even at four years old it was unsettling. Something subtle had been done to me—a simple change into pajamas—that I couldn't quite account for.

Jacob's brow furrows and he sticks out his bottom lip. "I don't think I mentioned Rafiki Island at all. I might have told Leo I'm a diver . . ."

"Is he?"

"A diver? No. Not that he said. They're both from London. They seem kind of . . . land-based."

"Not like us, then. Not kids who grew up in the salty sea." A long-buried memory of night swims with Cassia threatens to engulf me but I push it back, moving across the room to kiss Jacob on the lips. His skin is sour, like old beer kegs in the pub basement. But still he won't look me in the eye.

"They haven't been together long, you know. Tamsin said she only met Leo backpacking a couple of months ago in Zim. She calls Zimbabwe 'Zim,' like that reception guy back in Nairobi. She's posh." He yawn stretches, and yet his voice doesn't match the indifference. "She calls Kenya 'Keen-yah,' too."

"Okay," I say.

"Honestly, Stevie." He stands, picking up his T-shirt from the floor and dragging it over his scruffy head. "There's not much you missed last night. Just Leo and I bro-drinking. Tamsin wasn't even there for most of it."

Did I ask if she was? His flurry of information seems strange, as does his need to downplay it.

"Come on," he says, pulling on board shorts, too. "Let's go for a swim. Leo says it's a cure-all for a hangover."

What else did you talk about? What else did he say? I wonder, but I manage not to ask it out loud. It's probably time to stop fueling crushes. I grab my bikini and get changed. We have one day at Diani Beach. Then it's just me and Jacob again, and we can press on, find our bearings.

———

I t's an hour or two later that I see the two of them walking toward us on the beach. The sun is beating down, baking the top of my scalp through my sun hat, even though Leo and Tamsin seem unaffected. What strikes me first is that I can't tell which of them is the more attractive because Tamsin is literally turn-your-head beautiful. Jacob has been avoiding that little detail. Suddenly all his skittishness falls into place.

I stare at her from a hundred feet away, squinting into the glare. Her dark hair is tied up in a knot on the top of her head, and she has a gracefulness in her limbs that makes her seem like she took ballet classes as a kid. She's dressed in a cool red sarong-skirt and a simple white T-shirt, well-cut, the sleeves ripped away with designer-label scruffiness. She's one of those women who move through the world with such certainty, who've made an alliance along the way that so few people get offered. A pact with the world, I mean—an assurance that all will continue to work in their favor. She looks like a girl who's best friends with her life.

"Jacob," I say, nudging him as he dozes in the shade. "They're here."

"Who?" he says, as if he's completely forgotten where we are. But when he catches sight of Tamsin, he dusts himself down and gets to his feet.

"Hello," Leo says as they reach us, and the four of us stand in a circle. "How's everyone today?"

"Pretty decent," Jacob says. "Everything's good."

I say nothing. I can't help but stare at Tamsin. Up close, she's amazingly like Cassia.

"How's the head, mate?" Leo bumps Jacob on the shoulder. The two of them are exactly the same height, but Leo's more cut with mus-cle. "You were keen on the beers last night."

"I was?" Jacob groans and runs a hand over the top of his head. But weren't they drinking together? Leo couldn't look fresher. Wearing nothing but board shorts, and with those pectoral muscles, he looks like he's come straight from the gym.

"Are you Stevie?" Tamsin steps forward, smiling. "I'm Tamsin. It sounds like you and I missed out on a big night."

"I think we did," I say.

"It was a good time," Leo says, staring at me.

"Have you just been for a swim?" Tamsin edges closer. "The water's beautiful here. We were in Cape Maclear and there were hippos in the lake. We had to be really careful."

"We did a canoe safari in Zim. Tamsin's idea." Leo rolls his eyes, mock-annoyed. "Hippos and crocs everywhere. And the bloody canoe tipped! This one!" He grips his hand onto the back of Tamsin's neck, jostles her. "She's always getting us into scrapes."

"What did you do?" I push back the brim of my hat. "When you hit the water? Did you think you were going to die?"

"Oh," Tamsin says, surprised by the gravity of my question. I shouldn't have asked it. But it's so rare to meet anyone who might have been to the same dark edge as me. Not many people understand what it means to stare at your own mortality or to see others grappling with theirs. Jacob, for example, has no concept of it.

"Leo and I managed to stay fairly well in the boat," Tamsin says, her green eyes intent on mine. "But the other two completely fell out. We had to form a triangle of boats around them and haul them back in. One of them was huge, too, a bit of a fatty. It took us a while to get him back in, while the girl had to tread water. She was having a total 'mare. Shrieking and splashing. It was bonkers. The guide had his paddle in the air like this—" She mimes a raised hammer, as if playing Whac-a-Mole in an arcade. "Because, you know, when you're being attacked by a crocodile, it's helpful if someone hits it now and again on the head."

We all laugh—including Tamsin, whose whole face lights up. Those eyes, that dark skin. She's the spitting image.

"So, what are your plans for the rest of the day?" Leo asks. "More swimming? Is anyone hungry? I could murder a sandwich."

"We're pretty wide open," Jacob says. "Right, Stevie?"

I nod vaguely. My brain is rattling through images of Cassia, of high school, spooling all of them around my feet in a reel. All this time I've spent haunted at home, and here I am in Africa, staring at the actual ghost.

"We could go for a bite to eat in the hut," Tamsin suggests. "Or meet for supper later. Double date!" She smiles at Leo, but he doesn't return it. "Us two have one more night here before we head out to Rafiki in the morning."

"Head . . . to where?" I say, the sun beating hotter all of a sudden.

"Rafiki Island," she says. "There's this dive camp I heard about. Apparently it's all totally eco-cool. It's three months without electricity or running water, and you all live together in this big—"

"GoEco?" Jacob glances at me and then back again. "Did I tell you about that?"

"What?" Tamsin asks. "No."

"But you registered for the camp?" He sends me a *I wasn't a blabbermouth* headshake. I stare back at him, wondering what the hell is happening.

"We signed up yesterday," Leo says. "Or the day before? Can't remember. Tamsin's in charge of the planning."

"It's run by this guy called Duran. What a mint name." Tamsin grins. "Why, what do you know about the island? Oh, no, have you heard that it's rubbish?"

"No, it's just . . . well, it's where we're going, too." Jacob's smile is tentative.

"Jacob took a job there," I add, my teeth sticking to my lips. Everything feels slightly dreamlike and chaotic.

"That's the job you were talking about?" Leo laughs and all of his abdominal muscles contract. "Christ. Small world."

"Does that mean you'll be our boss? Our *instructor*?" Tamsin draws out each syllable.

"I guess." Jacob stares hard at his flip-flops.

"Well, come on, then!" Leo puts his arm around him, turning toward the eating hut. "Let's go and have a pint and sketch out the rules for being friends with Management."

They move away up the beach, leaving me standing alone beside Tamsin.

"Are you okay?" she asks, tightening the knot of her hair. "You're chewing your nails a lot."

I lower my thumb from my lip. Smile.

"You're panicking," she says. "You're thinking, *Oh my bloody God, my trip's just been hijacked by two complete nutters and I need to go and change islands immediately.*"

I laugh, can't help it.

"Don't worry. I think we'll have fun. I've got a feeling." She puts her hand on my forearm, her fingertips cool on my skin. "It's what I love most about traveling, you know, all the serendipity. The paths just keep crossing. I've said bye to people in the morning at a hostel, got on a bus for, like, fourteen hours through the most random towns, and then run into the same friends again later when they rock up at the same bar. That never happens at home."

But this is more than that, I think. It's more than just random coincidence. To me, Tamsin's presence feels pivotal.

Just then two little children arrive alongside us, holding out jewelry and trinkets. Their hair is swirled on their heads. Tamsin bends to see what they have, touches one of them on the nose so they giggle, hands them money she's hidden in the waistband of her sarong. She stands, holding two woven bracelets.

"Here," she says, passing me one.

"You bought that for me?" My throat is dry with echoes of Cassia.

"It only cost me about four pence. And anyway, Leo wouldn't wear it. He keeps telling me to stop buying tat. Says kids are bunking off school to make stuff for tourists. But I think it's good for the locals. It keeps their economy going. Leo can be kind of a downer; don't tell him I said so."

I take the bracelet, wrap it around my wrist, let Tamsin tie it on.

"There," she says, comparing her arm with mine. "Now we're peas in a pod."

Again the skin of my scalp tightens, and I gasp out a laugh. *Peas in a pod.* Whatever's happening, it's more than serendipity.

"Rafiki Island will be good," I say. "We can hang out and ditch the downers."

"We totally can," she laughs. "Because life's too short. Don't you think?"

We head up the beach together to join the others, and for the first time since we landed, I feel almost at home.

12

LEO

Everything's falling into place. We're a foursome now, but it won't be long before I whittle it down. Double date canceled. Tamsin, unbeknownst to her, is not at all in charge of the planning.

Jacob and I sit at the same table we were at last night, sliding onto benches opposite each other. Ever since he's found out that we're all headed off tomorrow in the same direction, his excitement has been palpable yet restrained: he's like a child with a Happy Meal, unsure if he's allowed to open the box.

"So, you're staying for the whole three months?" he asks. "Duran had space for you?"

"It seems so. You'll have to ask Tamsin about the fine print."

"And you have your dive tickets?" Underneath all his questions is a hum of nervousness. He keeps glancing at the door.

"What's on your mind?" I ask him.

"Look, I'm just going to say this quickly before the girls get here. It's great that you're coming to Rafiki and everything, but Stevie has this . . . this bee in her bonnet . . ."

I cross my arms, tilt my head. *Spit it out, Jacob. Let's get down to the nitty-gritty.*

"And I . . . I shouldn't have said all that stuff last night about being . . . you know."

I shake my head, feign confusion. I'm not going to make it easy for him.

"Curious," he says.

"Oh, about sleeping with other women?"

He widens his mouth and hunches as if to say, *Lower your voice, buddy, are you trying to get me in trouble?*

But the thing is, maybe I am.

"Don't worry," I say. "Your secret is safe with me."

"It's not even a secret." He rubs salt from his eyebrow. "It's not real. It's just something I think, not something I do."

"Isn't that just a matter of stages?" I ask. "Thoughts and actions? In my world, one thing invariably leads to the other."

"No," he says. "Not necessarily. I mean, I think most days at work that I'd like to slap my own father, but it's not like I actually do it."

You should try it, I think. *See where it leads. You'll be amazed at how slippery the slope gets.*

"So I'd appreciate it if we could keep that convers—"

"What kind of a bee in her bonnet?" I ask.

He shakes his head, trying to keep up. It must be hideous in here with a hangover. The hut is about a thousand degrees and Apologize hasn't brought us any drinks yet.

"Stevie? No, it's nothing," he says. "She just has this idea right now that nowhere is . . . safe. I mean, I get it. We've had some bad luck. But she's worried I told a whole bunch of people where we were going, and now with your plans being exactly like ours, she's—"

"Oh, that's a shame. It's no fun, going around feeling edgy like that." *I know more about her than you do*, I think. *Isn't that interesting?*

"Don't say anything to her about that, either. Her edginess, I mean. And if she asks, can you be clear that Rafiki was your idea?"

Poor Jacob. All these secrets stacking up on top of him like lumber. Pretty soon he's not going to be able to breathe.

The girls walk into the hut right then, Tamsin leading the way. They take seats next to us in the expected formation, almost as if joining opposing teams. As competitors, they'd represent different hemispheres: Tamsin from the steamy South; Stevie from the cool, true North. I wonder who'd win. Beside me, Tamsin pulls off her T-shirt, sitting forward in her bikini top, her skin lovely against the pale mint green of the fabric. I glance at Jacob and catch him looking. He immediately fixates on the table.

"Get the beers in!" Tamsin says, just as Apologize deposits four cold bottles of Tusker. Jacob swallows as if his mouth is flooding with saliva.

"I don't think I can choke down a beer," he says.

"Are you feeling that rough?" Tamsin smiles languidly. "But you know what they say. Hair of the dog and all that."

"Maybe some food with it, then." Jacob nods at Apologize, who returns with a plate of mealie meal and sauce, which Jacob prods at with his forefinger. The mealie meal indents like a sponge.

"You've bought bracelets," I say to Tamsin. "Matching ones."

"I know." She twirls the woven fabric around her wrist. "Aren't they lush?"

"Schoolchildren made them for us," Stevie adds, darting a blue-eyed, mischievous look at Tamsin. And it stings, to think they've bonded this way. That Stevie would choose such obvious branding.

"How do you feel about the impact of tourism on developing countries, Jacob?" I ask.

"The what now?"

"It is, at the very least, worth some kind of debate." As I fold my arms, I can feel my heart beating against my wrist.

"No, it isn't," Tamsin says. "Not now, anyway. We're making friends, Leo. It's meant to be fun, not debatey."

I wince and wonder if anyone saw it. Again and again, she makes me look bad. How come I'm never the fun one?

"Let's play a drinking game." Tamsin's lips are curved and dangerous. "Let's play Never Have I Ever. My friends and I used to play it all the time at school. It's the bollocks."

"Is that a good thing?" Jacob pushes his plate away.

"Leo will go first," she replies, ignoring the question. "He'll say something he's never done and then if you *have* done it, you need to drink. Go on, Leo."

Never have I ever gone to prison for murder? I think. *Because never have I ever been caught?*

"Never have I ever kissed a girl," I say instead, smiling as I take a huge swig of beer from my bottle.

"Le-o! You're meant to say something you've *never* done," Tamsin tuts.

"My throat's dry." I scratch at my stubble. "I needed to wet it."

All of us drink. *All of us.*

Jacob turns to Stevie on the bench beside him. "When did *you* kiss a girl?"

"See!" Tamsin laughs. "Amazing. I told you this game was the bollocks."

"Never have I ever seen a ghost," Stevie says, keeping her eyes low.

"Dark." Tamsin rotates her beer. "I like it." She doesn't drink.

"Unexpected," I say, lifting my own beer and sipping. "What? Everyone's haunted in some way, aren't they?"

Jacob stares at the table. There's a pause while all of Tamsin's fun threatens to disappear.

"Let's move on," she says. "Who's going next?"

"I'll go again." It occurs to me that this game presents something of an opportunity. "Okay, moving on from spirits and ghosts . . . Never have I ever watched someone die." *You have and I have, Stevie*, I think. *Wear all the woven bracelets you want; it's me who's your soul mate.*

"Oh, my God, Leo, you're doing it again," Tamsin says. Everyone stares at me. "He's too much. Isn't he?" She kisses me along the jawline. "It's lucky he's so good-looking. Okay, I'm changing that statement on account of it being bonkers. Here's a better one: Never have I ever done something on purpose that I know is wrong."

Now Stevie and I are the only ones who drink. Can't she see how in sync we are?

"What is going on?" Jacob nudges her, coloring. "Don't you want to play or something?"

"What? I'm the only one playing properly." Stevie looks from face to face. She has a point. "Do we need to go over the rules?"

"What have you done that's so wrong?" Jacob asks. "Or are you still talking about all the kissing with all of the girls?" He looks like his head is too hot.

"I was seventeen when I met you." Stevie drinks again, as if that explains everything.

"Okay, pressing on," Tamsin says, battling a smirk, "let's find some neutral ground, if there is any. Never have I ever had a relative who's completely and totally lost it." She sips immediately. "My great-aunt Veronica is off her head. She thinks dead people live in the attic, and never takes her eyes off the ceiling. She's amazing to sit next to at Christmas dinner."

Jacob smears one hand against the other in his lap. Condensation slips down the side of his beer, settling in a puddle on the table. Trouble is coming. He knows it and so do I. Beside him, Stevie drains her bottle entirely, sets it down, wipes her mouth.

"Wow," Tamsin says. "Your crazy relative must be a corker."

"Oh, she's a real treat," Stevie says.

"Everyone's got one!" Tamsin leans across and clinks her bottle against Stevie's empty one, grazing her breasts against the wood of the tabletop. "Who's yours, then?"

But Jacob holds up his hand. "Stevie, let's head back to the bungalow. It's crazy hot in here." But it's too late. We've already slid too far.

"My mother." Stevie's eyes are hard-cut ice. Tamsin stops laughing. "When I was six years old, she walked out on me in the middle of the night and never came back. I woke up and our apartment was completely empty. There was just a trail of her clothing across the floor, a shirt and a pair of pants I recognized. It looked like it was her, though, lying down, laid out for me. I was just little. I didn't understand how her body had vaporized."

"Jesus," I say. None of those details are written in her diary.

"I ran out of the apartment and went to my grandmother's house across town. I didn't even take shoes."

Jacob rubs his hand over his eyes and exhales.

"Holy shitballs," Tamsin says. "You win."

"Do I, though?" Stevie stands. "I'm sorry, guys, but honestly I don't think I like this game. It's not the right way to meet people."

"Let's stop playing," I suggest, with that same pit in my stomach I always had with my mother. If only I could reach her. If only I could get her on my own.

Stevie steps over the bench. "You go ahead. It's okay. But I'm out." She turns and walks straight out of the hut.

The three of us sit in silence for a minute.

"If Stevie was an animal," Tamsin says, her tone impressed, "she'd be covered in spikes. Is that what you like about her, Jacob?"

"Not spikes," Jacob corrects her. "Just armor. She's needed it." For the first time in twenty minutes, he picks up his beer and drinks properly.

I sip, too, watching Jacob over the lip of my bottle. Firstly, he's not going after her. And secondly, heavily armored or not, there's always a way in.

13

STEVIE

I walk back through the trees to the bungalow, past a ring of dread-locked backpackers playing hacky-sack and laughing. It isn't that I'm mad at the others. I just can't play drinking games like that. I guess I'm not very good at asking big questions lightly.

Nobody comes running out of the hut after me. Not even Jacob. Perhaps they're all giving me space. Or, more likely, he's fascinated by Leo and Tamsin. I get it—they *are* fascinating. They're both so drop-dead hot and seem so into being friends with us. Why? It's not like we bring much to the table. Tamsin can't know how much she looks like Cassia; she has no idea she's momentous to me. And the way she rep-resents Leo—he's a downer, he's not fun—it seems strange that they're even together. There's almost a tinge of anger about them. So, are they together because the sex is good? Before I can help it, the image of them in bed together fills my mind and I blink fast, trying not to dwell on it. Sex is definitely enough of a backpacker reason to be together. But are they swingers? Surely the possibility ought to have occurred to Jacob, too, except that he has no radar for unusual behavior. His parents have been nuts forever, and he doesn't seem to have noticed.

I first met his mom when I walked home with him that day in eleventh grade. His parents live in a crumbling old farmhouse, long since abandoned by any livestock. There are no other farm buildings around the property—no barns, no outhouses, no feeling of anything working or growing. Every time I'm there, it looks like everyone's left in a panic. We walked into the cottage that first day and stooped to take off our shoes, bumping together in the tightness of the coatroom, which smelled faintly of cat litter.

"How many people live here?" I asked. Every peg seemed to have four coats on it, each of them thick and quilted.

"Me, my mom, and my pop." Jacob tried to hook his backpack onto a peg, but the coats wouldn't let him get purchase. "Set your stuff anywhere. Come in."

We pushed forward into a small kitchen, the vinyl of the floor ringed with brown near the stove. All four plants along the windowsill by the sink were dead, their papery leaves hanging low from the plant pot rims, wispy like old hair. The sound of game-show cheering came from the next room.

"Mom!" Jacob opened the fridge and closed it again. "I have a friend here."

There was a clattering, something china knocking against a table and thudding to the carpet. The game show went quiet. I heard a hurried padding, like a pony trotting on sawdust toward hay.

"Holy moly." Jacob's mother rounded the corner of the fridge wearing track pants and an enormous sweater. "You never said you were bringing friends home." She patted her hair flat as she glanced around the kitchen, tallying clutter. She was small next to her son, and unlikely. Round where he was long.

"It's okay, Mom. We're going upstairs to paint."

"Well, it's a lovely thing having company." Mrs. Jones pulled the sleeve of her sweater low over her fist and swept her arm across the tablecloth on the kitchen table. I felt crumbs freckle my shins. "How exciting. Do have a seat." She looked straight at me, her head tilted. "Oh, goodness."

I bit my lip, unsure what she'd noticed.

"This is Stevie." Jacob stretched, his fingertips almost touching the ceiling. I could see the tight line of his stomach above his pants.

"Is it?" Mrs. Jones blinked, unsure of her next direction. "And what do *you* do, Stevie?"

"Ummm. I go to high school," I said.

She nodded once, then moved to the sink, where she ran all four pot plants under hard tap water. "You're not that girl from the paper, are you? Stevie Erickson. The one in the accident with the police and all?"

I cleared my throat. *Accident.* The town had packaged it so neatly. I said nothing.

"Mom!" Jacob shot her a pointed look. "Come on, Stevie. We're going to my room."

"No closed doors!" Jacob's mom shouted as he led me out through a living room that had an even lower ceiling. All the curtains were closed and magazines littered the floor, a variety of them open and faceup as if Mrs. Jones had spent the day listlessly kneeling to read each one. Another plant sat in the corner, brown, forlorn.

Once we were upstairs and inside his room, Jacob closed the door and leaned his back against it.

"Don't you ever bring friends home?" I asked.

"Why would you ask that?"

I shook my head, looking around. Every wall was white, almost institutionally. Jacob had a bed on the floor, a white pillow, a white sheet, a leather notebook, a copy of a Hemingway novel, a pen. On a table that sloped in the corner were a hundred loose sheets of thick paper. His windows were open, no curtains, no blinds, the breeze of late afternoon giving the papers a wash that sounded like the movement of water.

"My mom knows me. She's protective." Jacob stayed by the door, his hands behind his back. "But isn't that kind of the point?"

"I don't know what the point is." I stepped toward the papers on the desk.

"No—wait—don't look at those." He hurried over, but it was too late. I saw a hundred different outlines of a face, the cut of a jawline, some even closer-up images of the shape of pale eyes. It was indisputable: I was on his every page. When I turned to him, his head hung low, curls of dark hair shielding his face.

"It's not what you think," he said. "I'm not obsessed or anything." My breathing had quickened. "It's just a symmetry thing. Please don't leave."

"What does that mean?"

"You're beautiful." He shrugged. His eyes were clear and uncomplicated. "I like you. I just like you."

He said it so simply. No possibility of harm. He was standing in madness and it didn't seem to matter. At the time that was such a relief: I wrapped his security around me like a blanket.

But now I'm not so sure. Because Leo and Tamsin aside, something isn't quite right at this beach resort, just like it wasn't right on the train, or in the first hostel. Is it me? After all, with the exception of Jacob, I'm the only one who's been in all three locations. And yet I can't shake this feeling of being watched, of being followed. Jacob's radar has always been so different—he can't spot what's strange and what isn't, or perhaps he simply doesn't care. Nattie used to call that his "nice boy" approach to the world, his generosity of heart. *You stick with him, my lovely, he won't lead you wrong.* But was she right? He'll tell anything to anyone. And out here, is it really okay to be so open and trusting?

I decide not to go back to the bungalow, but instead head down the beach to the water's edge. There's a tree near the shoreline that's wider than the rest, with a perfect curve in its trunk to lean against. I sit quietly for a while in the shade, palm leaves whispering above me. Far offshore where the reef starts, little crests of waves break. Above me the sun bears down. It's unsettling to have sat in the hut just now showing near-strangers the most desecrated parts of me. Normally, the only person I'd have spoken to honestly about my mom would have been my grandmother.

In the years after my mother left me, I used to sit on the beach a lot with Nattie. It was never a beach like this one: it was bitter, and angry, like a metaphor. Nattie wore lace-up, mannish shoes and sat with her legs straight out, comically thick at the ankles. She liked the beach most in the winter, where we'd spend hours bundled in scarfs, watching the churn of the sea. It reminded her of Cornwall, she said, all the wildness. She'd grown up in England but had been wooed by an American GI in the war.

"Useless, he was," she used to say, "all talk and no trousers. And your mother's the same, I'm sorry to say, even though I raised her to be better. She chose complete pointlessness when it came to your father. But *you*, my love? We're breaking the cycle with you."

I knew my mother wasn't dead. From time to time, she sent postcards from random American towns with pictures of birds or monuments on them. Every Christmas, a parcel would arrive with a tired old grocery bag inside it full of ill-informed, cigarette-smoke-permeated gifts. A bra when I was only seven. Beer-flavored chewing gum. A Ouija board. Nattie vetted them after the first year or two and then canned them altogether. She knew that for me every parcel was just a beacon of not being wanted. Mom was alive. Oh, she was the life of the party. She just couldn't be bothered with me.

Growing up, my grandmother held me tight to herself, barely letting glimpses of the wider world in, but even so, there were years where she worried that the genetic cycle she dreaded hadn't altered at all. As I grew so did my anger, until I walked around so pressurized that even the slightest prod might burst me. And then came losing Cassia, and I was indecipherable.

So when I brought Jacob home one day in eleventh grade, Nattie's eyes popped clean out of her head. I pushed open the front door of her old cobblestone cottage and stepped into our living room. Beyond, in the little galley kitchen, Nattie was bending to pull a pan from a drawer. The backs of her knees were mottled and complex with veins. She stood up and turned, her baking apron fingerprinted, the tie of the apron dividing her body into two cardboard boxes.

"Where've you been?" Nattie said. "I was starting to think you were dead in a ditch."

"Sorry. Jacob and I took the long path home." I kicked off my shoes by the radiator, gesturing Jacob forward into the house. He had to duck to get in.

"Who's this now?" Nattie walked out of the kitchen, draping a dish towel over her left shoulder. "You're a tall drink of water."

Jacob stood uncertainly in his skinny pants, his slip-on skateboarding shoes he never went skateboarding in.

"This is Jacob Jones," I said. "He's in my art class. He walked me home."

"I thought chivalry was dead in a ditch, too." Nattie arched an eyebrow while extending a floury hand for Jacob to shake. He hurried forward, even bowing slightly as he said hello.

"Are you staying for dinner?" Nattie asked him.

"I don't think so." He pulled the sleeves of his sweater low over his wrists, almost making gloves. "Am I?"

"He's not."

"No, I'm not. I didn't think so. I'm actually . . . going now. I should go." Having been in the cottage all of a minute, Jacob turned to the front door and pulled it open. "It was very nice to meet you, Mrs. Erickson."

"I daresay we'll meet again, Jacob Jones. Close the door, you're letting a draft in."

Jacob hurried through the gap, widening it again at the last minute. "Bye, Stevie."

I raised a shy hand. Once the door was shut again and the sound of outside had clamped quiet, my grandmother poked me in the ribs.

"Well, then," she said. "That's more like it."

"What does that mean?" I blushed. Ordinarily, I'd have withdrawn to my room upstairs by now.

"He's elegant."

"He is?"

"Nice manners for starters and that's not a given these days. Put him in a tuxedo and give him a hairbrush, he'd be a showstopper."

"Normally you hate my friends," I mumbled.

"Well, I do, and I tell you what, I'm not wrong. All's you've brought home of late is a long string of reprobates and hooligans." She reached out and patted my forearm. "No, you mark my words. That one's different. Buy him some new shoes and I don't mind him at all."

I stayed longer in the kitchen that night, helping my grandmother peel vegetables. A bridge was forming, bricked fresh by the existence of Jacob.

I lean my head against the rough bark of the palm tree, liking the snag of wood against my sun hat. For a moment I feel entirely peaceful—the memories of my grandmother are soothing to sift through—when out of the corner of my eye I spot Leo heading out of the hut and down the beach toward the group of hacky-sackers. Is he coming to find me? I can't tell if I want him to or not. He reaches the other backpackers and their game stops. The boys in the group withdraw as the girls press forward. They cluster around him, vying to be noticed, the prettiest two of them all but shoving each other out of the spotlight. From where I sit, I can't hear what they're saying, but Leo's interested in a necklace one of the girls has around her throat. He leans in, his fingertips at her collarbone, breathing close to her neck. She preens, sweeps her long hair to the side, exposing her skin to him, desperate not to move him away.

And then, behind him and soundlessly, Tamsin emerges from the eating hut and stands there, watching her boyfriend. Her head stays very still. Leo touches the second girl on the forearm, then says something and laughs. I can see the indents of his muscle from here. Tamsin walks smoothly toward the three of them as my breathing quickens. Surely Leo is busted? Or does he really not know he's garnering a fan club?

But as she arrives at the edge of their circle, Tamsin does nothing very noticeable at all. She simply stands, taller than the other girls, exuding a kind of power that somehow alters every dynamic around her. The girls step away from Leo. The same girl shows Tamsin the necklace, at which Tamsin looks unimpressed. The other girl compliments her wildly, almost frantically, pulling at the thread of her T-shirt fabric, adoring the cut of her sarong. Tamsin absorbs the compliments—composed, regal. She says something light to Leo, who takes her hand and kisses it near the veins of her wrist. And when she walks away, he follows her, trotting behind her, a peon in the sovereignty of her train.

14

LEO

We have one more night at Diani, then will travel together to Rafiki in the morning. All afternoon, Jacob hangs out with me. For a man who drank heavily last night, he doesn't seem to be opting for a nap.

"I want to get fitter while I'm out here," he tells me as we sit on beach recliners, the sky filtering its way toward dusk. "The world responds differently to guys who are built."

"Yeah?" I say, watching Stevie and Tamsin on loungers twenty feet from us. "Gaining muscle is just science. You're already strong and tall. Eat what I eat. Do what I do. You'll be like me in no time."

He pauses, the first hint that this might be more about competition than I thought. But I haven't got time to worry about that. There's no doubt Stevie's forged some kind of bond with Tamsin. They're talking in voices too soft for me and Jacob to hear.

"They've taken to each other." Jacob follows my gaze. "It's a good thing. Stevie needs something to lock her in."

Yes, but it categorically cannot be Tamsin.

"This job on Rafiki is all we have," he sighs, continuing his need to tell me things. "There's nothing to go home to."

"What about your job with your father?" I ask. "Jones Boys' Boats."

He hesitates and inwardly, I freeze. He's never told me the name of his business. Stevie wrote it down in her diary.

"No . . ." He regroups, assigning it to harmless details thrown out over beers. "I wrote him an email the day we left. Told him it was unlikely I'd come back to the barnacle job."

"He's okay with that, is he?"

"He hasn't replied."

"Oh dear," I laugh. "Perhaps you've slapped him after all."

Jacob shrugs. "Maybe it's a rite of passage. At some point, we have to separate ourselves from our dads."

Yes, I think, *hallelujah*.

"Do you get on with yours?" Jacob asks.

"It's not a question I consider anymore." I sit up, rearrange the towel behind my back, which has wrinkled. "He died in February of last year."

"Oh, I'm sorry," Jacob says.

I'm not, I think.

He'd called me to the house the January before he died. I got out of my car, the monolithic stone frontage looming over the driveway, all the windows polished so zealously that they rejected any light rather than absorbed it. *It's only a matter of time*, I thought, *before a house becomes the very essence of its inhabitants.*

I hadn't been back for twelve years. Not at Christmas, not for birthdays, not all the way through medical school. In all that time, all I'd done was send Dad a few emails. Factual ones with short sentences, the full stops punched in like rivets. I banged hard on the front door, the weight of the old iron knocker familiar against my finger-tips. Footsteps squelched on the marbled floors of the hallway. When the door heaved open, I looked down into the face of a diminutive woman in her sixties wearing a white starched shirt. A gold name badge on her lapel read *Dolores*.

"Are you the son?" she asked.

"Yes. The prodigal one."

"Come in." She stepped aside. "He's been asking for you."

Why? I thought. It wasn't like he asked for me when I lived here.

At the door of his study, she stopped. It was surprising. I'd been told my father was ill, but I'd imagined a death bed, with pallor, tubes, and beeping. Wasn't this the point of the visit—for him to apologize, fully and hurriedly, before his time ran out? But when I entered, Dad was sitting at his desk. He was in his midfifties by then and had shrunk since the last time I'd seen him. His chest looked concave, his jawline haggard. And yet he sat tall with both hands on the lid of his laptop, still wearing a wedding ring, tidy at the collar and cuffs.

"Come in, Leopold," he said. "Sit down. Dolores, could you bring us coffee, please?"

"I don't want any. Thank you." I glanced at the bookshelves I'd destroyed. They'd been replaced, as if no damage had ever been done.

"Water, then," Dad said to Dolores. And then to me, "Please sit down."

Dolores left, and I did as I was told. We stared at each other. Finally, Dad cleared his throat.

"I'm very glad you came. It's been rather a long time." He raised his eyebrows, aiming toward gentle comedy.

That's not an apology, I thought. *Don't let him off the hook.*

"You look well, my boy. You've grown into quite the young man."

"I'm twenty-seven."

"Gosh, has it been that long?" He sighed and moved his hands from his laptop. I couldn't believe the casualness of the man. He was acting as if I'd been away on vacation, not banished from his life for over a decade. "Well, you look strong. Just as you should. What have you been up to? Why not catch me up a bit, give me the highlights?"

Oh, I don't know, Dad. Surviving military school, which was more or less a correctional facility, thanks for sending me. Making it into medical college, specializing, working my arse off without any help from you.

"I'm fine. I work in neurology. Things are good."

"Oh, great." His shoulders were strangely bony under his cashmere sweater. "A science man. I always said it. Good for you."

But that wasn't why he'd invited me over. He hadn't brought me out of exile to congratulate me.

"How ill are you?" I asked.

Dad's laugh wheezed. "Oh, I'm ill enough. Ill enough, thank you."

"Have you told Mum?"

A flicker of something unusual passed over my father's face. Was it regret? Vulnerability?

"She may have got wind of it."

I don't know how long my mother stayed with Dad after he'd sent me away. It was obvious she'd hated the plan but had been given no final say in it. *My darling, he won't be talked out of it!* she'd whispered in the dark of my bedroom, the night before I was due to leave. Every few seconds, she turned back to the door, terrified she'd be captured in enemy territory. *But don't panic. Listen to me: opportunities always arise. Just because you get put in a place doesn't mean you have to stay there.* The next day, she'd refused to come for the car journey to Kent, and the goodbye hug she gave me felt desperate. And yet it wasn't as if she'd arrived to rescue me at any point. I never did understand the vanishing act she'd done, too.

"Won't she want to see you?" I asked my father. "Or does she really not care about you at all?"

It was a cruel thing to say but I couldn't help it. Anything sharp I could think of I'd throw.

"Ha," Dad said. "No, I think it's safe to say she's moved on."

You haven't, though, I thought, staring at the ring on my father's fourth finger. *Sad old man, trapped in all the love you lost.*

"Here's the thing, however," Dad said, wrenching back some confidence, some textbook control. "Obviously your mother's out of the will. Oh, don't balk at me, Leopold. Of course she is. She married into my money and she married out of it. It's basic cause and effect."

"Okay," I said, starting to feel sick. The room was too hot, too small, too familiar.

"Which leaves my entire estate with really only one rightful recipient. Do you know what that means?"

I sat still in my chair. *Here we go*, I thought. The estate was worth millions, it had to be.

"Do you know what I think about as I sit here wasting away?" Dad leaned forward, light from the lamp behind him giving his skin a jaundiced glow. "I think about the most important moments in my life. And those who were alongside me at the time."

"Are you talking about me?" My heart was beating fast. It was the closest my father had ever been to contrite.

"What? I'm talking about life, Leo. I was in the military for thirty-two years. The Asia-Pacific region—Thailand, Indo, the Philippines."

"I know that. I lived with you, remember?"

"It was always dangerous work, but we were highly skilled, trained for typhoons or terrorists. We got chaps out of buildings, we got chaps in."

"Dad, I know this—"

"No, you don't." He sighed loudly. "You left before I told you anything interesting. Do you know that we helped people and hurt people, depending on the directive?"

"I don't know why you're . . . Hurt people how?"

"The real stories I have aren't social, Leopold. We were all doing the jobs that nobody else wanted to."

"Okay."

"I'm changing my will and leaving everything I own to the British army. My entire estate. I wanted to tell you in person."

My pulse beat in a steady drum at my neck while the inside of my head felt scribbled in red. My fingers were itching.

"I hope you can understand my position. I called you here simply to explain."

"That's so kind of you," I said.

Just then, the door behind me opened and Dolores walked in with a rattling tea tray. She placed a silver cafetière, a cup, cream, and sugar in front of my father. Then, turning, she put her hand to her lip.

"Oh. Water?" she said. "I forgot."

"It's fine. I didn't want it anyway." I watched as she left the room again.

"I appreciate you might be shocked. But to be fair, you haven't—"

I stood and moved toward the bookshelves, facing the war biographies with my back to my father.

"—featured in my life very much. I'm afraid you and I have rather missed out on the relationship I'd envisioned."

I snorted, turning around. "For the first fifteen years of my life, you were gone the whole time. And for the next twelve, you had no interest in seeing me. So, no, it hasn't quite been the bond of the century."

Dad moved the wedding ring on his finger, around and around and around. "I felt it best that you learn some independence out in the world. You were a pampered child. A mummy's boy."

"I was not," I said.

"At Ridings, I forbade your mother from contacting you. So, yes, I suppose you can put that on me." He paused while I battled to control my breathing. "However, the choice of that school was hers alone. She's the one who picked it for you. And I'm afraid her *continued* silence is something she's devised all on her own."

"Liar!" I shouted, the sudden loudness alarming even to me. "Fucking lies! She would never have done that to me! Never sent me away!" I should have left. I should have walked out of the room right at that moment, but I didn't. And from there, everything went wrong so fast.

"Leo?" Jacob prods me in the shoulder from his beach chair. "Did you hear anything I just said?"

"Gosh," I said. "Sorry. I got lost there for a minute."

"I asked you how your father died. But, you know, it's okay if you don't want to talk about it."

"Suspiciously," I say. "There was a whole court case. He was a rich man. It was a terrible business."

"Someone attacked him?" Jacob looks horrified. "*Murdered* him?"

I nod. "He was found dead in his stately home."

"Holy shit. And they caught the guy?"

"Yes and no." I shift on my lounger again, can't seem to get comfortable. "They caught him, but they couldn't convict him. Didn't have enough evidence. In the end, the man walked free."

"Jesus." Jacob exhales. "That's terrible. And I thought *our* lives were complicated. No wonder you needed a break." He pauses. "What was your last name again?"

"Asher," I say, holding out my hand. "Leo Asher. You're right. I've never properly introduced myself. This traveling lark—I tell you—you can spend weeks with a person and never find out the most basic facts."

"Good to meet you." Jacob shakes my hand, his smile kind. "Jacob Jones. But you knew that already."

What a great guy he is. What a champion. It's such a shame he's the one in the way.

15

STEVIE

On the horizon, the sun is melting into the sea, turning the sky to pastel. Tamsin and I lie on beach recliners next to each other, the murmur of the boys' voices behind us. For the past hour she's been telling me about her life at home—the job at The Ruin, a celebrity-hotspot gin bar in Soho where they serve drinks in china teacups and all the waitresses are models (*not me, though, get real*); the little sister she adores and would do anything for, even though she listens to rap music (*she thinks she's cool; who is she trying to kid?*); and the fact of her parents' wealth, the trust fund she'll inherit in less than two years (*you know, as long as I don't fuck up by then*).

"Does Leo know you're going to be rich?" I ask, and she shakes her head.

"It hasn't come up. When he met me in Zimbabwe, he just wanted to be with me. He followed me from hostel to hostel."

"That's sweet," I say, wondering if I mean it.

"He was so insistent we hang out," she sighs, enjoying his masterfulness in the story, even though from what I saw on the beach earlier, it's her who holds more of the power.

"Do you think you'll stay together your whole trip?"

"Oh, we're easy come, easy go." She laughs, dangling her hand in the gap between recliners. "We're a backpacking romance, after all. Playing it by ear. We're not really bothering with are-we-aren't-we conversations."

How undefined their relationship is, I think, wondering what that kind of freedom must feel like. Jacob has long been established as the savior of my driftwood soul. He's always seen me that way, as something to be helped. And yet it's not like I can blame him for that: I've always let him.

Beside me, Tamsin takes several pictures of the sky, then turns the phone and takes one of me. I don't have time to smile. She cups her hand around her eyes to review the photo.

"Hottie," she says, and I feel the blood heat up in my face. "I'm posting that. You should follow me on Insta. I'll tag you."

"Okay," I say, flattered. The only girl who ever called me a hottie before was Cassia. Something stirs in me, something that's been silenced for a very long time. I glance back at the boys, but the two of them don't seem to be talking to each other. Jacob's looking at Leo, who's lost in thought.

"What's he like?" Tamsin asks, glancing back, too. "Is he all soulful and sensitive?"

"Jacob? He's . . . yes, he's a thinker. An artist. He's quiet and . . . safe. In high school, he used to bring novels to class and read them when he was done with the assignment."

"Really?" She glances down at my ring finger and smiles. "You've been together since school and you're not engaged?"

I slide my hand under my thigh. "He hasn't asked me. I don't think we'll get married."

"How come?" The question is so basic it causes me to pause.

"I don't think we need to." But even as I say it, the sentence rattles and clangs. Something in me is lifting its head.

"Good for you. Marriage is an outdated construct anyway—it blatantly doesn't fit anyone I know. How could it? Who you are at twenty-five is never going to be who you are at fifty. It's like trying to draw a line around something fluid. I seriously don't know why people bother."

I find myself nodding. Jacob and I so rarely talk about marriage, but every time we do, I feel a clammy grip of panic. I feel it now, too, but it's coupled with a different fear—as if all the hidey-holes I've dug in my life are about to be busted open.

"Jacob's sensitive," she says. "Is that what you like about him? His *emotional availability?*" Her words come out slanted through a smile as she puts her phone away.

"He's not *that* available—"

"Does he cry after you make love?"

"Tamsin! 'Make love'?! Eww—" Heat gathers for real in my face. Talking about *sex* with Tamsin? I don't know if I can.

"Does he leave you love poems?"

"No—"

"Sculpt you out of clay? I bet every drawing he does is of you."

I hesitate. "They're not. Not anymore . . ."

"Oh, but they *were!*" She claps her hands together. "You're his muse! Oh my God, that's amazing. Completely unhot, though."

"Why do you say that?"

"Nobody wants to be hero-worshipped. Where's the challenge in that?" She leans over so that I can feel her words on my neck as she speaks. "What you need, sister, is a little less safety and a lot more chase."

I blush deeper, although I doubt Tamsin spots it in the fading light. Everything with her feels intimate. Is this just how she communicates? She's like a street performer I watched once with my grandmother, unfurling gold coins from behind the ears of children. *Look what I've found here*, went the act, *but no, no, you can't keep it*. I learned that day that magicians only offer their audience knowledge to further distract them. But that was okay—they could take what they wanted, if it meant I got to see magic unfold. Tamsin is no different. Here she is, turning us all this way and that, every movement she makes seamless and mesmerizing, until before we know it, we're totally caught up in the dance.

I stay longer on the beach with her than Jacob does with Leo. By the time we get up to go back to our cabins, the stars are on fire in the sky.

"See you in the morning?" Tamsin says, tracing her fingertips down my forearm as she peels away toward whichever is her bungalow.

"Checkout's at ten."

"Okay, sleep well. And no making love!" She stumbles away giggling, and I laugh, too, giddy as I make my way back to Bungalow 8.

Inside, Jacob is lying on the bed scrolling through stuff on his phone. By the door, his backpack is tidy and ready to go.

"Hey," I say. "Everything okay?"

"Yup." He frowns at his screen, doesn't look up.

"Are you looking up how to get to Rafiki?" I kick off my flip-flops, sit on the end of the bed.

"No," he says, glancing up. "I already know how."

"Okay."

"You've had fun." He stares back at the phone. Strange that it isn't a question.

"Yeah, I like Tamsin. I think I can be friends with her." Deep inside, whatever is waking up in me shifts again, but I tense all the muscles in my stomach, bat it back down.

"Good." Jacob scrolls. "Well done. That's great." His tone is super condescending. *You're making real progress, Stevie. What an important breakthrough for you.* "Have you noticed how she looks like your old friend?"

"Who?" I say, coloring. Because that's my ghost. She's mine to inhabit.

"Cassia." He sets his phone down on the bed. "Tamsin looks very like her."

"A little, I guess." *Back off, Jacob. Don't you dare get into it.*

He shrugs.

"Are you still hungover?" My voice is flat.

"No."

"Did you have fun with Leo?"

He sighs and sits up, buffs his pillow. "You know what? It's the weirdest thing. I've just been googling him and he's got, like, no online presence whatsoever."

"What do you mean?" I crawl toward him. "Why were you googling him?"

"He told me his name—Leo Asher—and said there'd been this whole media circus around the death of his dad last year. Or, at least, he said there'd been a court case. I thought British tabloids loved that kind of story. I was looking for a headline with his name in it."

"Why?"

"I don't know." He stares at me. "Am I being too nosy?"

"No, I mean why was there a court case?"

"Oh, he told me his dad was killed. I guess someone came into his house and took him out. Leo said it was about money."

"Jesus! That's horrible."

"Right? No wonder the guy's rethinking his life."

"And bird-dogging Tamsin from hostel to hostel." I bite my lip, aware suddenly that I sound way too jealous. *What do you care?* Jacob should ask me, and the question is valid. Why do I care? But instead he lifts the phone.

117

"He's been through a lot," he sighs. "I probably shouldn't be rifling through his privacy like this. It's just morbid curiosity. I wanted a few more details."

"I would have done the same," I say, lying down so my body's alongside his. "There's *nothing* online?"

"Nothing. No Asher court case, no murder inquiry, no Facebook account in Leo's name, even." He taps new letters into his search engine. "Maybe I should just try and google general headlines. Rich . . . guy . . . killed . . . in home . . . England." He types with his tongue peeping out, then balks as stories load. "Whoa. There's a shit ton of them. But nothing very mansiony or upper class." There's a pause while he thinks. "You don't think Leo would have made it up, just to get attention?"

"I doubt it." A lie that big would bury him. Take it from one who knows.

"Yeah, I feel bad even wondering that. He seemed choked up when he was talking about it."

"It's weird he isn't on Facebook, though," I say. "Isn't everybody?"

"No." Jacob smiles. "But the lack of headlines is odd. My bet is he's changed his name to be rid of the whole thing. Anyway," he shuts off the screen, sets the cell on the floor by the bed, "it's good you're hitting it off with Tamsin. I was worried you'd have nothing to do on the camp while I'm working. But you can totally hang out with her now."

"You're going to be that busy?" I ask. "Not, like, twelve-hour days, though, right?"

"Maybe at the beginning, while we set up the new recruits."

I raise my eyebrows.

"I told you that. I said it'd be flat-out at the start. But you'll be okay." He gets up, moving the wicker chair so it sits right up against the bungalow door. "Hey, and look, I'm leaving this here tonight. Just so you feel better about . . . everything."

"Thanks," I say, although my jaw muscle has tightened again.

There you go, Stevie, you little nutjob. Here I am, still looking after you. My mind snags back to how Tamsin described all her freedom. Thoughtful as he is, I don't want to be Jacob's project anymore. It's starting to feel like an enclosure.

He gets back into bed, gives my knee a pat. "I'm gonna get some shut-eye. Tomorrow will be big. And I lied when I said I wasn't still hungover."

"Okay." I press a customary kiss against the side of his face. "Are you okay that they're coming with us to Rafiki?"

He opens his eyes. "Leo and Tamsin? Yeah, I don't have a problem with it. Seeing as how it all happened by chance. Are you okay with it?"

"Yes, it's fine," I say, leaving it at that. I don't tell him it's starting to feel more than fine. Especially with one of them more than the other.

At reception in the morning, Leo is already talking to Wilson when we walk in to checkout. Leo speaks as if he's grown up with the guy, as if he'll see him again soon.

"Are you traveling indefinitely?" Jacob asks Tamsin as she hands in her key.

"Do you mean am I rich?" she says. "Rude. You're not meant to ask ladies about money."

"No." Jacob blushes. "I just meant you seem confident here. You're old hat with everything."

"I'm a what?" She turns. "What did you just call me?"

Behind Jacob, I shake my head and laugh.

"Do I need to sign any paperwork?" Jacob asks Wilson, who stares at him blankly.

"Mate, you don't even have your key, do you?" Leo slaps him on the back. "You're wasting your time in here."

There's a second where I think of the monkey in that tree again. It feels so unlikely, and the fingertip warning starts to tap in my head. Leo watches me, hands on hips, his T-shirt catching on the curve of his chest muscle.

"Are you okay, Stevie?"

"Yes, I was just—yes, I'm fine. Ready to get out of here."

"That's the spirit," he says. Wilson asks Leo something in Swahili, and he turns back to the desk.

"Look," Jacob says, "let me get all the bags into the cab. I'll take that job." He goes to pick up Tamsin's first. It's a small bag—carry-on size—and as he lifts it, a small, well-thumbed photo album falls out of the side pocket. Jacob picks it up and stares at one of the pages, his eyes widening. I edge closer, but Tamsin snatches the album away.

"*Ja-cob!* You're a right nosy parker." She stuffs it back into her pack and zips the pocket. "And by the way, Stevie and I don't need help carrying bags to the car. We're perfectly capable, thank you."

She motions for me to follow her as she heads outside, but I hang back.

"What were the photos of?" I whisper to Jacob, watching Tamsin get into the cab.

"Women," he says, the skin around his throat mottling. "Beautiful naked ones."

"Really?" I say. "The whole album?"

"I didn't see all the pages, but there was definitely more than one in there."

"Ready to go?" Leo puts his arm around Jacob. "I think we're all sorted here. Might as well hit the road."

Jacob and I raise our eyebrows at each other. He seems more embarrassed than anything, but I want to ask him more questions about what exactly he saw. There's no time now to find out, and the two of us walk stiffly to the car, both of us climbing in. Leo walks behind us, shoots me a quick glance through the open back window, then gets into the front seat.

All the way back to Mombasa, Tamsin's thigh presses against mine, our skin trading moisture and heat. Whenever she passes me a water bottle, I can't help but think about her lips having touched it. A slow fuse has been lit in my head. Again and again, I will my focus back to Jacob, the safest place I know, the man I'm with. Hours pass as I grapple beside her.

Once we get to Mombasa, Leo's rented a car to shorten the remainder of the road trip to nine hours—the bus can take ten to twelve—and I'm grateful for the forethought. All day long I want to ask him how he's coped with the death of his father—if he has any tips on grieving—but I don't. There's too much else to sift through. I sit quietly in the back with Tamsin, thinking about that album full of girls, wondering why she has it with her. We play I Spy. We eat corn on the cob we buy from the side of the road near Tanga. We sing "American Pie," looping through the verses because the radio doesn't work. The boys don't know all the words. Tamsin leans into me for every chorus and the whole thing also feels like a gift, a redo, a chance to ride in the back of a car next to an almost-Cassia, with nothing going wrong. Dust flumes from behind the vehicle as Leo speeds us closer to Dar es Salaam, and in the wariest corner of my mind, I imagine Tamsin with those girls, wondering if any of them look like me.

16

LEO

For hours, I watch Stevie in the rearview mirror, but she doesn't look back at me once. She's beautiful when she sings—newly lit, smiling— but as we leave Kenya and head into Tanzania, somehow it's not me she's shining for. It's boys in the front of the car, girls in the back, and the boundaries are being etched in stone. By the time we get to the docks in Dar, it's dark, my fingers are tight on the steering wheel, and my neck is aching.

"Go on ahead, find the jetty for Rafiki. I'll get rid of the rented car," I say.

I watch the three of them wend their way through the throng, past men selling oranges, women with babies strapped into the weave of their clothes. The girls lead while Jacob plods along behind. By the time I catch up with them, they've found a thirty-foot boat—a dhow—the wood of it hand-hewn, the sails stitched with hemp and raffia. The captain is a tall, muscular man who's wearing a Miller Genuine Draft T-shirt and no shoes. The bottoms of his feet are cracked and scuffed white at the edges with sea salt.

"This is Titus," Jacob says. "I think the boat is his."

For a second, I wonder if Titus has stitched it together himself, but surely that would have taken years.

"Are you taking us to Rafiki Island?" I check. "Tutaenda Rafiki?"

Titus bellows out a laugh and puts his arm around me. "Bru," he says. "Yes, we're going now." Then he thuds off to check the mainsail.

All of us get on.

"Listen, chaps," I say. "Don't copy him on the bare feet front. If you walk on wet sand without shoes, the jiggers will get you."

"The *what* now?" Stevie asks.

"They're worms that lay eggs in your toes, and you'll have to cut around the ridge of the egg sack with a knife."

"You've seen this before?" she asks, horrified.

"Oh, God, yeah. Happens all the time."

"He hasn't *seen* it," Tamsin cuts in. "He's heard about it from people in hostels."

"Whatever," I say, bristling. "Just keep your flip-flops on."

The two girls drift away to the opposite side of the boat and put their packs down, leaning over the side and chatting while they watch the water. They laugh close to each other's necks with an intimacy that's jarring.

"They seem very comfortable with each other," I say dryly to Jacob, who's standing alongside me. But he just shrugs.

"Girls are always like that," he replies. "She was the same with her best friend in high school."

"Was?" I say, as if I don't know the friend died. More information is always handy, even if I already have more than him. "They fell out?"

"No . . . she . . . her name was Cassia, and she was killed in a car wreck." He gestures to the deck with a nod, closing the subject. "Are we camping out here tonight?"

"Did you like Cassia?" I ask, leaning my bag against the side of the boat. Jacob exhales through his nose, doesn't want to speak ill of the dearly departed. "Got it," I say. "Understood." And I do understand. I totally hear what he's too nice to say.

"Tamsin can be annoying, too," I offer, sensing a new pathway.

But Jacob ignores me, calling across the deck as the dhow moves off from the dock. "Stevie! Do you want to sleep over here with us?"

She glances across at us, shakes her head a little.

"Okay." Jacob busies himself. "Well, it's good she's made a friend."

"Is it?" I snort. "I don't know, mate, I think you just got snubbed." Jacob's neck begins to redden. "Maybe you're losing your lover's touch?"

"She's allowed to hang out with whoever," he mutters and without him noticing, I roll my eyes. *Come on, Jacob. Get in the fight. It's only going to get harder from here.*

The journey from the mainland to the island is ten hours through the night, and by midnight, we're entirely at sea, no lights visible from anything onshore, just the stars above us. We pitch along in the boat, the only sound the murmuring of other passengers and the occasional soft laughter from Tamsin and Stevie. Waves slap roughly against the hull.

At around 1 a.m., Jacob arranges his pack as a pillow and lies against it. "I've had comfier beds. But the ceiling has never been this awesome." He sounds content, but he shouldn't be.

"I've been thinking about what you said about other women," I say, and he jolts. "No, don't worry—it's fine, they can't hear us. They've been quiet for a while now—they're both asleep."

Jacob leans up on one elbow, a long strand of hair hanging over his eyes.

"Listen, we're mates, right?" I say.

"Right." He sounds cagey.

"Why don't you sleep with Tamsin?"

He laughs but it catches in his throat and comes out as a single syllable.

"No, I'm not joking," I say. "I can tell you're attracted to her. You should go for it, mate. See what happens."

Now he really sits up. "Are you high or something?"

"It would break up their tight little club quite nicely, though, wouldn't it? I mean, why can't we be included in their gang? You might act like it's not getting to you, Jacob, but I'm going to say it for you: they're a little bit fucking annoying."

He waits, every muscle in his body tense. Then he bursts out laughing, pointing at me. "Ah, you nearly had me! Wow. For a while there I thought you were serious."

I laugh, too, slap him on the shoulder even though it's not jollity I feel. He exhales relief. "Your face," I say, shaking my head. "I nearly had you."

"You're such an asshole!" He rubs his forehead, grinning. "For real, though, buddy—man to man—I'd be blind not to notice your girlfriend. Anyone would. She's insanely hot and I'm not denying it. But I would never do that to you, and I'd definitely never do it to Stevie."

Liar, I think. *In a week or two, you won't even know what you're doing.*

He settles down, nestles his head in the crook of his arm. "*Lala salama*," he says. "Sleep well."

"How well do you know Stevie?" I ask.

His eyes open again. This isn't the lullaby he was expecting.

"No, it's just that—as a mate," I pause, "you know, *man to man*, I don't think she's quite who you think she is."

Now he sits up, clears his throat. "What's that supposed to mean, bro?"

I smile at the "bro," at the clear warning in it, like a flare sent up into the night. *Watch it*, he's saying, but it's a puny defense system. Jacob isn't scary.

"There are things she's not telling you." I open both palms. *Look, bro, I'm being as honest as I can here.* "Stevie's very complicated. And human brains filter and store things with great complexity. This is my field of work, Jacob: I'm an expert. So, I'm just saying, I think you should consider that there might be events she's not fully disclosing. Emotional events, I mean, as much as physical, since one often informs the oth—"

"Stop." He holds up his hand like I'm an errant pedestrian. "Stop talking. I'm not taking advice from you."

We stare at each other in silence for a few seconds.

"Why not?" He'd do well to pay attention, since the key to all romance is in listening properly. My mother taught me as much on my thirteenth birthday, preparing me for what she called "imminent adventures." *As a man, you've got two of these, darling*—her fingertips dusting the soft skin of my ears—*and one of these*—index finger smooth across my bottom lip. *What does that tell you?* Oh, I've learned to be a very good listener.

But color gathers in Jacob's cheeks and neck. Gosh, he's furious. I had no idea he had such a top gear.

"Maybe concentrate on your own girlfriend." He slams himself flat again, tugging at the zipper of his sleeping bag. "A minute ago you were pimping her out. Wouldn't that count as fucking weirdly complex, in your expert opinion?"

"Jacob, I'm just trying to—"

"Yeah," he says, turning so that his back is to me. "Got it. Thanks."

I watch his shoulders for a while, noticing the rigidity in them, the quickness of the breaths he's taking. But things can only bend so much before they snap. Ask my psychiatrist, Jacob. She'll tell you. We're all in trouble here, unavoidably, and I'm trying, I'm really trying, but all the voices in my head are shouting the same thing and I can't seem to make it stop.

I shift my gaze, leaning back against the hardness of the boat, hugging my knees. Across the deck, the girls snore peacefully in their sleeping bags. Their tranquility is a mockery. A sham. Along we all sway on a tar-black sea, while octopus tentacles creep up the boat. Somebody, for the love of God, do something. Shine a light, blow a whistle, sound an alarm.

Because otherwise, the devastation will be inevitable. All this space, Stevie, and you've never been more penned in.

17

STEVIE

In the dream, I was wrapped tight in a mosquito net, my face pressed so close against it that I could smell the DEET, see an array of calcified insects hanging from it mid-crawl. Somebody was watching me through the netting, hands pawing at me, and as I struggled, I saw fingernails, a man's hands, a stranger's, stretching out to touch me.

I sit up, gasping, the last flash of the dream a swollen face—but it isn't a man's features I see. It doesn't match those fingers. The face is Cassia's, as it always is, the pallid bulge of her cheeks above mine in the dark.

I rub my eyes, gripping my knees in my sleeping bag as I look around the boat. Everyone is asleep, an array of hump-whaled shapes on the deck. Jacob is curled in his sleeping bag next to Leo, and I think for a second that I should have opted to sleep next to them. But, bottom line, I didn't want to—and doesn't it always come down

129

to a bottom line? No need to overthink it. It was more fun over here. And I don't need Jacob with me the whole time. At the stern of the boat, I see a tiny tip of a cigarette glow and retract. Titus, the captain, is awake, quietly smoking a cigarette by himself. At least someone's steering us right. I take a deep breath, trying to shake off the remnants of my dream. Beside me, Tamsin is lying with the warmth of her forearm resting against my hip. Can I tell *her* about the nightmare? For some reason, I feel she might understand it.

At the beginning, the night terrors were only about being with my mom.

"Don't you worry about bad dreams," Nattie used to say. "They'll go, my sweetheart. Demons can't stay if you don't feed them."

When I moved in with her, she bought a bigger bed, so tight in her tiny cottage bedroom that she could barely open the door. I slept with her for years, needing to know it was her when I woke up in the night, not some new guy my mother had brought home from the bar, who'd leer at me from the doorway while Mom went to pee in the bathroom.

"Little unguarded soul," Nattie would say, stroking my hair at all hours of the night. "Don't you fret. Nobody's getting past me, my love. No more of that nonsense."

By nine years old, I'd recovered enough to move out of my grandmother's room. But at sixteen, the dreams came back, the cruelty of my subconscious now adding Cassia into the mix.

"What is it that you see?" Jacob asked me when we were together, seventeen years old and lying side by side in his bedroom. "Maybe if you talk about the dreams, they'll stop."

But I couldn't. And they didn't. Not until he gave me a journal to write in and swore that anything I wrote down in it would be private—and he stuck to that promise—did the dreams start to fade. But here I am again, back in the thick of them. Nattie was wrong about demons: even when you think you've got them cornered, they shape-shift. They mutate. They feed.

The sway of the boat is soothing, and I match my breathing to it, liking the occasional creak of the boom. It's 5:30 a.m., the light just beginning to sift overhead. Soon the night will surrender to day and the world will be more manageable again. I scoot back against the curve of the hull, careful not to dislodge Tamsin. But she moves in her sleep, lifting her arm away from me. I feel colder immediately. Reaching across, I pull her sleeping bag so that it covers her shoulder, and she exhales softly. And it's then that I hear the laugh.

Looking around the boat, I wonder if it's Titus, since we're the only ones awake—certainly the only ones sitting up. But then, diagonally across from me, I see Leo, lying on one side with his head on his hand, all of his focus on me. How long has he been watching me? His gaze is so intense it's almost a visible beam. Did he see me cover up Tamsin just now? I feel a wave of heat in my face, and quickly lie flat again. But I don't fall back to sleep. All I can see as I stare up at the sky is his knowing smile, his teeth glinting like bone under the leaching sky.

II

hashtag herecomesparadise

18

LEO

Stevie avoids me as we get off the boat. It was nice being awake with her as the sun rose, even if she hurried to change it. As soon as she noticed me watching her, she curled her body along Tamsin's. She's making her choice. It doesn't mean I can't unmake it for her.

Jacob steers clear of me, too, although he's doing it less directly. Taking opportunities to watch the approaching shoreline from angles that separate him. Sitting next to Titus, who already seems to represent some kind of a blockade. It's a basic technique. Nothing I haven't seen before. Nothing that will win him any proper cover.

Rafiki Island, when we reach it, is minuscule—a series of goat-track roads, a tiny village of mud huts, and a dock that's rusty with old nails. We pull into the harbor at 6:30 a.m., and every local on the island is there to greet us, a lot of them children running in the sand. There are women in brightly patterned sarong dresses sitting on a low wall under the trees, while men stand knee-deep in the ocean to unload Titus's cargo—great strong-shouldered locals who look like they've never eaten bad food or had a sleepless night in their lives.

I stand beside Jacob on the gangplank. He acknowledges me only with a slight raise of his eyebrows, turning when Stevie arrives beside him so that his back is to me. "How come you didn't want to sleep closer?" he asks her, his voice low.

She glances past him at me. "It wasn't a big boat."

"No, but are you doing okay? You look tired."

"I'm fine. Hungry. I'll go get us some food." She moves off toward Tamsin, who's buying samosas where the gangplank ends. She pays for two, hands one to Stevie. They nibble with their elbows touching. Two little mice now, not one. Neither of them looks like they're planning on moving back toward us.

"Jacob Jones?" shouts an American voice and I glance away from the girls toward a man standing tall on the dock. "Over here!"

It has to be Duran. He's midthirties, with graying hair shaved close to his head and a watch on his ham hock forearm that looks like it could get him out of any difficult situation imaginable, below or above water. There's no doubt he's ex-military. He has that swagger, that confidence, that alpha-male assumption that we're all here to follow his lead. My father had the same reckless self-confidence. Look where it got him.

Duran jogs to the boat, carving a path through the locals, and he and Jacob shake hands.

"Long time no see, Jonesy." Duran's fist dwarfs Jacob's. "I'm really happy you came." There's a grit to him, some telltale scars around the chin that seem more ex-boxer than ex-soldier, although perhaps the two aren't mutually exclusive.

"Yeah, it was time," Jacob says with a grin.

"You look older," Duran says, jostling him. "Five years of boat cleaning in the Atlantic will do that to a guy."

"I'd have come sooner," Jacob says, "but it wasn't . . . We couldn't."

"All good, man. You're here now." Duran looks around. "Where's this girl I've heard so much about?"

"Over there." Jacob points at Stevie, blushing. He seems gangly and awkward in Duran's presence, like a teenager intent on impressing him. I can't stand dynamics like that. "And this is Leo Asher," he adds, the introduction lacking an equivalent enthusiasm. "He's one of the volunteers."

"You ran into each other on the boat?" Duran turns to me. "What are the chances of that?"

"There's only one boat that comes here, isn't there?" I say. "So, fairly broad." I shake his hand, making sure to tense all the muscle in my arm and transmit it.

"Welcome," Duran says, his eyes narrowing for the tiniest of seconds. "Thanks for signing up. Okay, let's gather everyone up and head to the car. You can throw all your bags in the back."

Jacob signals to the girls, and we all make our way off the gangplank, blinking in the brightness of the beach. Duran's car is a scuffed old army Jeep parked at the tree line. Of course it is. We all pile our bags in while Duran hangs back to shake hands with Titus and have a chat, before striding up the sand to join us. He jumps into the driver's seat next to Jacob, his flip-flops so well worn against the pedals they're wafer-thin.

"Mike Duran," he says, turning briefly to shake hands with both Stevie and Tamsin beside me. "How was the trip? Kind of a red-eye?"

"No, it was lush." Tamsin's voice is honeyed and luxurious. "The girls' team slept perfectly. I don't know about the boys."

"That's good," Duran says, turning the key in the ignition. "If you can sleep without creature comforts, you should be fine here."

"Oh, I can sleep anywhere," Tamsin says, and Duran glances at her in his rearview mirror.

He drives fast through the village, raising his hand as he passes by a group of men playing checkers under a tree.

"Can you slow down, please?" Stevie shouts beside me. "There aren't any seat belts back here."

"*Polay-polay*," Duran says, lifting his foot from the accelerator. "*Polepole*, slow it down. It's all Titus ever says to me. But you're right—I'm sorry—I've been on Rafiki for three years now and I'm still going too fast for the place."

"Stevie's uncomfortable in cars," I say. "Aren't you?"

She darts a glance at me as if I've somehow slipped under her skin. But I have, and it's okay. It's right that I should know.

"How do you—?" she begins, but before I can tell her all the ways I'm invested in her, all the commitment I'm putting in, we arrive at the dive camp. Duran parks by a separate hut and shuts off the engine, jumping out to pat a short-haired dog on the head who's trotted over to greet him. The dog is young and mostly white, with mocha patches along his ribs that have yet to fully darken. Brown eyes. Floppy ears. Extremely waggy tail.

"This is Crusoe," Duran says. "He runs the camp, so stay on the right side of him. I don't know whose he is but six months ago, he decided he was mine. Feed him scraps if you like. I've been trying to fatten him up for a while."

"Awww, he's beautiful." Stevie bends and tickles Crusoe behind the ear and he immediately collapses onto his side for a belly rub, his tail thumping in the dust. *Animal-lover*, I think. *Check*. I should have spotted it from her Instagram.

"You win over Crusoe, you win over me," Duran says, and Stevie squints up at him from where she's crouching. Then Duran spreads his thick arms wide, turning in a circle. "So here we are, guys. Welcome to Rafiki Island dive camp, the beating heart of African eco-tourism." His smile broadens, elongating that scar on his chin. "I'll give you the tour and introduce you to the other volunteers."

"I like what you've done with the place," I say, gesturing at the mud walls, the mud floors, all the dust and dirt.

Duran stares at me. "Which one are you, again?"

"I'm Leo Asher. The late addition." I crouch down, join Stevie in pampering Crusoe. Our fingertips touch in his fur.

"Leo and I only booked a couple of days ago," Tamsin adds. "We're always fashionably late to the party."

"Have I met you before?" Duran asks me. "You look familiar."

"He gets that a lot." Tamsin rolls her eyes. "Everywhere we travel, people think he's a Hollywood actor. Sometimes they even ask him for autographs. Chris Pine. Chris Evans. All the Chrises."

Duran doesn't strike me as a man who goes to parties or watches television. His lip curls. "Come this way and I'll show you the cement floor where you'll be sleeping," he says. "And the long-drop where you'll be shitting."

He walks ahead, leaving the four of us wide-eyed.

"Blimey," says Tamsin. "I've met better-skilled concierges."

"He's just rough around the edges." Jacob hefts his pack onto his shoulder. "He'll warm up."

We follow Duran down a path that leads past one big hut, winding into the foliage of the jungle. Ants bite at all of our heels and we have to keep slapping them. We stop at a smaller hut—big enough for one person to squeeze into—with a roof that's shoulder height at best.

"This is the bathroom," Duran says. "Or long-drop." He gestures at a filthy hole in the ground surrounded by slow-crawling millipedes. "Keep your eyes open in here. There's a green mamba in the rafters. Doesn't often come out." He waits for one of us to gasp but none of us oblige him.

"Where's the sink?" Tamsin asks cheerfully. "Do you provide soap?"

"There's no running water or electricity on camp." Duran's tone is flat. "Didn't you receive the brochure?"

Tamsin inclines her head as if to say *Touché*, and Duran leads us back toward the sleeping hut. We duck inside. Along each side of the makeshift room are ten or so beds, six of them already filled with other volunteers sleeping, reading, or writing in journals.

"Breakfast isn't until oh-eight-hundred," Duran says. "People tend to sleep in if they can. That's if they make it past the rooster at first light. Jacob, you have a separate hut if you'd like it, out there by my Jeep. Or you can sleep in here with the others. It's up to you and Stevie."

"I think we should stay in here," Stevie says without much hesitation. Jacob falters but says nothing. Brilliant decision. Works for me.

"Where are you sleeping, Mr. Duran?" Tamsin asks him.

"It's just Duran. I don't stay on-site. I have a house across the island. But my office is here, and we store gear and data at camp."

As he speaks, three of the six volunteers stand and move to the entrance to greet us. They wait until Duran has finished talking. My first thought is how young they look, as do the ones still asleep. What are they all doing here? Have their parents sent them off, given them money, told them to go and save the planet?

A redheaded male steps forward, announcing his leadership of the welcoming committee. He has a double stripe of tattoo around one wrist and a T-shirt with the slogan *This Ain't the Big City*. I would have thought that was obvious.

"I'm Axel," he says, while the other two hover behind him. "From Holland. And these are really great Canadians, Greta and Ted." *Greta and Ted? Why are those names familiar?* "Really so great. And then they are French, these other ones. Manu, Hugues, and Louie. They don't speak so much."

"They speak to each other. We should probably brush up on our French." Ted emerges from behind Axel—shaggy-haired and blond, shirt two sizes too small for him—and the skin of my forehead recedes. I know this man. I know exactly where I met him.

"We've crossed paths before, Ted." I step forward, extending my arm for a handshake. "You and your sister were in a hostel with us a couple of months ago. What an unexpected reunion."

"Oh, *yeah* . . ." Light dawns on Ted's face and he clears his throat. "How's it going?" Beside him, his sister Greta takes a step back.

"Oh my *God*," hisses Tamsin beside me and I see her grip Stevie's T-shirt. "It's *her* again."

"How's it going, guys?" Greta asks, her chin wobbly and strange. "I didn't think we'd see you beyond Zim."

Tamsin sticks out her bottom lip. "Here we all are. How great."

"Okay, I'll leave you all to chat," Duran cuts in. "Breakfast's in half an hour and normally we'd do a morning dive, but since we have new recruits, we'll set out for the reef at fourteen hundred. Everyone needs to make sure their gear is ready to go. *You* and *you*," he points at me and Tamsin, "come over to my office and show me your tickets. You can't dive until I've seen them."

"Yes, *sir*." I mock-salute, but Duran has already turned and ducked out of the hut.

"Which beds are you taking?" Ted asks, shooting a harried glance at his sister. "We're down the far end."

"It's hotter down there. Not as much airflow," Greta says quickly.

"I'll stay near the exit," I say with a smile. "I was taught to sleep with a door in clear view. I'll take this bed." I put my pack on it, wondering which spot Stevie will choose. If I've guessed right, this angle will be perfect for nighttime.

"I'll take the one next to you," Tamsin says to me. "We could move the beds together."

"The mosquito net won't stretch," I mutter, while Jacob and Stevie choose the beds directly opposite. Exactly right.

"You guys were in Zim together?" Jacob asks.

Ted squirrels one hand over the other. "We took a safari on the Zambezi River. Same boat. It went badly, but these things happen," he says, eyes on Greta as she walks back to the far end of the hut. "I leaned the canoe too far and we fell in. Maybe let's not get into it, though: my sister's still kind of sore about it. She just needs time." He moves away, his shoulders angled downward.

"Time?" Tamsin says. "She might need a little bit more than that." Beside her, Stevie chuckles.

We unpack and move as a group out to the long tables of the eating hut. Breakfast is hot chai with chapattis on dented tin plates. The French guys don't speak much English, although Manu tries, tucking his blond hair behind his ear and asking questions only of Stevie. He wears beach-worn beads and smiles at her too often. Greta chews her food for ages before swallowing it, bovine and inward, shooting stricken, apologetic glances along the bench at Tamsin. Ted keeps pouring her more and more fresh cups of tea, which she sips.

"What have you been up to, Ted, since we last saw you?" I ask, tickling a frond of grass against the table. "Found any wonders of the world?"

"We mostly headed straight here," Ted says. "We ran out of cash."

"Ted lost a bunch of our money," Greta adds.

"I did." Ted wrinkles his nose. "I'm clumsy at times. As you know."

"Ah, it's normal. Things get stolen, especially when you're traveling." I roll the grass strand between my thumb and forefinger. "D-I-A, right? None of the locks work here. All the rules are different."

Stevie flinches like she's been stung. "What did you just say?"

I hold her gaze. "I said all the rules are different. Haven't you noticed?" A long, heavy silence swells between us. It's like that moment we shared at her window in Diani Beach. I love it when we lock in our wavelength.

"Do you have your dive tickets, Leo?" Jacob asks, and the moment bursts. "I think you were meant to take them over to Duran's office. If you're done with your food, I'll head over there with you right now."

"Is it all right if we pick our own dive buddies?" I stand slowly.

Jacob stares at me. Crosses his arms. "Mine will always be Stevie."

"Will it? What about the days you're not diving? You know, doing paperwork. Being managerial."

There's a sudden clattering of a plate, and Stevie gets up from the bench, walking away from the group without speaking. She heads straight toward the sleeping hut, everyone staring after her.

"I was only asking," I say. "I just worry that you'll be kept at camp administratively, and Stevie will need a plan B."

Jacob breathes in and out through his nose. For a second, I'm reminded of my father in his study. All the weighted silences, the fingertip tapping on desks, the displeasure. But really, with Jacob it's time things went up a gear. The clock is ticking, after all, and God knows time isn't infinite.

"Let's just be clear," he says. "*You're* not diving with her."

There, I think, *now you're getting it*. Welcome to the fight.

"That's a bit territorial, mate." In my peripheral vision, I can still see Stevie. "And I think you're coming at it all wrong. What if I was the perfect chaperone?"

"Leo—" Jacob draws himself up to full height.

"Let's go with plan A for now, shall we? Maybe your paperwork will be minimal, and it won't even be an issue."

His jaw clamps shut. I let him lead us on toward the office while I track every step Stevie takes. Girls love it when boys notice what they do. *Two eyes and one mouth, darling. What does that tell you?* Slowing my pace behind Jacob, I trace Stevie all the way into the hut.

19

STEVIE

It's quiet in the hut on my own. The light is softer. I know I should be out with the others, meeting people and making an effort, but ever since Leo laughed at me on the boat, I'm beginning to feel creeped out whenever he's nearby. I sit down on the bed, the rope scratchy beneath my thighs. Is Leo flirting with me or laughing at me? He seems to find it funny that I care about Tamsin, but I haven't done anything wrong. So how is it that I feel like I've been busted?

Leo also seems to know I'm uncomfortable in cars. It's as if he's managed to look inside my head, tallied all the ways in which I'm struggling, and decided to visit them one by one. I know Jacob told Leo I get claustrophobic, but he shouldn't be gifting him anything else, not when he doesn't know Leo's intentions. It could be he's not as charming as we first thought.

I open the top of my pack, roll out my sleeping bag, lie down on it. In the rafters of the hut are thick cobwebs, the clack of little creatures scurrying. At night, I'll need to get out my mosquito net. Maybe Jacob and I should go and sleep in the other hut, the smaller one Duran mentioned that's just for staff. But honestly, I'm not sure I want to. And there it is again: the persistence of a bottom line. Tiny flutters of warning start to pulse in my brain. *What is it that you really want, Stevie?* And the problem is, Leo might have gotten to the answer before me. All I know is I want to sleep near Tamsin. I close my eyes, flooded by a wave of panic.

When I was sixteen and my life exploded, Nattie gathered up all the pieces. But the truth is, she only handed me back some of them.

"Stop that now this minute," she'd say, old mottled hand on my knee as we sat in her living room, cups of tea beside us losing their warmth. "We're closing that lid, child, and we're not looking in there." She steered me through those days, a tugboat in the whirl of a storm, allowing me some instincts while outlawing others, tethering me to the sturdiest landmass she could find. Herself. And Jacob Jones.

In Nattie's defense, she was only trying to simplify. But what if important parts of myself got lost in the trade? I'm not as straightforward as she wanted me to be. I'm not. Already I can feel the edges she scored in hard black starting to blur. Something skitters in the rafters above me, a pattering of insect feet, too many of them all in a flurry. *Take a deep breath, Stevie, take another and calm down. Do not blow up your life all over again.*

Everything's fine. I'm in Africa. It's unfamiliar. I'm in mourning. I've been with the same guy for seven years. Tamsin is fun and exciting, or—even more powerfully—she thinks *I am*. All of this will shake down. If I take sensible steps and don't freak out, I can be friends with Tamsin. Choose the long-term option. The nonexplosive one. Build something lasting. But is it really friendship that I feel?

The inside of my head feels like a bag full of snakes, all of them writhing and wriggling, and just when I think I can't take it anymore—that I can't cope without Nattie, can't keep any of this within bounds—Tamsin comes into the hut. She squints for a second or two in the shadows.

"Stevie?"

"Over here." *Keep it together, keep it together.*

"Oh, hi." She stands by the side of my bed. "Shove over."

I shift and she lies alongside me. There's a second or two more of silence, while I keep all of my muscles tense, my body straight like a competitor in an Olympic luge.

"What are we doing in this hut?" she asks.

"Nothing. This."

"Are you okay?"

"Kinda."

"God, same. That French guy is hot. Have you seen him?"

"No, not really."

"The blond surfy one? Manu. So hot. Doesn't speak much, but that's fine. Oh, God, and I can't believe Greta's here. It's like *Casablanca*!" She shakes her head beside me, exhaling. "Of all the dive camps in all the towns in all the world, she walks into mine. Sorry to go on about it, but she and Ted are sniveling around me, desperate to apologize. How long are they going to do that for? They're massively uncool."

"Maybe just let them apologize, and they'll move on." I smile. "They probably think they scared the shit out of you in that canoe."

"They did! But, bloody hell. As if I want to go over and over it."

Her skin is closer to mine than it's ever been. She smells good—of summer, of coconut body lotion.

"Do you know who else is being uncool?" she says. "*Leo.*"

"Right?!" I turn onto my side, even though it means facing her. "Did you see that back there? Why is he saying the rules are different, and what is up with all the dive buddy talk? Is he saying he wants to be mine? It's just so weird."

147

"Leo *is* weird. He says strange things every day. But don't worry, he's harmless. I think he has a ginormous crush on you and doesn't know what to do about it. It's kind of sweet."

I lie still for a second or two, noticing tiny freckles on the bridge of her nose. "Don't you care? You're okay with him crushing on me?"

The sides of her mouth curve into a smile. "He might not be the only one."

My breath stops in my chest. She's doing it again. Throwing lit matches just to see if they catch. It doesn't seem fair at all.

"I don't want to be Leo's dive buddy." I turn flat again, my voice sounding shaky. There's a verge here and we're helter-skeltering toward it.

"Okay," she says. "Do you want to be Jacob's?"

I don't answer. Can't. Heat moves to the surface of my skin.

"Have a think about it." She pats my thigh, spangling electricity through me. "And in the meantime, I've come to fetch you. We've got to go over to Duran's office and take some quiz thing on fishes. He's waiting for us." She stands, brushing dust from her shorts.

"What? What quiz?"

"God knows. All new recruits have to do it. Apparently, we're all meant to be able to identify fifty species of tropical fish on sight. I don't even know one. Cod's not tropical."

"What if we don't pass it?" I get up, my mind still trying to separate this snake from that, let alone news of an unexpected exam.

"Duran says we can't dive until we know what we're looking at. It's so full-on, it's like being back in school. I'm going to get a detention."

We walk out of the hut together into the glaring sun, our palms to our foreheads as we move across the scruffy dirt to Duran's office.

"I'm underprepared," I say.

"Me, too."

"Are we just going to make up fish?"

"I think that's going to be my plan." Tamsin grips me at the elbow

148

for a second as we walk, leans into me like a disruptive kid on the way to the principal's office. For a moment, we're Stevie and Cassia back in tenth grade, kicked out of English class again.

"Were you a good girl at school?" I ask her.

She grins at me. "What do you think?"

We climb the three rickety steps to the office and knock on the door. Nobody's in there. Pushing the door open, we step into what appears to be a shipping container with a desk at the far end and charts of fish all over the walls. There are dive tanks lining one corner, and a few stranded wetsuits heaped alongside them. The whole room smells of sunbaked neoprene.

In the center of the space is a laptop hooked up to a screen. Duran has been running his fish exams already. Tamsin drifts to his desk, moves pieces of paper, peers at photographs pinned to a board behind his chair.

"Look at Duran here!" She points to an image of him standing in a crew of army divers, all of them naked to the waist in wetsuits. "He's so Jason Bourne. I bet he's snuck into embassies and has literally eight passports."

I walk over and take a look. It's true: he looks like an action hero. There are other photos on his wall of oil rigs, deserted beaches, reefs, wrecks, yachts, Crusoe, and several of one woman in particular. She's beautiful with a wide, bright smile.

"Who's this?" Tamsin picks up the framed picture on the desk. "Do you think she's the one he goes home to every night?"

Duran walks into the office at that moment, and Tamsin sets the frame down again. Crusoe has slipped into the office, too, and sits with his muzzle touching Duran's knee.

"Ready?" Duran looks from my face to Tamsin's. "This is a quick test, shouldn't take long."

"Why are we doing it?" I ask.

"You're helping out on the camp, right? Counting fish underwater.

We're recording dwindling numbers. Then, in theory, the government protects the reef." He opens the lid of his laptop. "But we can't sully the data. That's why I sent that link in the email when you signed up—the catalogue of most common fish life on this reef, etcetera."

"Right," Tamsin says. "Got that. Read it cover to cover."

"Okay, good. So come over here in front of the screen. There are answer sheets here"—he heads to his desk, hands us each an A4 sheet and a pen—"and it's twenty names for twenty photos I show you. I've selected them at random from the fifty you've studied. Sit down."

"Has everyone else done this test?" I ask, lowering myself into one of the two seats he's set up. "Has Jacob?"

Duran opens a file on his screen. "I figure Jacob knows his fish. He got the link, too. But he won't be counting out here. He'll be supervising you guys."

Easy for him, I think. Because I know for a fact that neither of us studied. It seems unfair that of the two of us, I'm the only one who's about to look like a moron within two hours of getting here.

"Are you married, Duran?" Tamsin's still standing behind the desk.

"Yes. That's my wife in the photo. Apollonia. She's from Rafiki. We've been married for twelve years."

"Twelve! That's bloody ages! Were you thirteen when you got married?"

Duran hesitates. "I was twenty-four. Can you come and sit down, Tamsin?"

"Twenty-four," she sighs. "I'd never in a million years marry the guy I was with at twenty-four. Would you, Stevie?"

"I'm twenty-four now," I say.

There's a silence, where it seems like Tamsin's still waiting for an answer.

"Perhaps you don't choose wisely, Tamsin," Duran says.

"Oh, I definitely don't. But I'm trying to change that." She slides into the seat next to me and I realize how hot I am, how much I need a drink of water. "Falling in love is a chemical drug, though. Nobody can choose well when they're tripping bollocks. So, basically, we all create versions of people that aren't real, and then the drugs wear off."

"Is that right?" Duran taps the pad of his laptop and a fish appears on the screen in front of us. "Mine are still working. But let's press on."

I can't even look at the fish. I'm wondering if Tamsin has a point. I don't remember feeling trippy when I first got together with Jacob. I just remember feeling safe. Does that mean I didn't fall in love with him, then? I rub at my temple, mad at myself. It doesn't matter what happened with Jacob seven years ago. It just matters what happens now.

"Emperor angelfish," Tamsin says suddenly, staring at the wall while I gape at her. Infinitesimally, she drops her eyes to a sheet of paper she has hidden under hers. One she's brought with her from Duran's desk, with Leo's name at the top. One that's full of answers

"Nice," Duran says behind us. "You did do your homework. But write your answers down, don't shout them out."

"Did you meet Apollonia when you worked in the Red Sea?" Tamsin asks. "No, I just saw that photo on your wall—it looked like you worked on a Laurence Sloane liveaboard before. When was that, then?"

Who the hell is Laurence Sloane? I think, wondering if I've slipped into an alternate universe.

"Laurence Sloane is, like, *the* kingpin of luxury dive travel." Tamsin touches my knee, making me jump. "British. Owns a shitload of yachts around the world. Celebrities flock there. They love him."

"He owns five," Duran says. "And yes, Apollonia and I worked for him for a while. Then we moved back here together."

"Friends in high places," Tamsin says. "I wouldn't have pegged you as a celeb kind of guy."

"Thank you," Duran replies. "Please write down the name of that fish."

"Threadfin butterflyfish," she says. "So you're still in touch? With Sloane, I mean?"

"No, not really. I hardly ever hear from him. Can you put your answers on the paper?"

"I think this test should be oral, Mr. Duran." Tamsin puts one hand to her chest. "It presents too much of a temptation. Stevie's copying from my sheet."

I watch her, amazed by the spectacle. Everything she does feels naughty, and I have that feeling again—the same one I always had at sixteen—where things are about to get completely out of control. In the old days, I lived for this exact kind of headiness.

Duran doesn't answer, just taps to the next image. Before it even loads properly, Tamsin shouts, "Picasso triggerfish!"

There's a weighted silence.

"Are you cheating?" Duran asks.

"Me?" Tamsin says.

"What do you have there?" He moves away from the computer. "Do you have Leo's sheet?"

"Yes, and how does he know the answers, anyway?" Tamsin throws up her arms. "He's a right girly square."

I laugh, can't help it.

"Maybe Leo's here for the right reasons. Did you ever think of that?" The vein near Duran's collarbone is starting to rise a little. Crusoe watches him.

"He really very much might not be." Tamsin glances sideways at me.

Duran slams shut the lid of his laptop. "We're protecting a reef, Tamsin, an entire ecosystem. You're not just here to look good in a bikini."

"You haven't even seen me in a bikini. But thank you."

"You can't count fish if you don't know what you're looking at." Duran snatches both sheets from her hands. "You might as well not be here."

"You're kicking me off the island?" Tamsin says. "This isn't *Survivor*. My tribe hasn't spoken."

Duran takes a deep breath to respond, but before he can, there's a knock at the door and Titus steps into the space. "Mr. Duran, we need help with the compressor."

Duran shoots a dark look at Tamsin, grabs keys on a lanyard from his desk. "Okay, both of you, I'll run this test once more tomorrow morning. Be ready. This afternoon's dive can be recreational, but you're not doing that every time. This isn't summer camp."

He exits the office with Titus, Crusoe trotting behind.

"Whoops," Tamsin says. "Might have pushed that one a bit far."

"I think you got us both a detention."

"We can study. All good." Tamsin gets up and walks to his desk, pulls the photo of Apollonia and the Red Sea yacht from the wall and stares at it. "Isn't it weird that Duran would go from that job to this one? I mean, what are the odds?"

"Because of the luxury he gave up?"

"Yeah. Exactly." She blinks as if out of a trance, sliding the photograph into the back pocket of her shorts.

"What are you doing?" As rebellious as the past twenty minutes has been, it doesn't feel right to steal a guy's photos. "Tamsin, you can't—"

"I'm only borrowing it. I'll put it back tomorrow, I promise. I just want to see if he values it, if he notices it's gone."

I'm quiet for a few seconds, watching her.

"What?" she asks. "Do you think that's miles over the line?"

"I think you're taking it for a different reason," I say.

She runs a forefinger over her bottom lip. "What's that, then?"

I lean forward, speaking close to her ear, matching her for danger. "I think you're taking it to put in your photo album of girls."

"My what?" She shakes her head like she can't have heard right.

"The album you have in your backpack. The one Jacob found. With all the pictures of beautiful women in it."

153

"Oh, my God! No! That album's not mine. It's Leo's. He calls it his 'art book.'" She bunny-ears mischievous quotation marks with her fingers. "Did you see it? I literally think it's a log of all the women he's shagged, but I can't bring myself to look in it. Why would I?" She cringes. "It would just make me feel shit about myself."

Sweat prickles at the base of my neck. That photo album is *Leo's*? When it was Tamsin's, I couldn't stop thinking about it. Now that it's his, it feels wrong. There's that whisper in my ear again. *Why the double standard, Stevie? There's no doubt you want something from her that you never really wanted from him.*

"Does Jacob have an art book?" Tamsin asks.

"I think his would be more of a flyer," I say before I can stop myself, and Tamsin laughs.

"Well, they can't all be international men of mystery," she says.

Like Leo is? I think, trying not to show the doubt on my face. He's not mysterious, he's just starting to feel gross. Was I right about all the bird-dogging?

"You don't think it's weird that he'd have a book like that?" I ask.

She shrugs. "I don't love it. But I don't think he's added to it in a while. Maybe any day now he'll throw it away." She pauses while I commiserate. "Let's go back to the hut. Who cares about Leo? We need to read the *Encyclopedia of Tropical Fishes* and outscore everyone tomorrow. Let's keep all of them guessing." She winks at me and we head out of the office into a bright wall of heat, Duran's photo still in her back pocket, my head hot inside and out.

20

LEO

Two weeks go by and I can't get to Stevie. She's within reach but always guarded, existing like an exquisite creature in an aquarium that I can only watch through a panel of glass. Jacob stays by her side when he can, but he's working more and more, leaving Stevie to wander down to the dock to read or write in her journal. As prime an opportunity as this might be, it's always Tamsin who capitalizes on it. She joins her, and Stevie always puts her book away, the two of them laughing and sunbathing for hours with their legs touching.

I wonder if Stevie's panicking. Sometimes there's the tiniest moment of reticence in her—all this attention from Tamsin must be having an impact. I've read her diary. I know how she felt about the other one. Still, I can't quite manage to intervene. They're calling it friendship—Does anyone really believe that? Does she? Does Jacob?—and they're inseparable on land and at sea. We've been diving

155

every day since everyone passed their fish test, but on the very first dive, the girls sat next to each other on Titus's boat, collecting gear by their feet as Duran assigned it.

"Guys, your dive tanks will be numbered," he said. "You're each responsible for making sure yours makes it on and off the boat. Stevie, you're tank four and this is your weight belt. We're starting to color-code them so I can tell who's accountable for what."

"Why is mine pink?" she asked. "Because I'm a girl?"

"That's a bit genderist," Tamsin said. "Why's mine purple?"

"Oh, for crying out loud." Duran ticked equipment off on a list as the boat swayed. "You're tank six, Tamsin. Just put the gear on, do the dive. Ted and Greta, check your gauges! Do it properly."

They dove together, as I worried they might. With Jacob manning the office while we were out on the reef, I was left with Axel for a dive buddy. *Axel.* All the way through the dive, I made sure I kept slightly behind Stevie and slightly above, so that everything she breathed out touched me, softly, a tickling bubble of intimacy. Only when the two girls held hands underwater did I descend and bump into them.

"*Leo*," Tamsin complained afterward. "Watch where you're going when we're down there. You'll crash us into something."

Oh, but I am watching, I wanted to say. Make no mistake. I'm doing little of anything else.

A few days ago, Tamsin even gave Jacob a haircut at camp, another way in which she excluded me. Her thighs brushed each side of his hips on the bench as she sat behind him, the warm skin of her smooth belly against his back.

"Why are you letting this happen?" I asked Stevie, and both girls stared at me. Jacob, for his part, refused to make eye contact.

"There you go!" Tamsin sat back in her bikini, admiring how short she'd gone, how fit he looked now with his six-pack coming in. "So much better! You looked like the Beatles before. Now you look proper lush."

"Holy shit," said Stevie, as Jacob ran his hand over his head. "Good job."

So, I thought, *now* Jacob's *a contender?*

I spend nighttime with Stevie, of course. I've got to be careful, but if I'm quiet, it's the best time to be with her. Several times I've smoothed out her mosquito net where it's snagged on the rough wood of her bedpost. The last thing I want is predators getting to her. She's beautiful when she sleeps—the way she lies curled like a child, palms tucked under her cheek, her lips relaxed and plump in the shadows. Still, these visits I make to her bedside are not enough for what I need—what *either of us* need. I want to talk to her, find out more about her, be her best one. At the start, the universe threw us together, so why is it blocking us now? It's only when Duran comes into the hut at the start of week three that it feels like the stars might finally align again.

It's rare that he steps into our hut. He mostly hangs out in his lab, or at the home he seems to have on the other side of the island. As soon as he enters, Axel and Louie stand up straight by their beds, as if he might be about to check the angle of their sheets for symmetry.

"Is everyone awake and had breakfast?" Duran looks around. "It's almost oh-nine-hundred."

Manu and Hugues shake their heads. They're brave. Either that or his tone is lost on them.

Jacob puts a forefinger into the page of his Tolstoy novel. "Is there something you need us to do?"

"Well, yeah—get up, for one thing." Duran kicks the toe of his flip-flop against the support beam. "I have to go get the tender from Dead Dog Beach." He pauses. Harsh name for a beach destination. Nobody points it out. "It's a twenty-minute walk through the mangroves. Who wants to come help?"

Ted busies himself with his shoes. I haven't even stood up yet.

"I can, if you like," Jacob says.

"No, I need you here to fill tanks in the compressor shed. Thanks, though." He grits his teeth like he's really spread thin. *But Duran*, I want to say to him, *you're the alpha male. What do you need us for?*

"I'll go." Stevie steps out from behind her bed. "I could use the walk."

Duran turns. "Okay, good. Meet me out front in five minutes. Wear dive booties. There are mangrove spikes."

"Actually, you know what?" I get up, stretch. "I'll come, too. I'd enjoy a little jaunt. This all sounds interesting."

Stevie pales a little, but Duran walks out before she can back out or anyone else can join in. My heart starts to thump, steady and heavy.

We set off from camp, Duran in front and Stevie following. I trail behind, and she turns from time to time. Perhaps she can feel my eyes on her. She ought to be happy about it: there are other girls I could have chosen. But I chose her. And I'm nothing if not committed. Most of the pathway is clear through the forest, and it's cooler, the light dappled. High up above us in the trees, the vervet monkeys shriek. Duran glances back every now and then to check we're still with him. After a minute or so, I jog until I'm beside Stevie.

"Why do you walk everywhere like you're late for a meeting?" I ask.

"I don't like to lollygag," she says, not looking at me.

"This isn't lollygagging." I look up into the trees. "You just blazed past a really cool lizard. You didn't even see it."

"I know what lizards look like, Leo."

"They're all different."

"No, they're not." She stops now, so I do, too. "They're quiet, and they tiptoe around, and they change colors to blend in."

I pause, scratching my head, which is caked and salty. She really doesn't like lizards. I need to add that to my list of things I know about her. But she doesn't wait for me to reply, she just takes off again, hurrying through the forest. I jog after her, my rubber booties squelching.

158

"You don't walk this fast when you're at home," I say. "In Anchorite Bay, Maine. You enjoy an easy pace. You take the time to notice the little details of the day there." The ravens, I mean. The stone walls. The storms.

She stops dead on the path, hands on her hips. "How the fuck do you know that?"

"What? No, I'm just saying—"

"What is your deal, dude? Your beady eyes are on me wherever I go. Back the fuck off."

"How do you know my eyes are on you?" I run my fingertips along the bark of a mangrove tree. "Wouldn't that mean *you're* watching *me*?"

She moves closer, but not in a friendly way. "Whatever you're selling, Leo, I'm not buying. You might have fooled me at the start, but I know exactly who you are. You're a player. And you're mad I'm not in your fan club."

"My fan club?" Now I take a step toward her. "No, you're the only one I—"

"Stop choosing me! Stop acting like you know me! Stop . . ." she motions to all of me, ". . . this!"

She's breathing hard. I can see her chest rising and falling under the fabric of her shirt.

"When we first met, Stevie, you thought I was gorgeous. We had a thing. No, don't deny it! You felt it, too."

"It wasn't a thing," she says.

"It was. You couldn't take your eyes off me in the restaurant at Diani. Or by your window that night. And it was mutual, Stevie. That's what I'm saying: it was totally mutual." My voice sounds shrill, like there's a string in my throat that's close to snapping.

"You're delusional," she says. "You think I want to be with you? That I'll sleep with you, and you can put me in your little art book?"

"What art book?"

"Oh, you're not the only one who's been finding things out." She sets off down the path again, and I feel the top of my head baking in the sun. My scalp is tightening.

"I know about *your* book!" I shout after her, desperate now. "I know about Nattie and your mum and Cassia."

When she turns, her eyes are so ice blue that they're almost translucent.

"You're so busy falling in love with Tamsin," I say, "you've totally forgotten about me. But we're the same, Stevie. *I understand you.* We might even be soul mates."

"How do you know about Cassia?" Her voice is quiet, like a trap setting. "You read my journal? When?"

"She died right next to you, in your arms. And every day since, you've wondered how you could have done that to her, to someone you loved. How you could have killed—"

She flies at me, wild, like an animal. Pushes me hard in one shoulder, knocks me off balance into a tree.

"I didn't kill her!" she shouts, tears welling in those lovely eyes. "Don't you say that!" She shoves at my chest, again and again.

"It's okay," I say, absorbing everything she's got. "No, we're the same, Stevie, that's what I'm trying to tell you. You and I, we're two halves of the same broken heart."

Why won't she admit it? I don't understand. I've read those pages, all the things she wrote down. How she was with Cassia in the back of the car; the way she put her hands across the boy's face who was driving; how it was all just a joke, just a gimmick; she didn't know he was going to swerve. Except she did know. She must have. What else was he going to do?

She stands, tight with fury, breathing audibly through her nose. "Stay. The fuck. Away from me."

"I'm trying to help you—"

"No! Don't come near me. You're so fucking creepy. I can't even deal." She rushes away, running now, trying to catch up to Duran.

"Tamsin doesn't know you!" I shout after her. "She doesn't care like I do." My heart is pounding. It's not only outrage I feel. And before I know it, I'm running, too, thoughts fluttering in my head like wings. It's too late, I can't stop it, I've lost her. I run, but Stevie's as fast as I am, and she's already nearing the tree line. I stop short of the beach while I'm still in the shadows, bend double, gather my breath.

There's only one thing to do now. One terrible card I can play. Here I am again, a moth in the darkness, and as always in my life, I've arrived at the flame.

21

STEVIE

I burst out onto the sand, run past a stone well with my legs pumping, breath heaving in great rakes in my chest. How dare he say that?
How *dare he*? I didn't kill Cassia. It was an accident. I was a child! A
sixteen-year-old kid, party-stoned, carrying on like I didn't give a shit,
angry at the world as I made my life's greatest mistake.

Every day since, I've relived the few seconds that I blocked Josh
Hollander's vision. Thought about it awake and asleep. And the same
day the car crash happened, I told the police what I'd done, said it
twenty different times in the interview room. But still they wrote it all
down as an accident, ruled it that way, closed the case. Yet now, here's
Leo, using the whole nightmare against me, dragging it up to the light,
playing on the remnants of guilt that remain. And where has he gotten
all this insight from? Not even Jacob knows the depth of the aftermath. Leo's stolen my journal and read it. It has to be what he's done.

Duran is waiting by the tender, which is beached by a rocky inlet in the shade. I run over to him, wiping tears from my face.

"Are you okay?" he asks instantly. "What's going on?"

"Leo's obsessed with me, Duran, and it's getting out of control—"

"What are you talking about?" His eyes dart to the tree line. "He attacked you?"

"No, but he's scary, and I can't even—" But Leo emerges then, jogs lightly toward us down the sand. "Duran, help me. He's not well. I'm not even kidding at all."

Duran braces, his hands on his hips. As Leo approaches, Duran steps in front of me. "What happened back there?"

"Where?" Leo says. "Nothing."

"Stevie came barreling out of the woods like a startled deer. Were you chasing her?"

"No, I—"

"Did you put your hands on her?" Duran advances so they're chest-to-chest. "In any way at all, Leo? I'm dead serious."

"No!" Leo's voice rises now. "Don't be stupid. I didn't touch her!"

"He stole my journal and he read it," I say.

"*That's* what happened?" Duran asks, glancing at me and then back to Leo again. "You did that?"

Leo squirms, scratches at a patch of peeling skin on the back of his shoulder. "Not all of it. Not cover to cover." He holds up both palms, a parody of innocence. "Look, mate, the diary ended up in my hands—it was a misunderstanding—and I opened it before I gave it back. That's it—that's all. Anyone would have done the same thing in that situation. Been curious. Even you, Duran."

Duran studies his face. "She says you're obsessed with her."

"I'm not." Leo shoots me a lovestruck glance, a *How could you?* like I'm letting him down. He's insane. "It's not like that."

There's another beat. "Okay," Duran exhales. "Guys, let's get on with it. This boat needs to be in the water."

Wait, that's it? That's all he's doing? What the hell kind of help is that? And why, when a woman is in trouble, is it so often *a man* she has to appeal to?

"But Leo's . . . He's broken camp policy," I say, my mind desperately scrolling now. Has he done more on paper than steal my diary? There are so many moments I can't prove.

"Oh, for heaven's sake," Leo says. "I haven't laid a finger on you. I haven't done anything except follow you on Instagram, along with two hundred other people."

"And read her journal," Duran adds, moving to the back of the tender. "Which, for the record, I would never do."

"Yeah? Okay, then. Sorry, Captain America. Clearly we're not all flawless like you."

Duran's jaw is set as he takes one side of the boat and Leo takes the other. I help out but I cannot look at Leo. Everything I ate for breakfast is lodged high in my throat. It takes a lot of hauling to get the tender down the beach —we have to put some real effort into it—and I tug at the ropes, channeling my hate, until my forearms are striped red from the rubber siding. Once the boat is afloat, I clamber in, leaving Leo at the stern in the water. Duran sits down by the motor. But he doesn't pull the cord to get it started.

"Leo, is your name short for anything?" he asks. "Leonardo . . . Le—"

Leo stands still. "No."

Duran scratches his stubble. "And you said your last name's Asher?"

"Yes. Why?"

"I swear I've seen your face before. You're from the UK? Which part? I spent a couple months over there with my wife last year. It would have been around springtime."

Leo takes off his tank top, scrunches it into a ball and throws it into the boat. The thought of his skin makes me sick. My sarong is drenched and clinging to my legs but there's no way I'm taking it off. "I'm from London," he says.

"Huh." Duran shakes his head. "We didn't hang out in the cities."

"People always think they've met me before." Leo's eyes are a darker blue than I've ever seen them. "I'm a lot of different people. But let me know when you place me."

"I'll do that." Duran pulls the cord with the vigor of a man accepting a direct challenge. The engine roars and Leo tosses his dive booties into the tender, but Duran leans forward, picks them up, and flings them back onto the sand. "You're walking," he says. "I'll wait for you on the beach by the steps."

"I'm . . . what? No, I'm not walking—"

"You're walking," Duran says again. The air between them is loaded and thick. *Wow*, I think. *That's better. Maybe Duran's getting it after all.*

"Because of the diary?" Leo's face colors like a wrongly accused child's. "Or just because she's Jacob's girlfriend? Duran, listen to me, they shouldn't even be together—"

"Stop!" I shout at him, because God knows what else he's about to interpret from the pages he never should have read.

"She's afraid of you." Duran squints at him in the sun. "And until I find out exactly why that is, I'm taking it at a human level. I don't care whose girlfriend she is."

Leo's whole face is tight and hateful. But when he turns to me, all the fury dissipates. It's like one of those crazy mimes, where the sad face turns happy under the sweep of a white-gloved palm. It's terrifying.

He reaches toward me with his fingers, making me arch back in the boat. "Safe journey, Stevie. Catch you back at camp."

Immediately I look over at Duran. *See?* I'm telling him. *Do you see what I mean about him?* It's not that he says horrible things. He says nice things horribly.

Duran maneuvers the boat quickly out of Leo's reach, and I exhale little by little. We travel in silence for a few minutes, until he's not even a speck on the shore. The farther away we get from him, the less chalky my mouth starts to feel. Duran banks a wave and a fine spray of seawater covers my forearms like glitter. He cuts the engine and we idle, a wave passing underneath that raises us both like an inhale of a breath.

"When did he first start bothering you?" Duran asks.

"The day we got here," I say. "Or maybe on the boat journey over."

"He follows you? Reads your stuff? Just . . . what? Creeps around?"

"Yeah. Yes, all of that." I shudder involuntarily.

"Have you told him to stop?"

"Just now I did. I told him to back off."

"Okay. No, that's good. And he's never laid a finger on you? He's being truthful about that?"

"Yes. He hasn't touched me. But, Duran, I feel like he wants to."

He nods. "Have you told Jacob?"

"Not really." In truth, I'm starting to lose track of the things I haven't told him. "I mean, I've mentioned I feel uneasy generally, I guess, but things are so hard to . . . to pin down."

Duran looks out to the horizon for a minute. "Okay, here's what I'm going to suggest. I can't kick Leo off the camp for reading your journal. But I will speak with him, and tell him to clean up his act, and give him an official warning. He only gets one. I'll isolate him for the afternoon, and you and Jonesy should move in to the instructor's hut. Put anything personal in the safe in my office. With measures in place and me watching him closely, he should settle down and pull his head in."

"Okay," I say doubtfully. It's something, I suppose. But how isolated can Leo be on an island of this size? Mostly I just want him to go away. "If he's not who he says he is, can you kick him out of camp?"

Duran smiles. "Let's just see how we go for the next couple days.

I'll monitor him. You have my word. If he's a pest, we'll can him for sure."

"Good. Thank you. Okay." I pause. "Do you really think you've met him before?"

"No," Duran says. "But there's something. I can't put my finger on it." He revs up again and we ride in silence for a minute. "Dead Dog Beach, man," he yells. "There's always trouble."

"Why?" I shout back as our camp comes into view. "Why is it even called that?"

Duran cuts the engine and we steer toward the shore. "When we first set up here, the locals were worried we were going to ruin their income. You can understand it. If we protect the reef, we stop the dynamite fishing and the European ice boats waiting at the edge of the reef all go away. Ultimately, the locals make less money. It's always been hand-to-mouth out here, but it was never this difficult until Westerners interfered. Anyway, the villagers threw a dog into the well to poison our water supply." He says it so matter-of-factly, as if he's seen too much of what the world can do.

"Ugh. That's horrible. For everyone." I saw that well at the top of the beach, ran past it when I was fleeing Leo. What a ghostly gravesite. I feel surrounded by turmoil and grip the edge of the boat.

Duran raises his eyebrows. It's clear from his silence that he has stories—war zone ones, the ultimate inhumanity. "The main thing is to try and talk things over. Sometimes there's a way through."

I swallow hard. "Was the dog dead when they threw it in?" Why? Why do I always ask questions like this? It's like I actually *want* to feel worse.

"I don't know. Titus and I got him out. He's buried behind the rocks where we moor the boat. Nobody goes back there anymore: the locals say it's filled with evil spirits." Duran jumps out and pulls the tender until it scuffs in the shallows. "We had a meeting with the villagers. We figured it out."

"I guess that's something," I say, sliding over the edge to help.

"Look, go find Jacob. Tell him you're moving huts. Tell him why. Leo won't be back for another ten minutes or so. I'll intercept him. We'll figure all this out, too."

"Thanks, Duran." It's a nice idea, after all. But I can't help thinking that Leo's wilier than Duran realizes.

I run up the beach, hiking up my sarong to take longer strides. I won't have much time. I take the steps two at a time, sprinting once I reach level ground, past the office where Jacob will be, past the fire pit, past the tables where people are milling about, playing cards. I edge into the sleeping hut, my eyes adjusting, making sure no one's lurking at the back. Leo's backpack is leaning against his bed, a smaller day pack tucked underneath it. I pounce on it, fumbling with the buckles, my fingers wet and ineffective on the clasps, which are done up as tight as they can be. *Hurry, Stevie*, I think. *Get the evidence yourself. You need more than a journal that's been read.*

There are a bunch of things stashed in the day pack. A wallet— folded, leather, no time to look in it—and a cell phone, locked with a password. There's a photograph, curled at the edges, of a woman and a little boy standing in front of an enormous house. I almost drop it to the ground as I hurry. And then, tucked away at the back of the pack, there's his passport, like I knew it would be. For a guy hiding who he really is, there's no way he'd hand over his passport to a communal safe.

It's crisp at the corners. Maroon. Embossed with a gold coat of arms. I take it, put everything back, stow the bag where I found it. My knees are trembling. Leo will be here any minute, and he'll be coming straight for me. I crouch by his bed, holding my breath, and shakily flip to the back of the passport, my fingers itching to find the page that's glossy and laminated. And only then do I exhale, in a rush.

There's his photo. Handsome, upstanding, trustworthy. The kind of face that'd fly business class, that you'd sit next to, clink glasses with, and tell all your stories. And there's his name, in legal, indisputable print. LEOPOLD JAMES CAVENDISH. Not Asher at all. Not anything like what he said.

I cover my mouth with my hand, stare into this man's expressionless eyes. Leo Cavendish. Liar, stalker, creep. But then a new thought strikes me, with a fresh pinch of fear. This is a man who's certain I've killed someone. And yet, he thinks I'm his soul mate.

He thinks we're exactly the same.

22

LEO

I only walk until the tender is out of my view. After that, I run. I can't afford to let Stevie slip away. That bastard Mike Duran. Sticking his nose where it's not wanted. He has no idea what he's dealing with.

I fly along the sand, leaving only the lightest of footprints. Where will Stevie go when she gets off the boat? Straight to the arms of lily-livered Jacob? She won't find the slightest bit of solace there. Every cell of my body is straining to follow her, chase her, make her see. I'm fueled by the anger I feel. I don't think I've ever run faster. My fists are clenched and it's clear to me, looking down as they pump: here I am again, and the universe has decided I'm the villain, when everything I'm doing is right.

Below me, my feet thud on harder sand. The faster I move, the more rapid my thoughts, as though they're keeping a synchronized beat. Duran can't stop me. He can't, he won't. Flex all the muscles you want, throw as many dive booties as you like out of the boat, even tell me off in front of Stevie, but you know what, Duran? You're not better than me. You're twisting things. You're filtering them. Dad did that, too. And then look what happened.

I slow for a minute to catch my breath. What is it about stories that people always need to change them? In the weeks when I went back to see my father, those visits when I drank his tea and ate his biscuits, we talked a lot about my childhood and the parenting role he'd played. Except that as he talked, he altered everything. All the light he threw on himself was golden, all his choices utterly sane, as if, all along, he'd had a clear outcome in mind. There I stood, a grown man of twenty-seven, self-sufficient, successful, on course to be rich. Hadn't my father done well? Wasn't I a product of great decision-making? Not once did he lay claim to any of the cruelty he'd doled out.

"You were never a good boy, Leopold," he told me that February, a couple of weeks after my first visit. "Your mother always thought you were, but I knew better. I saw all the recesses inside of you where you hid."

"Because they're yours," I said. "I got them from you."

"Oh ho," he coughed out a laugh. "Perhaps you did. Remember that time you hid those cigarettes at the back of the cutlery drawer? You were—what? Nine?"

They were Mum's. I took the blame for her. Dad was back from a long tour overseas, kicking down every aspect of the life we'd built together while he was gone. Mum smoked one cigarette a day at 5 p.m. while she sat between our rosebushes by the pond. She enjoyed it. She inhaled luxuriously. I watched her lovingly each time, unseen.

"I made you smoke all the cigarettes in the pack, one after the other." Dad chuckled again, his face so smug as he waited for the memories to hit me.

In a flash, I was nine again, so defiant, refusing to break eye contact with him as I worked my way through the tobacco. Then, when I was sick on the carpet, he wouldn't let Mum help me clean it up.

"I remember, Dad." Oh, I remembered. Everything had been catalogued and stored.

"They were your mother's," Dad said, and I flinched. "Oh, spare me. She set you up your whole life. In you came on a valiant steed until she stole it from you, and poof! She was gone."

My jaw muscle was so tight I couldn't speak. That wasn't how it went at all. If the light he cast on himself was unbearable, the ugly shadow he cast over Mum was worse.

"Look at you!" Dad's chest was wheezy. "You act like she was the perfect mother, Leo. She might as well have had snakes for hair."

Still I said nothing. But things can only bend so far before they snap.

I continue walking along the beach, breathing hard as I round the corner into camp. *The prodigal son.* At my father's house, Dolores ended up calling me that as a nickname, never fully understanding the nuance in it, all the latent rage. Because, really, does anyone care what the young man in that story has been through? I mean, why has he even come home? Nobody bothers to ask. I pause as I see Duran sitting at the bottom of the beach steps. Here we go again. The nickname was fitting then and it's fitting now: all alone, a long-discarded soul, approaching a homestead that will soon wash its hands of me. And nobody's as worried as they should be about my point of view.

"You made it back," Duran says, blocking the lowest step. "Faster than the average walker."

"I ran."

"Okay." He stands, a hair's breadth taller than me. "Come with me. We need to unload the boat."

But it's not about chores or helping him out. He's like a groovy teacher—the one at school with the light-up Christmas sweater—who'll do his disciplining while pretending to be your friend.

"I need to go up to the huts," I say. "I'm thirsty."

"Nope. You need to stay here with me." He wades into the water and pulls items out of the tender: empty water jugs, a diesel can, ropes. I stand like a mule, resentment silently building while Duran packs more and more weight onto me.

"Can you take this one, too?" He holds up a length of chain.

"No," I say. "I want to go." I need to get to Stevie, to stop her from doing what I think she's doing right now.

"Listen, I'm hurrying, too, man. I have shit to deal with." He climbs into the boat, secures the motor, checks the tank. "Shit like running this camp, for instance, and keeping all the kids happy, figuring out what's going on between you and Stevie."

"Nothing's going on." Nothing that's any of his business.

"Look, I get it." He doesn't. "She's a pretty girl. And you're all out here, in the tropics, living young and wild and free. You think I don't know what happens between the recruits on camp? I've been running these things long enough." He pauses as if I'll enjoy his newfound relatability. "But why read her journal, man? That's over the line."

"Sorry," I say.

"Are you attracted to her?" He crosses his arms now, angling his fists beneath the biceps so that they bulge imperiously. "Do you think about her all the time?"

"What?"

"You heard me. Do you have romantic intentions?"

I pause, blinking. That was a word my mother used a lot. *Romantic*. The same night I'd rescued her over the cigarettes, she slipped into my bedroom and woke me as she got into my bed. It was past midnight: light through my curtains cast her cheekbones as almost skeletal.

"My darling." She kissed me near the eyebrow, her eyelashes butterfly soft. "How brave you are! I had to come and say thank you. My wonderful white knight." Her throat smelled of lilies and warmth. "Do you know that girls adore it when boys are brave? When they'll do anything for them?" I nodded, my hair raspy against the pillow. "And you"—she kissed me again—"are the very best at it. Age nine and you see everything about me, don't you?"

"Yes," I whispered.

"What do you see?" She lay her head flat. Our noses were an inch apart.

"You're beautiful," I said, and she made a noise that was similar to a purr.

"Am I? That's lovely, darling. What else?"

"And you're clever."

She paused, and my eyes widened in the gloom. Had I got it wrong? Been too vague? She seemed to like it best when I was specific.

"You know who isn't clever, Leo? Who can't see anything properly?"

I waited, misery spreading.

"That one next door." She put her palm against my cheek and I exhaled. "Your father's the troll under the bridge. Do you know that when he snores in the night, all the windows rattle?"

Now I giggled and she grasped me closer, the whole outline of her body against me through her nightdress. Her ribs were like the wire of a cage; I liked the enmeshment.

"Gosh, sometimes I just want to eat you up," she said. "Do you feel like that about me?"

"Yes," I said, although I wasn't sure I'd ever considered such a thing.

"Good, then it's decided." She moved away from me, getting out of bed, leaving traces of her heat on the pillow. "My little romantic. We're for each other. And you'll do anything for me."

"Leo!" Duran's arms were still crossed. "I asked you a question, man."

"What? No, I don't have intentions toward Stevie. Not bad ones. Not at all. I read something I shouldn't have. End of story. Job done."

"I'm documenting it," he says, climbing out of the tender, all semblance of chumminess gone. "Consider this an official warning. Get another one, and you're out." He nods once, confirming I've understood, but I don't like his tone. Blood begins to fizz in my head like a foam. "And from now on leave Stevie alone. You so much as *look* at her funny and I'll be watching. Am I clear? There will no longer be situations where you two are alone together. And I'm putting you on boat watch for the next few hours. Here on this beach. You'll be kit guy with Titus today while the others dive."

"Boat watch?!"

"Sit in the shade, guard our gear. We've been losing stuff left and right."

"Oh, for crying out loud, this really isn't—"

"Nonnegotiable. It's this or head back to the mainland. You choose."

We start to walk up the steps. Behind him, I clench and unclench my jaw.

"Which do you want?" Duran says, turning.

"To stay here," I mumble.

"Okay, then. So we understand each other." After a few seconds, he stops. "Can I hear you say it, please?"

"For fuck's sake! Yes, I understand you! I'm not four."

He waits, bites his bottom lip, won't let us move any farther up the steps. "When you lived in London before, Leo, were you on TV at all? Could I have seen you in a show while I was over there?"

Drop it, Duran. You're getting warmer now.

He won't budge. "Or on the news?"

I let the water jug fall to the dirt, wrench the rope off my shoulder, toss the diesel can. "You know what? Carry your own shit." I push past him, making sure to bump his shoulder. "This is fucking bollocks."

"Leo—"

"No, I never signed up to be your packhorse. I'm thirsty. I'm getting a drink. Then I'll come and stare at a boat in the water for three hours. See—I'm doing everything I'm told, okay, Staff Sergeant?" I move up the hill before he can answer. There's limited time now. He's just slowing me down.

I'm almost at the top of the stairs when I run into Titus coming down them. He's a big fellow and he blocks my access. He even steps to the side when I do, as if it's a game.

"What?" I glare up at him. "Could you please get the fuck out the way?"

He grins. "*Polepole.* Slow it down, my bru."

I try again to get past him. But he shuffles, wagging his finger at me. "I've been hearing things about you. Two weeks now, I've been hearing things."

Needles and pins start to prick at the surface of my skin. "What things?"

"I see you."

I draw level with him, stare into his eyes. He has that look that says he knows me, that he's got me all figured out, and it's the same way my father looked at me in his study that final day. Before the doubt came, and then the fear, before his arms went slack by his side in the chair and the last rasp of his breath rattled quiet.

"We need to talk. You and me, my bru." Titus tugs at my shirt, pulling me into the scrub of mangroves where the ground is uneven. But I don't want to go in there, don't want to be with him, don't want anything that exists on this camp except Stevie. And I've had it, I've had it up to here with people's judgments and assumptions, so I shove him with the full force of my hands—just like I did with Dad—ramming him into the gnarl of a mangrove tree, pushing him back with my shoulder in his chest until he bellows. Titus checks the skin on his shoulder blade with his fingertips, and when he holds his palm up, they're bright red.

And I stare at him, horrified, because I know right then that this isn't the end of something, it's just the beginning. Like a whistle that's been blown, a red flag: this is it, we're in motion now. Here is the first of the blood that will flow.

23

STEVIE

I run so fast from the sleeping hut to the office, I barely register who's in camp. All I know is there's no Leo. I scramble into Duran's office—empty—and then remember, tanks, compressor shed, so I run there, halfway back down the steps, noticing the outline of Titus a little farther down in the scrub of mangrove bushes, although I don't know what it is that he's doing. I hurry across to the small wooden hut, the passport tight in my fist.

"Wow," Jacob says, looking up from where he's crouching in the dirt beside a dive tank. "Where's the fire?"

"Jacob, I need to—" I begin, but then I stop. Tamsin is kneeling next to him, silky hair brushing against his arm as she blows sand from the tank valve, the neckline of her tank top drooping. "What are you two doing?"

Tamsin sits back. "Filling tanks. It's well boring. What's the matter with you?"

I swallow, throat dry, as a sudden image of Cassia projects in my head—how she flirted with boys and never wanted any of them. *They're so basic I could cut them out of cardboard.*

"Tamsin offered to help me in here." Jacob looks a little clammy, but I can't tell if it's heat, guilt, or excitement. Would anything have developed if I hadn't walked in? I feel a plunge of betrayal, of indignation at being left out, but again—just like at Diani Beach—I don't know who I'm aiming it at.

"I need to talk to you," I say flatly. "I've found something out."

"You need to talk to me?" Jacob points to his own chest, which has grown considerably in the past two weeks. He's been getting up early to go running, does push-ups beside the bed each night.

"Tamsin, too. This affects her."

"Blimey," Tamsin says, bracing herself.

"Leo was really scary on the walk to Dead Dog Beach," I say, moving away from the wooden door of the hut.

"Scary how?" Tamsin brushes grit from her hands. "What did he do?"

"Did he hurt you?" Jacob stands.

"No, but he said things that suggest—"

"He wouldn't hurt her—he's crushing on her." Tamsin smiles up at Jacob, who frowns.

"Jacob, he read my journal. He knows all about my mom, and Nattie, and Cassia. He thinks Cassia's death was my fault, and now he's saying that we're soul ma—"

"Who's Cassia?" Tamsin's head tilts.

"Your fault?" Jacob says. "Why would he think that?"

"Did you tell him anything about me?" I ask, my voice rising now. "Have you spoken about the car accident?"

"No!" Jacob matches my tone. "He's been really annoying lately. I haven't told him anything at all."

"Well, he freaked me out. And I told Duran, and he thinks we should move huts so we can have some privacy." I avoid making eye contact with Tamsin. Somehow it's now me who's betraying something. "He's probably talking with Leo on the beach right now. He wouldn't let him ride back in the tender with us."

"Oh, Leo's getting *told*," Tamsin says. "His little heart will be broken."

Jacob and I look at her. How is any of this funny?

"But Duran can't kick him out of the camp for just reading my journal and crushing on me, so I—"

"Wait—kick him out of the *camp*?" Suddenly Tamsin clambers to her feet, too. "That's actually a thing?"

"He's stalking me, Tamsin! This isn't a light-hearted crush. This isn't normal behavior." Jacob's and Tamsin's faces are identically pale. "And so I looked in his bag."

"In Leo's?" Jacob widens his mouth like I'm going to get tossed off the island, too.

"I found *this*." I hold the passport up. For a second, they both stare at it, like I'm gripping an old piece of toast.

"His passport." Tamsin reaches for it and I hand it over. "This should have been in the safe. Is that what you mean?"

"Open it," I say.

Jacob takes it from her loose grasp and flicks to the laminated page at the back. His eyebrows shoot up. "Leopold *Cavendish*?"

"Who?" Tamsin snatches the passport back. "He never said his name was that."

"Didn't you notice?" Jacob asks. "You didn't look at his passport photo? I thought all couples did that at the airport."

"No, I did—and his photo is lush like *GQ*, look at it—but he must have had his thumb over his name." She looks more closely at the small print. "Not surprisingly. I mean, who the hell wants to be called *Leopold*?"

"Why would he be traveling with a fake name, Tamsin?" I say. "It has to mean he's hiding something."

She waits for a few seconds. "Like what, for instance?"

"Well, how much do you really know about him? You only met him about four months ago. He could have told you any old story about where he came from, or who he is."

Tamsin recoils, takes a strand of long hair and starts to suck the end of it.

"It must link back to that court case he spoke about," Jacob says. "Jesus, I don't want him anywhere *near* you, Stevie, if he's—"

"We need to get rid of him," I say. "Right now. Today."

"Axel's not using his first name," Tamsin mumbles. "He told me it's his middle name. He's trying it out over here."

"What?" I shake my head. "What's his first name?"

"I've no idea," she says. "But it's not unheard of. Going traveling, reinventing yourself. I know there was a court case, but Leo's traveling to get over his grief. That's what he told me." Her lips seem to stick on her teeth. Poor Tamsin. She's trying so hard to make it innocuous.

"Okay, look," Jacob says, turning off valves, unhooking hoses hurriedly. "We need to google him. We'll use the laptop in Duran's office."

But as we hurry out of the hut together, we bump straight into Duran, who's struggling up the beach steps with ropes, a chain, and two heavy diesel cans. He looks salty and too hot.

"Leo Asher isn't Leo Asher," Jacob blurts, holding up the maroon passport.

"No?" Duran doubles over on the sandy step, hands on his hips. "Who is he, then?"

"Leopold Cavendish," I say. There's a second while I wait for the name to register with Duran.

"Okay. Maybe that rings a bell? I still can't place it. And *you* didn't even know?" he says, looking at Tamsin, who's sucking her hair again. "Well, let me speak with him. He's getting a drink, then I've assigned him to boat watch, although I was hoping Titus would oversee it. But he took off down the beach just now and wouldn't speak to me." He pauses, exhausted. "Okay, I'll have a word with Leo again before we set out for the dive."

"No, but he's—" I begin, but Duran cuts me off.

"Hey, I don't like that the guy read your journal any more than you do, but I ironed all that out with him just now. He's compliant. He knows how he has to behave."

"But he lied when he registered." My voice is starting to sound whiny, but I can't help it. Nobody's taking Leo seriously enough.

"GoEco's a volunteer program, Stevie. People can sign up for it under any name they want. We don't ask for birth certificates. We're not recruiting them into the army."

"That's what I said," Tamsin mutters. "Any name you want."

"But what if he's—" I try one more time, but Jacob nudges me and I stop.

Duran wipes sweat from his forehead with the back of his hand. "Instead of getting a posse together—pitchforks at dawn—can you please help me out with this gear? It needs to go up to the wetsuit rack."

All of our shoulders drop. One by one, we all pick up an item.

"What a shitty day," Duran says. "Everything's a fight."

We move behind him without speaking. Tamsin, beside me, seems lost in thought. Jacob still has Leo's passport in one hand, and when he shoots me a glance, I agree with him. This isn't the time to move slowly. If only Duran would sense the urgency, but his strides are as slow and deliberate as a donkey's on a mountain incline. And none of us have the confidence to push past him.

24

LEO

Stevie's found my passport. I knew she'd go looking. It has to have been her: she was retaliating, invading the privacy of my personal belongings. And she's the only one who really thinks like me. If Duran hadn't made me walk or kept me on the beach holding diesel cans, I'd have intercepted her and finally everything would have changed.

I ran away from Titus as soon as I could, looking for Stevie, but when I got to the sleeping hut, my bag wasn't how I'd left it. The passport was gone and obviously she had it, but where was she hiding? It was possible she was in the compressor shed, but I couldn't really go looking—not right away, at least, not until Duran had come back to check on me and made sure I was on the beach, behaving like a good boy as promised. Right on cue, he arrived just now touting the knowledge of my real name as if it were his own discovery. But that's the thing about Duran—we're all meant to believe in his supremacy.

But it wasn't him. He's completely lost. And every question he asks is wrong.

"Hi," he said, back in buddy mode, as I sat watching the boat motor from the shade of the only tree. "Are you doing okay down here on your own?"

"Yes," I said. "Marvelously, thank you for asking."

"You have enough water? I know you get thirsty."

I lifted my water bottle. Pointed it at him. A *cheers*. A *touché*.

"Okay, well, don't let anybody on or off the boat. That motor cost—"

"I know," I said. "It's European engineering."

Duran put his hands on his hips, standing on the lowest beach step. "Leo, I've found out that you didn't register for this program under your actual name."

He waited, but so did I. At that point, the less I said the better. It was like all those times as a child when my father called me into his study to ask me questions about Mum. *What does she do while I'm abroad? Is there anything you need to tell me?* he'd ask while he stacked money and papers into his safe, trying to fool me into thinking our conversation wasn't his real focus. I stonewalled him then, just like I'd stonewall Duran.

"Leo, it's not regulation that you sign up with the name stated in your passport. I mean, we're a pretty relaxed outfit." Again, I said nothing, but Duran's chummy-teacher approach was transparent. It didn't even work the first time. "Can you explain why you're using an alias?"

"Yes."

"Okay." Duran frowned. "So . . . it's for . . . personal reasons? That you'd rather not talk about?" I raised my eyebrows but didn't respond. Duran scratched at his ear. "Okay, well, I just wanted to flag it. Not a big deal. But just so you know, I know."

Do you? I thought. *I wouldn't be so confident.*

"I have to help the others sort through the gear from the boat," he said. "You won't need your kit since you're not diving. But holler up if you need anything."

I raised my water bottle again. As if I cared about his stupid dive. He took my salute as a goodbye.

Five minutes go by while I stare at the boat and its motor. The important thing right now is precision. I was always too broad at crucial points with my mother—too foggy, too young, too vague. If I'd told her specifics when she'd asked for them—been better, done better—perhaps she'd have realized and stayed. And I shoved Titus earlier with the same muddled sense of intent: I didn't mean to hurt him, but I'd done it all the same. *You're a bad guy*, he shouted, wanting to hurt me back, but knowing he couldn't. It was a moment my father would have been comfortable with, all the ugly power within it, all the presumption. The very essence of imperialism, housed in the swiftest of seconds. He took off down the beach steps while I ran up them, my mind already on other things. Because with Stevie I need to get it right. Everything has to be exact. And now that she knows my name, it's only a matter of time before she finds out my history, adding it to the growing list of sins for absolution.

I make sure Duran has gone before I follow him up to the camp. The compressor shed has been left open, the rickety door hanging wide on its hinges. A hundred feet away by the drying rack, everyone is already gathering gear for the dive, Duran, Stevie, Tamsin, and Jacob busying themselves untangling the rope and chains they must have carried the rest of the way from the tender. Jacob seems newly alert and energized. Too late, though. Sorry. He won't be able to block anything now.

Nobody notices me as I walk. I've found, in all aspects of my life, that if I move with a certain sureness, people never question me or ask me to stop. I slip into Duran's office, which is empty. What an unimaginative space. He hasn't put any character into it, short of a few crinkled photographs stuck to the wall that, again, denote epic heroism. But I can't hang about cataloging all the ways in which he's predictable, so I grab a couple of sheets of paper from the printer, a pen from his desk, and then heave his big filing cabinet away from the wall. Bending, I disconnect the Wi-Fi modem for the internet and push the cabinet back again. It'll buy me a little time. Enough for what I need.

When I jog back out of the office and down the steps toward the beach again, everyone's still working on the boat gear. It's possible Axel sees me, but he's not the sharpest tool in the box. I doubt he'd dare interrupt Duran's work, anyway. Some guys are deer in the headlights when there's an overinflated army guy running the show.

Once I've set up in the shade of the beach tree again, I lean with my back against a smooth rock and take a deep breath in and out. Focus, Leo. Focus. Stevie's passport discovery demands a multitiered, rapid response. I might be a moth at a flame, but I am not without a sense of purpose. And writing things down brings clarity. It leads to a tidier finish.

This is where we're at now, Stevie, this is what it's come to. We're for each other, but you forced my hand, went looking for facts in all the wrong places. You might have my passport, but if you really want to know me—and I think you do—for better or worse, you'll have to read this letter. I lay my legs flat in the cool sand, liking the warmth of the rock behind me. How comforting it is that stone holds on to heat like a memory, and yet, leaning against it, there's only ever the inference that the memories it holds on to are good. It's simple for the rock: it's all just been sunshine, after all. If only people had that luxury.

Dear Stevie, I write, and then I stop. It's tempting just to leave it there, since it encapsulates everything. What else is worth saying? She's dear to me. It's such a throwaway beginning, one we all write without thinking at the top of a page. And yet for me, when it comes to her, it's so romantic. Tears well up and I press them away with the heel of my palm. Stop it, Leo. Stop it and be a man. Write the next sentence and get on with it.

Dear Stevie, I am very sorry about the things I've done.

Overhead, a bird cries out and I look up into a porcelain sky. I wrote my father a letter like this, too, explaining myself away before I killed him. It was about a month after I'd first seen him in his study, that fateful day he told me I wasn't set to inherit a penny, and that my mother had abandoned me all on her own. Dolores let me in. It was a Tuesday in late February, soft rain tapping at the windowpanes like the ghosts of old fingertips. My father was sitting in his chair.

"Hello, Leopold. Back again?" He pointed a weak arm at my doctor's bag. "What's in there?"

"I've come straight from work, Dad." I set my belongings down. "I've brought something for you."

"Oh, goody," he said, like a child expecting a cupcake.

When I opened the bag and handed him the letter, he looked unabashedly disappointed. But that letter. It was a stroke of genius on my part, because it took his mind off what was actually happening. It busied him. It gave me the opportunity to act without him looking at my hands or my face.

Dad, I'd written, *I don't forgive you for anything. And now look what you're making me do.* When he finally glanced up at me, his eyes were watery and young like a boy's. I waited with my arms behind my back because I knew he'd have to read the whole page twice. He was a military man. It's always about precision. I stood still until he got close to the final sentence. Then I unlaced my hands and moved toward him in his chair.

I regret my father's death now. Not the fact of it, so much as the speed. He exited without any real ownership of the damage he'd done, and I should have gone slower, made him work more, shown him how wrong he was about everything. Because in the end, I freed him. I was his deliverance. I might have sidestepped prison, but he got away with so much more than me.

Of course, after it was done, I burned that letter. What I'd written was just for me and for him—it was so layered, so rich—and had anyone else read it, the intricate weave of the ways in which I hated him would have been lost. And I knew they'd come looking—all the policemen, the forensics, the media. The letter couldn't become part of the trial. Nor could the vials of chemicals. They would have been a death blow for my lawyers and me.

This letter, though, this one is for Stevie. She knows my real name. As long as she understands what I've done, and what I have to do now—here, tonight, on this island—then we're as connected as we always have been. The loudest voice in my head will be heard. See how much progress I've made? My psychiatrist would be very proud of me.

25

STEVIE

We organize our gear for the dive, backs turned to the beach steps. Every few seconds I stop and check the tree line for signs of Leo. Duran said he's on boat watch down on the beach, but is he really? I haven't seen him for over an hour—he definitely didn't come up here to get water—and part of me thinks he's sneaking in and out of places unseen. There's a slick kind of shiver on the surface of my skin, an animal instinct, telling me to get ready, to stay vigilant. It's all I can do to untangle the ropes.

Duran set us straight to work as soon as we made it up from the compressor shed, and now, even after he's spoken with Leo, we still can't get into his office because Greta is in there with him. She's demanded some kind of private conference, her face as flat as a slap.

"What's her problem?" Jacob mutters, putting away diesel cans and supplies as the office door shuts.

"She's always in some kind of mood," Tamsin says quietly. "You should have seen her in the last place."

"Let's stow this gear quickly, then there'll be free time," I say.

But the ropes are tangled, the chains are in greasy knots, and everything is taking so long.

"You don't need to keep scanning the trees." Jacob grinds his thumb into another knot. "Leo isn't in there. And Duran has it covered—he'll be following camp protocol. There are steps."

"Can't he just jump to the last one?" I ask.

Jacob stands, rests his hand at the nape of my neck. "We'll check our phones in a second. No way I'm diving before doing that."

Good, I think, although I'm aware vaguely of Tamsin watching me. She's standing by the wetsuit drying rack, running her thumb and forefinger along the stitching of the neoprene, withdrawn-looking and dazed. I shift away from Jacob's touch. For two weeks I've been edging further and further away from him, chancing at something truer in me and harder to find. The closer I am with him now, the less honest I feel.

"Okay, are we all set?" Duran arrives beside us, rubbing his hands together. "Jonesy, can you bring my fins? I'm going to go fetch Titus back and get him to help me load tanks from the shed."

"Greta's okay?" Jacob asks, and Duran shrug-nods.

"I'll tell you later," he says.

"Is everyone diving?" Tamsin drifts out from between the wetsuits. "Is Leo?"

"He'll be on the boat. Supervised. All good."

Tamsin's arms are by her side but there's a glassiness to her. Is she angry, deflated, or in denial? I can't seem to get a clear read.

"We just need to check something before we head out," Jacob says, glancing over at me. "Stevie and I will catch up."

"Me, too," Tamsin says.

"Five minutes." Duran heads off to the steps. "No pitchforks at dawn."

The three of us run to the sleeping hut; each of us digs for our cell phones. Mine is almost out of power, but I type *L-e-o-p-o-l-d C-a-v-e-n-d-i-s-h* into Google—like the others do—all of us hunching over our screens, fingers fumbling and full of adrenaline. On my phone, the search engine wheel spins and spins.

"Shit," Jacob says, looking up. "There's no signal. Are you getting anything?"

"Nothing," Tamsin says.

"The internet must have crashed." Jacob exhales heavily. "Duran says it happens all the time—"

"How long will it be down for?" My voice feels shrill. It's as if the universe *wants* Leo to escape.

"Shouldn't be long. A few hours maybe? It'll be working again when we get back from the dive." Jacob shoves his phone into his bag.

"And if it isn't," Tamsin says, "there have to be other places on the island that have Wi-Fi." Is she hoping for proof or vindication? Mostly she just seems sad.

"Right," I say. "God, though. Of all the bad timing."

We leave the hut, jogging down the steps to the dhow. As we crest the hill, it's clear Leo is already on board. I can't bear to look at him, even though he's standing with his arms crossed, a sentinel, waiting for me. Everyone's loading gear, including Titus, who must have wandered back to help out. He's brooding. Silent. We hand our wetsuits and fins to Manu, then clamber onto the boat. As I pass Leo, he leans in toward me.

"I read your diary," his words waft over my skin, "but did I *tell anyone what you wrote*?"

My face wheels up at him, disgusted, but his expression is serene, benevolent. Does he actually think he's done me a *favor*? I push past him to the far end of the boat, fingernails clenched, ready to claw off all his magnanimity.

We take off from the dock toward the deep wall of the reef. The water is soupy as we go, viscous and thick as mercury. Manu and Louie sit up on the edge of the dhow, and everyone's quiet, liking the flow of air, but my mind isn't on the dive. Or if it is, it's in terms of the predators, the fast ones that'll be moving up from the deep. All at once, I'm aware I'll have no sense at all of what's beneath me.

"I don't think I can dive," I announce suddenly. Everyone stares at me.

"That's fine. You can stay on the boat with me." Leo smiles.

My vision starts to blot like it always does when I feel flooded, and I breathe in and out, in and out, just like after the car crash when I was alone in the dark with Cassia.

"Hey, we'll go together," Jacob says, and immediately the view widens again. Old safety. Familiar pathways.

"Let's keep this short," Duran says. We've reached the dive site and Titus has lowered the mainsail and tied to a buoy, wincing at an injury he's patched on the back of his shoulder. "The current's flowing, so watch your gauges, don't go deeper than twelve meters. I want you guys back in the boat in twenty. Stay together. Keep track of your time and put in a safety stop." There's a general setting of dive watches, checking of straps. Duran spits in his mask and rubs the saliva around the glass before rinsing it behind him in the ocean. "Greta and Ted, you're diving together. Manu and Louie; Axel and Hugues. Tamsin, you can buddy with me."

She looks up at the sound of her name, her eyes tired. "Great," she says, glancing my way. "Double date."

Two by two we jump into the water, arms pressed across our fronts to keep regulators and masks in the right spot. I tread water, eyes on Leo, who leans on the rim of the dhow like a parent who's proud that I can swim. I'm desperate to escape from his view, and so after a quick buddy check, Jacob and I descend, bubbles puncturing the surface until our lungs are too deep to feature. As soon as we're below the surface and my ears have filled with water, I hear nothing other than the clicking of plankton. As with every dive, the quiet comes like a reprieve. It's immediately calming.

We're caught by the current straightaway, and Jacob takes my hand. His fingers in the water are firm and strong. Just ahead of us in the flow are Duran and Tamsin. I can see the long flex of her calf muscles as she fins. Next to them, a little farther from the wall, are Greta and Ted, struggling with their buoyancy. Along we all whip, smooth and streamlined, and at one point I find a turtle with an old, wizened face that reminds me a little of Nattie. I hold the memory of her as long as I can, flying along beside the little guy before he sweeps away and the image dissipates. Soft coral flumes as if in a heavy wind.

We're about ten minutes into the dive when Greta suddenly begins to flounder, wheeling her arms back like she's trying to preempt landing from a great height. She clutches at Ted, who flaps, too. *No air*, she's signaling, her flat hand slicing frantically at her throat. *No air.* Her eyes through the glass of her mask are wide white circles. Jacob and I fin over to her and he grips both her fists, holds her down as she tries to kick for the surface. She can't—she mustn't—she might get the bends, and there's no decompression chamber on the island.

She claws at her mask next, looks set to rip it from her face, and the four of us careen like formation skydivers straining to form a circle, trying not to cartwheel, trying not to panic. Jacob reaches for his tank, finds the spare reg, jams it toward Greta's mouth. As soon as she gets oxygen, she stops pawing at her gear. Jacob holds her like a lover in the force of a gale, and the two of them stay like that, pinned together at chest and hip, Greta's pigtails billowing sideways, her eyes intent on his. They breathe as one, calming down, surfacing slowly. Jacob signals for Ted and me to do the same.

As soon as we're through the surface, noise hits me like the flat blade of a shovel. Greta has her mask around her neck and is gagging, coughing out sobs and saltwater. Her inhales sound like a terrible sickness. Jacob is blowing his dive whistle and yelling for Titus to come: we can see the boat, but it's a ways off, and we huddle around Greta, inflating her buoyancy compensator device so she's head and shoulders out of the swell.

Jacob keeps checking her face and his watch. "You're okay," he keeps telling her, wiping hair from her cheekbone. "Deep breaths, in and out, good girl."

She looks limp and terribly pale. Below us, the water is who knows how deep. Our legs dangle in the blue and I tread water, trying not to think about what's down there.

Titus pulls the boat alongside and the three of us haul Greta up to him. She scrapes her knee on the edge as he heaves her in: I see the streak of blood mix like oil with the water on her skin. Leo helps me in next—I can't stand that our hands are interlinked, even for a second—and I wrench away as soon as I'm back onboard.

"What's happening?" he asks. "A spot of trouble?"

We ignore him as a foursome, dump our gear, toss fins, wriggle out of our tanks and BCDs as Titus hurries to get the first-aid kit. Jacob undoes Greta's gear, unclips her dive belt, drags the tank off of her. He grabs her gauge and looks at the bars of air, compares it to his own, Ted's, and mine. We're all at around 150 bar; hers is beyond the warning level of 50, the needle sitting dead at zero.

"There's no way she used it all up," Jacob says to me, while Leo hangs back by the bow. "There can't have been more than 20 bar in that tank." He unzips the red pouch, then looks up straight at me. "Did I padlock the door to the compressor shed when we left it?"

We lock eyes, as Duran and Tamsin surface and Titus pulls them onto the boat.

"What's happening?" they both say at once. "What's wrong?"

"She ran out of air," Jacob says. "We managed a controlled ascent, Duran, but there wasn't a safety stop."

Tamsin kneels, sweeping a strand of Greta's bangs gently to the side. Greta's eyes move, but nothing else.

"How did she—" Duran turns, noticing Leo, who leans with his back against the gunnels.

"She's not looking too good, is she?" Leo says. "She's going into shock. You might want to warm her up a little bit."

Duran intercepts Titus with the first-aid kit, while I wrap my arms around Greta, who hasn't said a word since we got out of the water. Jacob bends, too, and he and Tamsin help me peel off Greta's wetsuit. She shivers, her breathing rapid. "Jacob," I hiss. "Greta spoke with Duran earlier today. Do you think it was about Leo?"

"I don't know, I don't know." Panic's hitting him now. Greta's body is limp. She doesn't move a limb as we pull the wetsuit away.

"Maybe she knows something about him and he—"

"What are you all whispering about?" Leo asks, and Tamsin looks horrified.

"Take your wetsuits off, too, and lie down with her," Duran says, returning to our side of the boat with a tinfoil blanket. He bites at the plastic wrapping, flaps the blanket open, holds it wide.

"I should lie down?" I ask.

"She needs skin-on-skin." Jacob nods but his teeth are gritted. "The body heat and the comfort. Hug her, guys—Ted, you too. All of you. Cuddle in."

"Not you, Leo," Duran says. "You stay right there."

Leo crosses his arms, watching with what looks like derision as Jacob makes a pile from the wetsuits we all stamp off, raising Greta's legs and resting them on top of it. Tamsin and I go to one side of her and Ted goes to the other; we wedge ourselves along the damp, puckered line of her. I try not to think of anything other than helping, try to ignore Leo's gaze and the smell of Tamsin's coconut moisturizer, the smooth tanned press of her back against the front of my body as we spoon. Jacob lays the crinkly blanket over top of us and tucks in every edge.

After five minutes or so, I hear Greta say something and raise my head. "What did you say? Are you okay?"

"Stevie," she repeats, licking dry lips. "Help me."

I shift, my throat acid-raw, and a billow of clammy heat escapes from under the tinfoil blanket. Oh, God, Cassia said exactly those words—*exactly them*—and I couldn't help her, I didn't. And they wrapped me in a rescue blanket just like this one, shone a flashlight in my eyes, all the firefighters working around the crushed shell of Josh Hollander's car after the hour I'd wriggled out and lain alone by the wreckage. But there's something else in the memory, something darker that's starting to rise now, like some kind of monster creeping out of a cave. What is it? What can't I see? More heat gathers and my airway is starting to constrict.

"Stevie?" Tamsin shifts, looking at my face. "Are you okay? Don't worry, we *are* helping."

Greta weasels under the blanket and a sob builds in my throat. I clamber out, crawl on all fours to the stern. Jacob hurries after me, guides me toward the edge of the boat where I take huge lungfuls of air. Behind me, Axel and the French boys are surfacing from the dive now—they climb aboard, stowing gear, shooting glances at Greta, Ted, and Tamsin who lie like cutlery in a drawer.

"We're having a problem, guys," Duran says to the group. "Jacob, are you good? We need to get back to shore."

Jacob checks that it's safe to leave me alone, then returns to Greta's side, crouching there with Duran. The two of them check her as they huddle, their conversation hushed and urgent. Everyone else takes a seat on the deck, frightened, a low-level hum of confusion around the boat as Titus steers us back toward camp. Only one of us remains standing, staring out from the bow with his back to us all like a proud nautical figurehead. How interesting it is that Leo's fine. He doesn't seem rattled at all.

26

LEO

Of course they think I emptied Greta's tank. Isn't it obvious? I had access, intent, and motive. But, as is beginning to be a pattern with me, it isn't very easy to prove. Try as they might, they can't quite pin it on me.

All the way up from the dhow, I offered to carry things, but nobody was really speaking to me—especially Stevie, who made a point of hanging back, muttering with Tamsin all the way up the steps from the beach. Greta's going to be fine. She's had a shock, of course, but with that many divers around her, it was never going to be life-threatening and there won't be any lasting damage. Once she's had a drink of water and half an hour in the shade, she goes straight to the sleeping hut and begins packing her bags. Smart girl. At least she's realized what this camp is really about. She seems to be the only one with her eyes open.

I stay in the eating hut, tidying plates and mugs. The key for me now is to be valuable, so they won't kick me off the island. Being essential is a must. It's the same as when my mother came to me when I was fifteen, a few hours before that summer party where I burned my father's bookshelves to the ground.

"Darling," she'd said, turning her bare back to me, holding up her hair with one hand. "The guests will be here any mo', but could you do me up, old boy?" I fumbled with her zipper, the satin of her dress slippery under my fingertips. "That's perfect. Now, how do I look?"

"Lovely." A bubble gummed in my throat and I coughed to clear it. "Like a film star."

"Sweet boy." She put her palm flat against my cheek and I tilted my head into it. "You don't look so bad yourself. You're getting quite muscly and girls love that. Although you could stand up a little straighter. Flatten your hair." She hesitated, studying me. "Leo, there's something I wanted to ask you."

"What is it?" I opened the top drawer of my dresser, searching for a comb.

She inspected the flawless paint of her nail polish. "Do you happen to know the combination to your father's safe?"

I turned. Said nothing.

"No, it's not urgent—and I could ask him myself, but you know what he's like. I don't want to wake up the troll! And I just thought, since you're in his study so often, you might have clocked the combo. You're such a watchful boy."

"I don't know it," I said.

Something changed in her eyes, the slightest glint of something colder. "Gosh, it's not very romantic or, or . . . *heroic*, is it, to fall apart at the first sign of a quest?"

"Mum, I don't—"

"Don't, can't, won't. It's all the same thing. And that's fine, Leo. I understand. Clearly I need to reevaluate your position." She swept out of the room, leaving me still holding the comb.

I failed her, I think all over again, as I reorganize the crockery in the hut. *Would she have disappeared if I hadn't?* Behind me, I hear Stevie exhale and I turn around, hoping above all else that she, at least, will properly understand how I feel about her. The letter I've stowed for her so carefully will mean history can't repeat itself. Surely she'll open it tonight.

"Leo, that's my mug and plate. Stay away from them." Tamsin's sitting so tightly next to Stevie on the bench that she might as well sew the seams of their clothing together.

"Or what?" I reply, beaconing such hatred at her that it seems impossible she wouldn't feel it on her skin.

She shifts, readjusting, gathering courage. "Stay away from me, too. From both of us."

"You know how your dad keeps getting divorced?" I reply loudly and her face turns to chalk. "I was thinking about it, and maybe it's *you* he's leaving. Again and again, he's just trying to get further away."

She stands, her eyes watery, and stumbles away toward the beach. *Good*, I think. *Keep walking, don't stop 'til the water's above your head.*

Stevie glowers at me. A second later, she's gone, too.

It isn't long before Duran comes to speak with me. It's so obvious a move that I'm hunched forward on the empty bench waiting for him, forearms resting on my thighs, fingers interlaced.

"My office," he says. No *hello*. No *how are you*.

I walk behind him across the dirt, noticing once inside the office that the filing cabinet is still flat against the wall. Nobody's worked it out yet. Duran takes a seat behind his desk, aiming for headmasterly control, with that same kind of condescension around his eyes that my father always had in this situation. I've stood here a hundred times.

"Leo, did you go into the compressor shed?" Duran asks.

"When?" I reply. "Is it completely out of bounds? I don't remember that being in the Welcome to Camp litera—"

He leans forward. "Do you have some kind of beef with Greta? Have you been following her? Reading *her* journal?"

"No," I say.

"She was in here earlier. Your name came up."

"In what sense?" Whatever he's driving at, he'll never get there in time. He's like a child on a tricycle at the back of the pack, pedaling as fast as he can.

"The most likely conclusion I can draw about today's incident on the boat is that it was a freak accident." He sighs heavily. "These things happen: tanks can leak. Our equipment isn't brand new."

"Exactly," I say. "Faulty tank."

Duran chews the inside of his bottom lip. "That said, I'm asking you to leave GoEco."

"You're what?" There's a flash of bright-red light inside my head, which sweeps to fill every space inside of me. But I need to keep calm. Deep breaths, Leo. If I go home, what will become of my little white mouse?

"You're bad for group morale," Duran says. "Or, to put it more frankly, nobody likes you."

Is he trying to make me snap? Of course he is. He's trained for this; they all are. And Duran can handle himself, I can spot it a mile off. If I punch him like I want to, he'll twist like he's fluid, catch me in the gut with a returning hook, then fill out the paperwork.

I take a deep, restorative lungful of air. He's asking me to leave, not telling me. He still doesn't have enough strikes. "I'm not going anywhere," I say.

"I've seen a million boys just like you, Leo. Lost little rich boys, swaggering around in the world like it owes them a favor. The recruits who come out here, the clientele on the Laurence Sloane boats. You're all the same. Dime a dozen."

"You think you know me, Duran?" I take a step closer and he

tenses. Part of him is wary of me. I can see that, too. "This isn't swagger. Maybe you should think twice before insulting me."

He stands up behind the desk, leaning on his arms so his triceps show. "If you're staying, Mr. Cavendish, watch your step. One wrong foot and I'll drive you to the harbor myself."

I turn and walk out of the office just like I used to at home: breathing hard, blinking away everything he meant and said. Three steps across the dead grass and I'm fine again. I've washed my mind clean because I'm good at this. I'm essential. I'm resilient.

Over by the eating hut, all the recruits have gathered to say goodbye to Greta and Ted. They must be heading to the ferry with Titus.

"Are you sure you won't stay?" Jacob is saying. "It's past noon: there might not be a boat."

Ted hesitates, his blond hair disheveled. Clearly he's not as keen to leave as his sister is, and rightly so. He's not the one who had the terrible fright.

"We're going." Greta's voice is hoarse; she looks fragile. "Ted, get in the Jeep."

"Does anybody want my email address?" Ted glances around the group. "Or I'm on Instagram @TeddybearTremblay—" The look Greta gives him could have sliced him in half. Ted stops talking and climbs quietly into the back seat.

"Let me help you with your bag." I arrive just as Greta's about to lift it into the trunk, but she wrenches the backpack away, horrified, as if I'm about to set it on fire. "Stay the hell away from me. Get the fuck off."

Her bad manners are jarring. She doesn't have to be so publicly unladylike. I'm about to tell her that there are ways to talk to people, there are rules, when she suddenly veers left, grabbing Stevie at the wrist, pulling her away a couple of steps and whispering in her ear.

From the back of the Jeep, all I can see is the ugly clench of Greta's chin, the stiffness in her posture.

"What?" I call out. "What are you saying to her?"

Stevie frowns, but Greta's moving away now, into the Jeep, banging the door shut. As Titus drives out of the yard, I keep my attention on Stevie. She's thinking hard, processing, but that's okay. I'll find out the secret. She'll confide in me tomorrow when I'm valuable. When there's nobody else left to tell.

27

STEVIE

Tamsin and I bring our dinner down to the dock. It's quieter. It's away from Leo.

"But what did she mean by that?" Tamsin asks, prodding at a limp piece of fish with her fork. "*It wasn't an accident—either time.* That's all Greta whispered?"

"Yeah." I can't eat my food either. "She was super grippy, too. Like, it actually hurt my wrist." I put my plate down on the dock. "She must think Leo did it."

Duran's ruled the diving incident as bad luck—*a freak accident, guys, this is why we have insurance*—and Jacob is following his lead. Why are they both being so ineffective? Obviously, Leo knew that Ted and Greta never check their gauges properly—we all know that, we've been diving with them for long enough. But Leo left her with just enough air that she'd only realize once she was a long way from the surface. He might only have meant to scare her, but the coldness and the precision is horrific.

"Why would Leo go after her, though? And what is the 'either time' bit? Has he been doing *more things* we don't know about?" Tamsin pulls her hoodie over the hug of her knees.

"I think she . . ." I pause, noticing how much younger Tamsin looks tonight, how much more bewildered, more dazed. "I think she might have meant the canoe safari. Leo was in that boat, right? Wasn't he at the back?"

She makes a noise that's very close to gagging. All these months she's been traveling with him, sleeping by his side, a kitten lying next to a python. There can't be much more she can take.

"But why would he do that?" Her voice sounds small. "He'd tip it to teach Ted to sit still? But *I* nearly fell in!"

Leo doesn't care about you, I want to tell her. *He never did.*

A fresh hideousness pops into my head, followed by a horrible billow of certainty. "Tamsin," I ask quietly, "you know in Diani Beach when you first had beers with Jacob? Did Leo sleep next to you in your bungalow that night?"

She turns her head. Her fork's trembling. "He was in and out. Unsettled. Why?"

"Nothing." Bile sours my throat. *He was in my room. Watching me.* "How much do you know about the death of his father?"

"His— The court case?" Tamsin's eyes widen even further. "Just that it was a media nightmare. He never speaks about his dad."

Oh, God, I think. *You don't know the first thing about him.*

"You think Leo was involved in it?"

"I don't know," I say. Except I'm lying. Ever since he cornered me in the mangroves earlier, I've known he was dangerous. *We're the same, Stevie*, he said, but what he meant was, *You've killed someone and I know what that's like.* If only I could have explained the conversation in more detail to Jacob, without him thinking I'd—

"We need to get out of here, Stevie." Beside me, Tamsin covers her face with both palms. "I'm serious. At first I thought all this Leo stuff was funny, I thought it was a crush, but it's so much worse. And this island is so tiny and claustrophobic. I feel trapped. Do you know what I mean?"

"I do." I put my arm around her and she leans against me, breathing out shakily. Every time I'm near her a little more doubt in my head sloughs away. Even in the midst of panic—or maybe because of it—it's becoming clearer how I feel about her.

"So will you come?" she asks, glancing up at the pinpricked sky. "I have enough money for both of us. Zanzibar's only ten miles away. We could steal the dhow or something, follow the North Star."

"Okay, Galileo," I say, and I can feel her smile against my shirt. But can I leave? What about Jacob? As mad as I am at his soft approach right now, Nattie would turn in her grave.

"Oh, God, I'm a total idiot." Tamsin sits up straighter. "I just keep thinking, how didn't I see all this?" She pulls up the hood of her sweatshirt so I can only see wisps of hair and the tip of her nose and chin. "I watched this documentary once on TV. It was about this guy who stalked women and strangled them. He killed, like, eight of them and he kept trophies from them in a suitcase under the bed. You know, a necklace, underwear, fucking *teeth*. It was rank, the things he kept. But when he finally confessed, do you know what the first thing he said was? *Please don't tell my wife.*"

"That's terrifying," I say.

"Right? His wife was sleeping right next to him for all those years. He'd, like, go and murder someone and literally cut out their molar and then come home and cuddle. I swear to God, that's always stayed with me. We don't even know the people we're with."

Around the dock, dark water swells and slaps. "Maybe the wives don't want to know," I say. "Their own lives on the inside are enough to be dealing with."

In the moonlight, Tamsin's eyes seem more gray than green. "Stevie, what happened to you on the boat today? Why did you freak out when we were under the rescue blanket?"

I hesitate as a lid creaks inside me. I haven't opened this crate in so long.

"It was an old memory," I say, my heart knocking against my ribs. "I'm— I get stuck sometimes in the past. It's a whole thing."

"Is it something to do with the girl you kissed? In Never Have I Ever?" Tamsin smiles, recalling the game. "Whoever she is, she's sacred and hidden in you. Jacob didn't even know about her."

A wide wave of sadness sweeps me, and for a second I consider jumping off the dock, just to be surrounded by anything else. But I want to talk—I need to. Because the memory *is* sacred and there's never been a freedom like this before, even if it all feels swirly and on the verge of being critically, irreparably changed.

"Her name was Cassia," I say.

"Cassia," Tamsin repeats, the name sounding perfect in her accent. She moves her hood back a few inches. "That's the name you said was in your diary."

"She was beautiful. Olive skin. Long dark hair." *Exactly like you.* "Her mom was Peruvian. Cassia was cool, too. Kind of distant."

"And when you kissed her?" she asks.

"I meant it." It's all I can say.

Tamsin puts one hand to her throat like I'm the cutest thing ever, but her eyebrows shoot up when she sees that I'm shaking. "Oh, shit, Stevie, I wasn't trying to upset you. I just wanted to know you more."

My face crumples. There's so much that needs to come out of me. And it's finally time to be who I am and say what I did. "I caused a car crash when I was sixteen. It was my fault—no, it was—even though nobody would let me take the blame at the time. We'd all been drinking and the boys in the front were shouting for me and Cassia to kiss. Like it was fun for them, like we were only there for their sexual amusement."

"Boys are disgusting." Tamsin takes my hand. Her skin feels warm.

"I've buried so much of this," I say. "Fought it down over the years, driven it deep. Nobody wanted to look at it with me, and there's more—there's . . . something about it I can't reach." *A fist on a steering wheel? Loud music?* I squeeze my eyes closed, trying.

"It'll all work its way out at some point," Tamsin says. "It has to."

"Yeah, well, you don't know my town. Things stay stifled. There are rules about everything." I look down at my knees. "Anchorite Bay is tiny and there's only one way to behave. I'd been handed a label and told to stick it on."

Tamsin nods, gripping my hand even tighter.

"But in that moment in the car," I say, "I realized that who I am can't really be fixed. Nor can whether or not I'm attracted to someone. I react differently to every person I meet."

"Of course you do," Tamsin says. "It's chemistry. It does whatever it wants."

I pause, take my hand back, press both arms around my ribs, wrapping myself up. "When I kissed Cassia, I didn't want to stop. It was like depth perception in a photograph: everything apart from her was a blur."

"That's sweet."

"It wasn't, though. It was the worst environment imaginable to discover something delicate like that. The boys were howling, whooping, looking back over their shoulders at us, telling us to take off our shirts."

"Ugh," Tamsin says.

"So I put both palms across Josh Hollander's face." I mime it for her, covering my own eyes. It's a while before I lower my hands again. "I just wasn't thinking."

She stares at her shoes, tugs at the frayed lace of one of them. "Cassia didn't make it."

"No." I breathe in and out. "No, she didn't. And I think about that a lot. The boys were okay."

"Oh, Stevie. You haven't told Jacob any of this?" Tamsin leans her head on my shoulder.

"I squeezed myself into an easier shape for him. After the accident, I mean, an easier shape for everyone. That's who Jacob knows me as. But I don't think it really fits. And it's been so scary, figuring that out."

"You don't have to be any shape at all," Tamsin says. "Especially not ones that other people come up with."

It sounds so simple when she says it. But perhaps she's further down this road than me. She doesn't strike me as a woman who'd take a label even if she was handed one.

I sit up. "Have you ever done anything bad?"

She cringes. "I stole money from Ted's wallet when he left it lying around the hostel in Zim. No, but I thought he'd been such an arsehole that day, almost dumping me out of that canoe and blatantly scaring the shit out of me, so at the time I felt I was owed some kind of compensation. God, I got everything wrong. I did pay him back, though, the first week here. He hasn't noticed."

"Thief," I say, but there's no conviction in it. I'm tired. I just want the ocean to lull us.

"Stevie." She takes my hand again and brushes it to her lips, jolting me with the electricity. "That car accident wasn't your fault. Don't feel scared of yourself. You're awesome, and you need to get off this island with me."

"Okay," I say, meaning it, because I can't watch her go. I've loved her since she gave me the friendship bracelet and said we were peas in a pod.

She pauses for a while, looking down at the jetty again. "Have you really only kissed one girl?"

I nod, my heart hammering. Her slate-green eyes are steady on mine.

"I want to be the second," she says.

In the beat that follows, it's me who leans forward first, who tries my lips against hers, just to see how that will feel. I've been thinking about it. I can't lie anymore. In that moment where I fall, I let the whole of me crash in the darkness. I'm a mouth and a heartbeat. I don't know anything other than her. She breathes softly into me, lips as warm as the night, tongue liquid smooth as the silken sea.

28

LEO

The walk along the sand to Dead Dog Beach is silent and unhindered. I move swiftly, my footsteps light, jogging as I round the first bend in the cove. So much has happened in the past hour, it's hard to believe things have taken shape as they have. Finally, finally the universe is on my side.

Jacob was climbing the beach steps when I first saw him—he'd been looking for Stevie, was going to take her a plate of sliced mango for dessert, but he must have been thwarted midway because when he came back, he was still clutching the plate in one hand. He didn't return to the group by the fire but headed into Duran's office and I watched him through the window as he paced back and forth in the dark.

Duran had already left his office and gone home for the night, having told Jacob and Axel to keep an eye on me. His security system is laughable. As soon as Duran was gone, the French boys got out a spliff and started singing along to Manu's endless guitar renditions of Simon & Garfunkel hits. Only Stevie and Tamsin were unaccounted for, and I wanted to know as much as Jacob did where they'd gone. Tamsin was on boat watch at ten on this beach—that much I knew—the roster for the evening having been clearly established by Captain Duran before he left. I wasn't on the list, which I presume he'd done as punishment, not that I cared in the least. It went Tamsin, then Jacob, then Titus. But what was Tamsin doing until then? It was pushing past nine when I stood and headed toward the office, noting with a smile that Axel was singing "The Sound of Silence" with his eyes closed and hadn't even registered I'd gone.

When I opened the door to the office, Jacob froze midstride. The plate of mango was sitting on Duran's desk.

"Are you okay?" I asked, noticing with alarm that the filing cabinet had been moved back away from the wall and the internet plugged back in. "What are you doing in here?"

"Nothing." Jacob's whole demeanor was sharp. He ground the heel of his palm against his eye socket. "Thinking."

"About what?" I asked.

"Those *girls*." His face shone like porcelain in the shadows. "I saw them just now. What the hell do they think they're playing at?"

"What's happened?" I leaned with my back against Duran's desk, blocking the laptop and Wi-Fi from Jacob's view. "What did you see?"

"Them," he said, his mouth hanging agape. "You know. To-*gether*." It was all he could do to spit out the second half of the word. "God, and after everything I'm doing for her! Everything I've done."

For a second I was stunned by the image of Stevie and Tamsin kissing. Or had he seen more than that? Hurriedly I pushed such notions aside. There was no time to dwell on them. If there was outrage in me—if there was absolute fucking fury—there would be a perfect moment to expel it. This wasn't it.

"It's Tamsin," I said quickly. "She's the cancer around here and always has been. She's the one that needs cutting out."

He let out a long, anguished sigh. "No, Stevie's mad at me. I know it. She's upset that Duran and I haven't kicked you off the camp. She called me a follower. And weak."

Well, you are, I thought. *But what else was she expecting?*

"Duran's already the leader around here," I said. "If you tried to push to the front, the troops would just get confused."

"Right," he said. "Exactly." He began to pace again, shooting me furtive glances.

"Look, Jacob, you don't need to kick me out of the camp. I didn't hurt Greta today." He stopped still. "Her tank leaked. That's it, that's all. And this whole fake name thing that I know you know about—" I paused, watching to see if he'd contradict me, "—I just . . . I didn't want my father's death to follow me out here, I suppose. It was all so consuming. I wanted a fresh start. I took my mum's name." I shrugged with my eyebrows high. *Look, I'm a nice guy. Completely transparent.*

"Why did you read Stevie's journal?"

"I found it by accident. I didn't engineer it, I promise you. And you're right: I shouldn't have read it." Again I paused. Would he go for that? "And when I told you to sleep with Tamsin on the boat, I was just trying to palm her off on you. I apologize for that, too. But I'm telling you, she's a fucking nightmare. She's the one you should be angry with."

"Why were you with her, then?"

"I don't know. Love's a maze, isn't it? There's no marked entry or exit."

Oh, that one he agreed with. His entire body deflated.

"I'm losing Stevie," he said, his voice raw. "I can't lose her. I can't."

"I know." In fairness, he'd lost her the first time I set eyes on her in the Nairobi hostel. But it wouldn't pay to point that out. "We were friends at the start, Jacob, you and I. Remember? You used to tell me things. I was someone you trusted." I kept my voice soft and he looked at me, his eyes red-rimmed and bereft. "I'm still that guy. I'm solid. And you look like you could use a friend."

He nodded, rubbed his nose with the back of his hand. "What are we going to do about the girls?"

And bingo. I had him.

The beach is a wide canvas as I round the final corner, keeping near the tree line where the shadows drift. I can't quite make out Tamsin yet, but know she'll be sitting alone on the wide swathe of sand, isolated, vulnerable, exactly how I want her. It's all in the approach now, just like it was with my father. Situations like this demand deftness, calmness, a clarity of focus. It isn't heroic to fall at the first sign of a quest. Of course, the environment in which I dealt with my father was so much more controlled: I'd planned it for weeks, seen every moment of it play out in my head. This opportunity is less calculated and therefore more volatile—it's Tamsin, after all, and as enemies go, she's unpredictable. But at least I have a teammate this time. It's a far less lonely enterprise. Jacob and I are allies, not that I really spelled out the plan for him. It was best that I kept things vague.

"What are you going to do, again, exactly?" he asked, sitting down in a chair in Duran's office.

"Get rid of Tamsin. For good."

"Yes," he sounded uncertain. "But how?"

"It's nothing bad, Jacob," I said. "Nothing wrong or upsetting. I'm simply going to ruin things for her. Cut her off. That kind of thing."

"Oh, right," he exhaled. "Financially. Yes, that's a good approach."

"It'll work," I said. "She'll be gone. Don't worry."

As I left him in the office, Stevie was approaching the fire pit, the logs by her feet burning white like the bellies of crocodiles.

"Have you seen Jacob?" I heard Stevie ask, her beautiful back to me as I stood on the porch steps. As a response, Manu passed her the rolled-up joint.

"*Laisse-toi aller,*" he said. "Relax."

Before I could stop her, she took a huge drag, then another. She made a noise that sounded so sensual as she stretched out her shoulders.

"*Ça te plaît?*" Manu grinned, tucking a strand of hair behind his ear. "It's good, no? *Tu vois, ça fait du bien.*"

But it wasn't good. Now she'd be stoned while she thought about Tamsin's lips against hers, their *tongues* together—oh, God, were there tongues?—and her whole body would feel tingly and delicious. Meanwhile, the image of them together scraped in my gullet like thorns.

"Why is that you want Jacob?" Manu looked up at Stevie with a crooked smile. "You can sit wiz me."

Louie and Hugues both laughed. *Careful, Manu*, I thought. *Do you really want to get in the game this late?* Luckily, Stevie handed him back his spliff.

"If you see him," she said, "can you tell him I'm in the sleeping hut?"

She hadn't moved out of it, not yet. *Good girl*, I thought, walking down the office steps and toward Tamsin's boat watch. *There's a meaning in that.*

I reach the well of Dead Dog Beach and crouch by the rocks, my fingers twitching. There seems to be a figure down by the shore, sitting alone on the sand. Is it Tamsin? I can't tell from this distance, but I can imagine her huddled under the starlight, luxuriating on the events of her night. She's really pushed it too far this time. Moving in on Stevie, stealing such intimacy from her and from me. Did she think I wouldn't find out? The anger in me spikes again and I advance, keeping my footsteps deathly quiet.

———

The absence of life in a body is the strangest thing. Where does all that animation go, all the vibrancy? What becomes of it? All that's left behind is a shell, a sack, like packaging ready to be recycled. And yet the skin carries the imprint of the life that was just in it. A dead body is a map if you read it properly. Take this one, for instance. This dead body. Look at all the muscle tone. The skin color. The health. This person was a testament to living well.

The ocean is battering at my feet and shins as I sit down on the sand. It's such a gentle night, with the movement of the palm fronds behind me and the continual push of the surf. The tender still bobs to my right, moored where Duran tied it, although Tamsin isn't watching it anymore. But it's so peaceful here, the moonlight rippling over the water. Nobody on the beach but me. Me and this dead person, this discarded packaging facedown in the surf, a lumpy thing, draped and saggy. Every time a new wave breaks, the arms billow in rhythm with the tide.

I'm definitely in shock. No question about it. Everything that strikes me seems irrational—a darting new thought with every fresh blink, and none of them of any use to anyone. And yet my brain can't seem to stop the churn, like a computer pumping out pointless spools of ticker tape. I thought I had everything under control, but it all spun away from me in seconds. The problem with my plan was the environment, all the contingencies, all that unknown. I didn't factor in anyone else's input, or the urgencies to which they cling.

I stare at the body, at its limpness where seconds ago there was fight. Like a switching of screens in my head, I'm back in the study with my father, creeping toward him with a syringe behind my back. I was the only one in the room—it was quiet, there was order—and yet still my hand shook as I plunged the needle in, as I watched his eyes, the absolute sweep of fear in them that I hadn't expected. *Leo,* he gasped, and he clawed at me, the gnarl of his fingers so dreadful that I broke away from his grip, wheeled backward a few steps, letting him retch and jerk in his chair. Dolores didn't hear it. She didn't come. I returned to his side in the end, so there must have been a moment when he surrendered, a benevolent momentary sense for me of things being right. But what did I do next? How did I get out of there? I gathered my things, hid the letter, took the vials. I was methodical. I was a machine.

That's exactly what must happen now, I think, forcing myself up to my knees, running a shaky hand through my hair to feel wetness, wondering for a second whether it's saltwater or something much worse. In front of me, the face scrapes against the sand—a face that held nothing but passion and ferocity, all the way to the finish. What a duel that was! I didn't expect any of it. But I need to get rid of the body now. I don't have a choice.

Should I bury it in the mangroves? Throw it into the well? Take it out in the tender and slide it into the depths of the sea? Dead bodies are so much heavier than when they're alive. I learned that with my dad. There's some kind of conspiracy, a stony slump, as if the dead organs gather the full weight of the injustice and absorb it as they collapse. I wash my palms over my face, rub my knuckles into the sockets of my eyes until my vision spots with kaleidoscope stars. *Think, Leo. Think.* What would your psychiatrist tell you to do? What would Mum say? I was doing so well before. Now where is my loudest voice?

I'm still resting on my knees, the water breaking around my hips, when I notice Jacob moving bare-chested toward me along the beach. Jacob. Ally. On my side. He's in surf shorts, hurrying, stress still tight in his elbows like windshield wipers moving too fast.

"Jacob," I call out. "Thank goodness."

"Oh, Leo, I didn't know it was you." He breaks into a jog. "It's my shift now. Has Tamsin already gone? You managed to deal with her?" In the darkness, he gets to within ten steps before he stops, his ankles in the surf just as a wave breaks that washes the bumping corpse against his shins. There's a second where he peers down at the water, his brain sorting through things it could be. Not a buoy. Not a package. Not debris. No, it's none of those things. Slowly I get up from the sand.

"Holy fuck! Jesus! Fuck!" He drops to a crouch, flounders in the surf, pulling at the neckline of the T-shirt so that his hands sink into the cleft of that hideous gash. The back of the head is entirely caved in. Jacob turns the body, dipping and cradling it, as if this were the grand finale of a ballroom dance. Duran's dead eyes stare up at him. Water seams from the cavern of his mouth.

"Listen to me," I say. "We have to think fast."

"What the fuck have you done?!" Still Jacob's cradling Duran, a strange kind of humming coming out of his throat.

"It's sad," I say. "I think that, too. It all went a little bit wrong."

Suddenly, Jacob stops hugging the dead body and springs at me, fists in my face, and I rake at his neck as he knocks me backward into the surf.

"Stop it!" I push at his forearms. "What are you *doing*?"

"Fucking *MONSTER*! This wasn't the plan!" he shouts, grappling me. It's not the first time I've been called that name but still it stings.

"Get off me!" I yell, shoving him. "Where's Stevie? Have you left her all alone in the sleeping hut?"

The question somehow halts him, and he staggers upward, backing away from me with both palms up as if I'm trying to run over him with my car.

"The thing is," I say, standing, breathing hard, licking salt from my lips, "people lie and they hide things. Why don't you know that yet?"

He retreats, aghast, and his foot snags on the weight belt that's still on the sand. The one clogged with hair and skull tissue.

"Where is she?" I ask again and he heaves, one hand over his mouth now. Why isn't he helping me more? *Jacob*, I want to tell him, *I'm valuable, remember? We're teammates here.* But before I can say anything else, he turns and runs, flying away into the darkness, feet flinging sand.

III

the predator

29

STEVIE

Jacob speeds us away from camp, taking corners in Duran's Jeep that make me press myself back in the passenger seat.

"Jacob!" I shout, but his eyes are on the rearview mirror. He has sand all around his hairline and jaw and he doesn't speak until we get to the harbor. There are lights on in a bar farther down the beach, little kids cartwheeling on the sand even though it's too late, it's too dark.

"We need to get out of here, Stevie. I'm not fucking around." It's so rare that he'd even swear. He shuts off the engine, still watching the curve in the road, as if another vehicle from the dive camp might come flying around it.

"What's happened?" I ask, my hand on his arm. I have so much to tell him, but he's not himself: grief floods his face and he gets out of the truck, grabs the packs from the back. By the taillight, he stops. Exhales as if all the life in his body is leaving him.

"Duran," he says. "Duran has been . . . Oh, God, Leo's killed him." His chin wobbles as he says it and his eyes are brimming with tears.

My face feels like it's been chemically peeled. "Duran?" The name quivers out of me. "No, he can't be dead! He's not—"

"I saw him." Jacob covers his mouth with his palm, and I stare at him, horrified, just as he lowers his wrist and sees something shiny matted into the hair of his forearm. "No, *no*—" He paws at it, but it's not coming off, this mealy smear of blood and tissue caked hard onto his skin like coral.

"Jacob!" I go to steady him but he lurches away, one hand against the Jeep, vomiting near the back wheel as he sobs. When he's done, he stays there, concave, spitting in the sand while I try to dig in my pack for some water, my mind reeling. Leo. A murderer? *But you knew this, Stevie*, my mind flashes. *You've known it since the passport, since the mangrove swamp.*

"We have to hide," he says, turning with bloodshot eyes. "We can't stay out here in the open. Come on."

"Wait." Blood roils in my head and I stagger. "Did you see Tamsin? She was there on the beach, watching the boat—she would have been there."

He breathes out slowly. "She wasn't." Without another word, he picks up his pack.

Before I can even gather another question, the gaggle of cartwheeling kids surrounds us, pulling at our clothes, urging us toward the bar fifty meters away. From here I can see that it's lit with lanterns. Bunches of bananas hang outside the main entrance and a few tables are set up on the deck. The kids are shoeless around us, giggling and bright faced, their hands young and perfect as they tug at us.

"*Nzungu*," they shout, high and soft. "*Nzungu*, come."

"No, we can't—" I begin, but they prod at me and I move, a mechanical being carried along in a tide, hearing very distantly the sounds of their laughter, the easy innocence of it. They sweep between Jacob and I, separating us like an eddy of water.

"Jacob!" I shout across to him, because the whole world's gone mad, but he's looking down at the children's faces.

"Do you have rooms?" he asks them.

"Yes, sir," a boy of about ten replies. "For you, for you."

We let ourselves be herded up the steps and into the bar, which is empty, save for a woman cleaning up, stacking chairs.

"*Nzungu!*" the children shout again, and she turns. Her face is maternal—broad and calm.

"Go to bed," she says to them, each word balanced and weighted like a metronome. "It is past your bedtime."

"A room?" Jacob asks her as the kids bump past him. "Until the boat?"

She pauses. "We are not really a hotel." She rolls all the *R*s, enunciates everything so richly. But I'm desperate now, I can't bear it, I grab Jacob by the T-shirt.

"Please," I say. "Jacob, we have to go back or get help—" Tamsin's face. Her eyelashes. The water-smooth warmth of her tongue.

"We're not . . . I'm not putting you in harm's w—" he begins, but I cut him off.

"Leo attacked her! Or he was trying to. Duran must have intercepted— Jacob, we can't leave."

He shrugs me off, angry, as if he'd rather just push me over. "Do you guys have Wi-Fi?" he asks the woman, and she points to a password on the wall of the shack. He pulls out his phone, walking the few steps to a table and sitting down heavily. His hands tremble as he punches in the code.

"Stevie, I saw you two kiss. I saw you and Tamsin on the dock. It was . . ." He shakes his head while my knees rattle. "I was choked. But the plan Leo said wasn't this. It wasn't. I swear to God, I didn't know—" He squeezes his eyes tight, then sniffs, trying to concentrate on his phone.

"Jacob—" I begin, because I'm so sorry, but what plan? He teamed up with *Leo*?

"All I know right now is that he's coming for you. There's no way you're staying on the island."

I lower myself into a chair at his table, my breathing ragged and damp. Inside of me, my heart is breaking, great clots of it being carried off as my blood pumps. Oh, God, Jacob, I never intended any of this. But *Tamsin*. She was alone on the beach when Duran must have come walking along it. What kind of horror did he stumble upon? He sacrificed everything trying to help.

"Holy shit." Jacob stares at his phone like it's suddenly caught fire. He tilts the screen toward me as my eyes struggle to focus.

DADDY KILLER, the headline reads. And below it, a smiling photo of Leo.

"Jesus!" I grimace as Jacob scrolls through the article, past the picture of Leo in an expensive suit, coming out of a rain-battered court building with two lawyers. There are other headlines, too: POSH BOY SLAYS OWN FATHER AT HOME, and COURT DATE SET FOR MANSION MURDER.

"Fucking loads of them," Jacob whispers, in shock. He clicks the phone shut, stands up. "We're leaving. And we need to call the police. I don't care about any of the other stuff."

But outside on the road there's the sound of a car approaching, the grit of sand under wheels that are braking too fast. A stripe of headlights cuts across the wall beside Jacob's head, turning the top half of his face to wax. He steps in front of me just as a car door opens and slams closed. And then there are footsteps, the smack of flip-flops, the heavy tread of someone muscular rushing up the steps onto the deck of the bar.

30

STEVIE

Jacob stands with his hands at each hip, like a gunslinger waiting to draw. The beam from the car's headlights still cuts across his face, his dark eyes lit with stress. Behind him, I back away from the door.

There's a flash of motion, a shape in the doorway, then a fast-moving body inside of it, and Titus charges into the bar, looking wildly from right to left. When he sees us, he flails forward, his arm outstretched.

"Jonesy, you're okay," he says.

"I'm okay." Jacob takes a shaky step toward him. "Duran—" he starts, and his face creases again.

"I know, I went for boat watch and Leo was there, dragging—" But he can't finish the sentence, either. "He is a bad, bad guy. I thought *Titus, you should fight him*, but he's wild. So I ran back to camp and we both came here to see if—"

"Both?" I ask.

"—to see if you guys were safe," says a voice in the doorway, and standing behind Titus is Tamsin, pale and disheveled, eyes big and round, tinier-looking than I've ever seen her. A noise escapes me that I know sounds like love, but I can't help it. I push past Jacob and throw myself into a hug, Tamsin and I both exhaling all the air that we have. Relief floods me and my knees give out.

"Hey, I'm okay," she says, pulling back, looking at each of us in turn. "It's so scary, though—it doesn't seem real. And I don't know who he'll go for next."

"I do," Jacob says.

"Did you run from Leo on the beach?" I ask. "I thought Duran must have helped you—"

"No, I don't know what happened. I ditched boat watch." She widens her mouth at the admission. "I came back to the camp through the mangroves and didn't see Leo at all."

"Titus," Jacob says, turning his shoulder away from Tamsin. "We need to call the police. Leo's level-ten scary. We should all get the hell out of here."

"The cops are up at the camp. We called them. You can't go." Titus is blocking the door. Even if we wanted to leave, I don't think he'd let us.

"We need to give statements," Tamsin says. "And they've canceled all the boats to and from Rafiki, anyway. Leo's somewhere on the island. Probably he's trying to get off it, too."

"Oh, God." Jacob looks nauseous again. "Nobody knows where he is?"

We stand in a circle, none of us speaking. My stomach feels splashy and sour.

"We stay together as a group," Titus says. "Come with us now. It's the safest."

Slowly Jacob bends and picks up his bag. "Are you sure the police are up there?"

Titus nods and we walk out of the bar into the velvet dark. But as we're moving toward Titus's truck, I hear a man's voice call out from the trees fifty meters away. *Hey*, the voice says again, *Stevie!* and I flinch, pushing myself into Tamsin's side.

A shaggy blond head bobs toward us and Ted appears, smiling. "Hey, guys! You're all here? We're sleeping over there under the palm trees. The boat never came—sheesh—D-I-A." He sighs, delighted at the great adventure.

"Ted!" I put my arms around him and he makes a surprised sound, but something about the sheer terror of the night is making me hug everyone. "You need to come with us back to camp. You and Greta—where is she?"

"Over there," he says, pointing. Very faintly we can just make out another shape under the palm fronds. "But she won't go anywhere. She's kind of hell-bent on getting out of here. She won't say why."

"There aren't any boats." Jacob's hands are rigid on his hips. "Something's happened."

"There's a strike?" Ted asks. But instead of replying, Jacob puts his arm around Ted's shoulder and walks him over to the palm trees where Greta is sitting. They gather her up along with their stuff.

Tamsin, Titus, and I reach the truck, where Crusoe is sitting patiently in the back. His tail thumps against the metal rim as we approach. I ruffle his head, stare into his soft eyes. *You win over Crusoe, you win over me*, Duran told me the first time I met him, and I feel the sudden urge to cry.

"We are *not* going back to the camp." Greta drags her feet behind us, her movements jerky and stiff.

"Fine. Sit here and wait for Leo," Jacob says. "I'm sure he'll be here any minute."

"Are you okay, Greta?" Tamsin's tone is gentler. "Don't worry; there won't be any more dives. But you're very vulnerable here. Can you see that? You could so easily be picked off."

Greta's breathing is low and shallow. I can't tell if she's going to scream fury or faint.

"Come on, sis, she's right. This is serious. Jacob says there's safety in numbers." Ted climbs into the back of the truck and sits down on his pack as Crusoe licks him. "I know you want out of Africa, but we need to be smart."

Greta keeps her head low. A few seconds later, she climbs up there, too, and sits hugging her knees.

"What did you mean about Leo earlier?" I tilt my face toward her in the moonlight. "When you said *either time*, did you mean the safari?"

Greta stares at me like I'm a total stranger. "I didn't mean anything. That's not what I said, anyway."

I frown but let it go for now. None of us are coping, not at all, but Greta must barely have gotten over the last shock. Titus squeezes in behind the steering wheel, Jacob climbing into the passenger seat beside him. Tamsin and I sit behind them like bewildered children kept up too late, and quietly I move my pinkie until it brushes against hers. She takes my hand, our fingers secretly interlacing, and we bump along like that all the way back to camp, terrified, brittle, holding on tight.

31

STEVIE

The fire is ash gray as we sit around it. It feels mournful, like a wake. It's close to 4 a.m. now, all the recruits on benches beside the pit, none of us talking. Manu and the French boys look like they were barely asleep before being woken again. Axel's gnawing his thumbnail. The coroner's van is here, as well as the entire island police attachment—six guys standing in a circle with Titus and Jacob by the top of the beach stairs.

"Why didn't they fucking bring dogs?" Tamsin says, kicking at the dust with her shoe. "Leo can't have gone far. It's a tiny island. How hard can it possibly be?"

I take her hand again and hold it. For the past hour while we've been told to wait, we've speculated in hushed tones about why Leo would have murdered Duran. It had to have been something Duran found out—*The headlines?* I said, and Tamsin paled further because

233

she hadn't read them yet—or the fact that Duran was blocking Leo in some way.

"It's that," Tamsin said. "That last thing. We both know what Leo wants. I mean, ultimately." I stared at her, fear creeping up my neck like a vine. "He wants you, Stevie. And he'll hurt anyone getting in the way."

It was true. Horrific and true. And now, here we are, without any clue of where Leo is so we can't even properly escape him.

"We should have left sooner." I shoot a glance across at Greta, who'd surely been ahead of the game. She hasn't spoken a word to anyone but Ted since they arrived back at camp. "Greta, do you know more about Leo than we do? He wanted you off the camp, so you must know something."

"Where is it that he hides?" Manu asks.

Greta flutters her head, moves another inch closer to her brother.

"That's the thing, though, isn't it?" Tamsin's still kicking at the fire pit. "He's good at this. He's been hiding the whole time."

I think back to the way she'd first described him when we lay on those sunset recliners at Diani Beach. Leo was so romantic in that version of the story. *He followed me from hostel to hostel.* It doesn't look chivalrous now.

"Oh my God, I'm her," Tamsin says suddenly. "I'm that woman."

"What woman?" I ask, feeling her shudder beside me.

"In the documentary. I'm the wife. Lying in bed while he stashes trophies under it."

"But how could you have known?" I squeeze Tamsin's clammy hand, catching Greta's eye. *Greta knew.* We both did. And quite suddenly, like the tiniest glimmer in my head, I feel in touch with the voice in me that tells the truth. All those years, Nattie forced me to mute that voice. Told me marriage was endurance and love a straight line, solid and low like a hum. But it's so much more jagged than that. And so am I. Sitting here holding Tamsin's hand is like holding my own, too.

"Here we go," Ted says as a young police officer walks across the camp toward us. He's skinny in his uniform, his belt cinched to the closest notch. He looks from face to face.

"Please, we need your passports now," he says.

"What?" Tamsin shifts on the bench just as Ted unzips his day pack and gives his passport to the policeman. "Ted! You can't just hand that over! That's a breach of—"

But she stops talking entirely as the coroner moves into view, pushing the gurney with Duran's body on it. They don't have an official body bag, but they've wrapped him loosely in a thin plaid blanket. As the gurney's wheel hits a divot in the dirt, Duran's arm slides out and lolls as he's wheeled past us all to the van. I can see his hand, the slight curve in the fingers, the gold of his scuffed wedding ring. His poor wife, I think. Apollonia. The girl he followed home to this island.

"*Bordel de merde*," breathes Manu, covering his eyes with both hands.

Tamsin stands, blinking back tears, her frame shaky. "The other passports are all in the safe, Officer. I'll go get them."

"Wait—" I stand, too. "I'm coming. You'll need the code from Jacob."

Together we walk over to the top of the beach steps. Jacob's sitting alone with Crusoe now, staring out at the reef. It's a glittering, starry night, but when he turns to look up at us, his face is death-haggard and gray. He smiles, the kind that would rather be weeping.

"Jacob." I sit down next to him, give him a hug, but he keeps one arm by his side, the other ruffling Crusoe's ear. "Are you doing okay?"

He looks at me with such puzzlement, as if the question's ridiculous, then glances up again at Tamsin.

"We need the combination to the safe," she says. There's a pause. "Sorry."

He tells me it—0-0-7, 0-0-7—and I smile, because it's Duran's last nod to being a superhero. "Shall I stay here with you?"

He raises his eyebrows. "Do you want to?"

I didn't mean the question to have such broad terms, but that's how he's taking it. There's so much to talk to him about, so much to say, but Tamsin is standing right behind both of us and we're all too exhausted and scared.

"I'll catch up with you in a bit," he says, standing and heading off to the fire pit.

Tamsin and I walk over to the office, and on the porch steps, I watch the huddle of six cops around the coroner's van, Titus talking with Manu and Axel. It's like the aftermath of something truly terrible, with all the accompanying trauma, and yet none of us have really gotten through it yet. Leo's still here. He's around. I can sense him with every fiber of my being. He won't have left the camp because he won't leave *me*. And of all the people blocking his path, Duran was only one of them.

Stress rasps in my throat and I pull open my day pack, looking for my water bottle. Behind me, Tamsin is waiting by the dark office door.

"Ready?" she says. "Let's get this over with. God, last time we were here together, it was shitloads happier."

I push my water bottle back into my bag, but it's then that I see the corner of a white sheet of paper sticking out of my journal like a bookmark I didn't put there. I tug at it, unfold it. It's a letter, the handwriting educated and fluid. *Dear Stevie*, I blink at the first line, a thudding starting to fill my head, *I am very sorry about the things I've done. In England, especially, but also out here.*

"Tamsin!" I turn, the letter radioactive in my hand, when suddenly through the window of the office, I see the swing of a kerosene lamp. Somebody's in there. Somebody good at being quiet. "Stop!" I hiss. "Don't!" But it's too late.

She's already twisting the handle.

236

32

LEO

I waited for so long in the mangroves, hid there for hours, oftentimes up a tree, moving from spot to spot while they searched. People so rarely look up. My father taught me that. *Evade and survive.* It's surprising the things I've learned.

But once they'd given up looking and I was left with my thoughts, it struck me that I had to find something out. What had spurred Duran to even be on the beach at all? What exactly had he found out when he'd plugged the internet back in? It felt imperative to know what I was up against, so I jumped down from the branches and began to tiptoe back through the forest to camp.

By the time I reach the clearing, it's close to 4 a.m., new unfamiliar noises replacing the dead of midnight ones. Every few steps, I stumble on a tree root, all my instincts jangling. I mustn't get caught. They'd lock me up for months like they did when they found Dad dead on the floor of his study. As I awaited trial, lawyers visited me, wardens were wary of me, and nobody replied to any of my letters. I duck low as I crouch in a glade of knotted mangroves, just able to make out the side of the eating hut, the fire pit, all the befuddled recruits herded into a row, waiting like cows in an abattoir. I can't quite see Stevie, and so I don't emerge. Instead, I circle around, coming out of the trees beyond the long-drop, then creeping around the back of the sleeping hut to the edge of Duran's office steps.

Timing has always been everything. I wait until they've wheeled out Duran's body, upset momentarily that they've actually gone ahead and disinterred him. I'd taken such trouble over the burial. I'd even said a prayer. I did that for my father, too, and it seems to have helped in the aftermath. Dragging Duran up the beach had been ghastly: I didn't like having to get so close to the damp, mulchy part at the back of his head, and it took a long time to erase the features of his face with sand. All the while I was dragging him, I felt certain he would start awake, burst free of my restraint, avenge all the terrible wrongness. I dreaded it and longed for it equally.

Nobody sees me steal into the office and shut the door. I wait, hunched by the side of the desk, ready for the ambush that will surely come. But there's nothing. Again and again, people go ahead and do whatever they want in the world, and nobody seems to stop them. Still, the fact that I'm crouching in a dark room on my own—in a country a million miles from my home—suddenly feels rather pitiful, and I lean all of my weight against the wall, slithering down it for a minute.

There are so many things I should have done differently. When I trace it back, the trouble all starts when I set fire to my father's bookshelves—or was it later? It could have been the day when I first saw him sick, when he lied about my mother's betrayal and I stepped forward and shoved him hard in his wiry chest. I wish I'd just walked out. He careened backward, landing with his hips up against the mahogany of his desk.

"Leopold," he gasped, smoothing strands of waxy hair back into the correct formation. "I need you to listen to me."

"Why, Dad? Why would I listen? You hate me, you called me here to tell me I'm nothing—to *anyone*—and you're cutting me out of the will. If all you want to do is hurt me, you could have just left me al—"

"I need your help." He was taking hard, rattling breaths, and his beady eyes locked onto me. "I know we don't have the channels of communication necessary for this. We've been silent for so long."

I took another step toward the door.

"But you're my son," he blurted. "And you're the only one I can ask."

"What?" I turned with my arms wide. "What do you want? How many more ways can you think of to demoralize me?"

"I need your medical skill." He fiddled with the cigar lighter on his desk.

"My what?"

"Your scientific brain, my boy. Your prowess." His voice was the softest I ever remembered hearing it. "I'm not getting out of this alive."

"None of us are, Dad." *Do not feel sorry for him*, I thought. *He's doing it again. Do not let him in.*

"I'm dying, Leopold. But I refuse to be a man who withers like this. I will not do it. Nietzsche wrote that we must choose the right death. At the right time, with courage. We must not squander our souls. *Verily I do not want to be like the ropemakers: They drag out their threads and always walk backwards.*"

I stood with my arms limp by the doorframe. Why the hell was he quoting Nietzsche all of a sudden? The world was topsy-turvy, and everything felt mad.

"Do you understand what I'm saying, son?"

"No. Not even remotely."

"Yes, you do." He crossed his arms at his chest. "Stand up straight. You do understand."

I kicked the heel of my shoe against the door. "I'm not doing it. I'm not helping you like that."

"I haven't asked for anything else from you once," he said. "Not a single damned thing. All your life you took your mother's side, even as she raised you to be some kind of suitor. And look at you! Forever spurned—"

"Stop! All you ever do is ask things of me, you just do it silently, at a great distance, with ingrained fucking endless disappointment—"

"Leo—"

"No! I'm not doing it."

"Assisted suicide isn't wrong. It's a dignified, self-directed exit, one that intelligent men through history have—"

"It's illegal in the UK, Dad! And it's . . . it's crazy! You're being crazy."

"I'm being smart. We can fix this so that none of it falls on you once I'm gone. We won't leave any kind of trail. And so, you see, I *can't* have you named in the will."

I stared at him, my jaw slack. "This is seriously why you invited me over? To ask me to kill you?"

"To ask you to help me."

He looked so weak, racked in bony misery against his desk, waiting for me to release him from the days that would get worse and worse.

"I feel sick," I said. "I need to go home."

And I left, right then and there, but a week later I went back. Just as he knew I would. And little by little, he talked me around.

I stand up in Duran's office, run a hand through my hair, walk carefully to the other side of the desk. His kerosene lamp is there, still burning weakly from hours ago, when he must have been online. It's tipped sideways, as if he ran off in a hurry, and I have to right it. His laptop's askew, the lid open. What would his password be? I try several, pausing between each to stare at photographs from his wall.

Everyone uses passwords of their lifetime's hallowed things. *Apollonia*, I try, but it doesn't let me in. *Diving. Water. Rafiki. Crusoe*—and bingo, I'm in.

There's an open email in his in-box. I read it twice, then move onto his Google search, stare at it, gape at the things Duran filtered and knew, the tabloid headlines *I'd* never even seen before that sent him running along the beach, fatally misjudging things, handing over his life. No wonder he was in such a fury. But he wasn't the alpha on camp, he wasn't the real contender, and the realization of that flickered in his eyes as he died.

I lower the lid of his laptop just as I hear noises outside on the porch. Stevie's voice, unmistakably. I fumble the kerosene lamp in my haste, almost toppling it, before creeping carefully, carefully to my side of the office door. With my ear to it, head tilted, I think I hear Stevie hiss something, but whoever's standing closer already has their head only a few inches from mine, their palm identically flat on the wooden paneling. If you took away the door, we'd be partners in a waltz.

I wait with a wildness padding under my skin, watching the door handle glint as it turns. The door pushes inward, and instinctively I take a step back. Get ready, Leo. If ever there was a quest, it's this.

Tamsin's face when I see it is innocent. Pallid. Young. For a second, I take in the sculpture of her bones—just as I did when I first met her—the wonderful green eyes, the messy perfection of the signature topknot. She doesn't speak; she doesn't breathe. But when I lunge at her, teeth bared, face twisted with all the hate that I feel, she shrieks, turning and grabbing for Stevie. The two of them hurtle down the office steps, running for the beach, my fingers clawing just a few inches behind.

33

STEVIE

I fly down the steps behind Tamsin, breaking the strap of one flip-flop as it scuffs in the dirt. I leave it, stumbling on, while behind me are heavy footsteps, gaining, gaining. We fly down the steps so fast, disappearing over the crest of the hill to the beach. With two steps to go, Leo is upon us, hurling Tamsin to the ground and grabbing my wrist, pulling me away. I look up the steps. No one is coming. Not even Jacob's noticed we've gone.

For a few paces, Leo yanks me along, a kid trailing a summer kite, as I lurch and trip behind him in the sand. He's all-out sprinting, separating me from Tamsin, and struggle as I might, it's only when we're around the first bend in the cove that I'm able to break free.

"No!" he shouts, lips sticky against his incisors as he launches for me a second time. But I bring my knee up, catch him hard in the groin, double him over.

Tamsin runs toward me and together we're away again, both of us running barefoot, a high, feverish noise in my throat. We burst around the corner to Dead Dog Beach, scramble up high to where the rocks are, floundering toward the shelter of the trees. Should we keep going into the mangroves, circle back to the camp? Tamsin stands, shimmying with indecision, panicked at the thought of heading into the dark shadows with Leo behind us.

"What's farther down the beach?" I pant.

"He'll catch us, he's too fast. We have to hide—quick—in here—" And the two of us barrel into the trees, hoping at least for some cover. Farther down the flickering path we go until both of us stop dead. Leo has circled inward, found a track, and he stands ten feet from us in the gloom.

"It's okay." He moves slowly toward us, palms outstretched as if we're the predatory beasts. "Let's all take a nice, deep breath. Everyone slow down for a second."

Tamsin grabs my hand. We edge back toward the beach, still facing Leo, our bodies grafted together at the shoulder, the hip joint, the thigh, like sisters in a terrible grip.

"Stevie, come here," Leo says, following us step for step out of the mangroves. "I'm not going to hurt you. Come closer."

"You're insane!" I yell at him, spit landing on my chin. "You're a killer! Get away from me!"

Tamsin tightens her grip. "She doesn't want you, Leo. You did a bad thing."

"I know." Still he advances, maneuvering us back against the rocks by the well. "I admit it. It was hurtful. I broke the rules."

He's crazy, completely crazy, I think. We need to run, but Tamsin angles herself in front of me, holding me tight.

"The number *one* rule, Leo," she says, and I think yes, yes, the most important commandment ever in the Bible. *Thou shalt not kill.*

It's then that I notice she's holding something in her other hand. A metal thing. It glistens against the fabric of her shorts.

"No, you're right," Leo says, palms still raised. "Absolutely right. The number one rule: *Don't develop feelings for one of the players.*" I stare at him, sound suddenly static in my head, because something is happening that I don't understand. In a teeter-totter of madness, I can't tell who's defusing who. "It was meant to be a fun game, wasn't it?—meaningless—something for you and for me."

"You changed it," Tamsin says, her chin sullen. "You took out all the fun."

Fun? What kind of conversation is this, and how is Tamsin following it? Sweat falls into my eyes and I smear at them. "Hey," I say, but she won't look at me. We're penned in while Leo inches closer.

"But this isn't about the game, is it, Tamsin?" Leo's only three feet from us now. "I saw the email Laurence Sloane sent to Duran. Asking him to take his old job back, so that Sloane could step away and mourn the loss of his daughter."

"You shut up," Tamsin says.

"Minta Sloane, celebrity socialite, drank gin all the time at The Ruin. Invited you to her Notting Hill town house. To party. The same night she died."

"I said shut your mouth," Tamsin says. "I didn't do anything. It wasn't my fault."

"What are you talking about?" I say, and Leo and Tamsin both turn to me as if they've completely forgotten I'm here. Leo's eyes bulge at me, but I'm in a bad dream where people's faces morph as I look at them, and nobody's who they were at the start.

"So you've told her about all this." Tamsin moves her hand away from her thigh, the dive knife gleaming. Did she have that the whole time in her bag? "You wrote all about Minta in your sad little *letter.* How into me she was, how obvious about it, too, how she came to

The Ruin four nights a week just to tip me. It was fun at the start—she was carefree, Leo, and noisy where you're so unbelievably *tight*. But my parents are straight—in every sense—you know that. What was I meant to do? I couldn't let her fuck up my trust fund."

"I didn't tell anyone about Minta," Leo says quietly. "I knew nothing of it. You got us out of the UK so fast."

The UK?! But didn't they meet in Zimbabwe? I try to slide away from Tamsin, but her sweaty palm is locked around my wrist.

"Stop judging me, Leo. I can't stand high horses. You're a killer, too, remember—and so is she." She nods her head at me, sneering. "We're a right little club. Duran, though. Who would have predicted that one? Of all the dive camps in all the towns in all the world. He told me he wasn't in touch with Sloane—hardly ever, he said—hardly ever, my arse. And the arrogance of the guy! I mean, did Duran actually think he could just jot a note to Interpol? *Oh, hi, guys, found her, here she is.* That I'd be okay with that?"

"It has to stop," Leo says. "All of it. The games, the hiding, the lies—"

"Does it?" She points the blade at Leo, and then me. Back and forth she wags it while my brain jars desperately on new facts. *Tamsin hurt Duran?* It's like a newsflash, blaring and bright red, so that I can't focus on anything else. "All these people saying they know who I am. My father, Duran, and now you two." The knife stops moving. "Well, maybe none of you get to decide."

When she pounces, it's Leo she goes for, but somehow he's ready, stepping to the side and throwing her back, slamming her into the rock.

"RUN!" he yells at me, trying to hold down Tamsin as she flails, but her one arm is free and she raises the knife, bringing it down hard, the entire blade disappearing into the flesh of Leo's back. I scream at the top of my lungs as Leo bellows and huffs, and the two of them drop to the ground, rolling and twisting away from me, a dark trail mottling the sand.

34

LEO

I feel a sharp gouge more than anything, one that aches more than most and seems to spread like hot liquid across my spine. But as I struggle on the beach with Tamsin, pinned with her in this crocodile death roll, my body heats up more and more. I'm slippery in the chafe of the sand.

The ache is flooding into my arms now, and I let go of her. She scrambles to her feet. In her right hand is a dive knife, the tip of it caked with a crimson grit. My vision is hazy, but I can't tell if it's me or the sky. I think I see Stevie, but she's a silhouette more than anything.

"No," I say, my voice further away than it should be. "Don't hurt—" But Tamsin is looming over me, hair lank where it's matted with blood. My blood. Spreading out from under me like a velvet cloak.

"What a hero you are," Tamsin grins, smearing her chin with her forearm. "What a handsome white knight. Your mum would be super proud of you, Leo. Even though she couldn't stand you and left." She brings the knife down into my knee as she spits out the verb and I yell, rolling onto my side. "Look at you, sneaking around—tiptoeing here, tiptoeing there—trying with all your might to help the ones who want you the least. Everything about you is pathetic. Even how you die." She raises the knife again. Behind her back, I see Stevie moving. There are other figures running but they're blurred, all their edges leaking into each other, stopping in a chorus to the side. "You were weak to the very end. What a disappointment. At least Minta and Duran put up a fight."

"Stevie," I rasp to the shadow behind Tamsin's head. "Run."

Tamsin turns then, knife high, just as Stevie whips a fistful of sand into her eyes. Some of it scatters onto my chin and shoulders. Tamsin staggers, screeching, then barrels full tilt at Stevie. With the last of my effort, I try to get up, try to stop Tamsin but I drop to all fours, my head low. Two pairs of hands help me, and I turn to see Jacob's face right beside mine.

"I was helping," I say, "I was trying to be the best—" But I'm losing all strength in my arms, my vision folding inward like a crêpe paper fan. As I pitch forward into the sand, I hear a woman's scream—high-pitched, echoey, and harrowing—before Jacob lets go of me and the whole world goes black.

35

STEVIE

I wake up in a white-walled room, a bamboo ceiling fan circling lazily over my head. Big window, no curtains, no blinds. Chair by the door. Jacob slumped in it, fast asleep, his hands loosely curled like summer leaves.

When I go to move, there's a tweaking tug at my pelvis, and I see a fat bag of liquid hanging from a hook on a trolley beside me. They're hydrating me? Draining me? Who did that and when? My right hand is bandaged all the way to the elbow. When I frown, the skin above my left eye feels tight.

"Jacob," I say, and he sits up. He looks haggard, as if he's aged twenty years. "Are we still on the island?"

"Yes, you're in the hospital," he says. "You lost blood. Careful— you have stitches over your eyebrow right there." He stands by my bed, his voice gentle, but he doesn't bend to kiss me. Instead he pats my arm like Nattie used to when I had the flu.

"What did I do?" I ask, but in the space it takes for him to answer, everything slides back into my head like wet cement. *Tamsin*. Oh, God, it's that summer before eleventh grade all over again: I blinded someone and caused a gruesome death. I inhale with a sob, and tears run down the sides of my cheeks, tickling at my neck.

Jacob holds my gaze. "Stop, Stevie. She tried to kill you. She murdered Duran. And she ran at you with a knife."

"But it was me! I did that. It was all my fault." I wriggle, desperate to pull out all the beeping wires that have been attached to me.

"You have to lie still! Look around: you're not in trouble. Nobody's guarding your door or arresting you. Everyone understands what happened."

But I can't hear him. All of a sudden, I'm back in the cottage with Nattie, home from the police station after the car accident at sixteen. *She's dead because of me. It was me.* But Nattie won't listen, won't allow it. *Stop that, put a lid on it. It's those boys' fault for taking you out there. Cassia's always been a bad influence on you. It was just a terrible accident. Everyone understands what happened.* But my brain is wrestling now, pulling on the end of a fetid string, and here comes an image up from the gloom, hidden for so long that it dangles and drips as I gasp. My hands are on a steering wheel. The car stereo is furiously loud. Cassia is beside me in the passenger seat, shouting at me to slow down.

I shake my head, *no, no*, and my mind cleaves open with one final dusty heave. I covered Josh's eyes, but he'd thrown my hands off, laughing, and kept on driving up to the clifftops. When both boys had piled out, I clambered into the driver's seat, yelling at Cassia to get in beside me. *It'll be fun, it's a prank, we'll show them.* We peeled the car away, leaving the boys stranded at the top of the hill. I can see it now, the whip of the bent trees as we hurtled back down the road. Faster and faster I drove, and Cassia began to scream at me to let her out. But I didn't, because—why? Because I was angry with her.

The realization hits me like a hideous lock of a cog. She hadn't wanted my kiss, hadn't felt it or needed it at all. No, she'd *laughed* afterward, like she agreed we were part of the night's entertainment. She had sided with the boys. *Stop it, Stevie! Stop!* she shouted beside me, but my heart was broken, and my teeth clamped. I pressed my foot all the way to the floor. I couldn't drive well, had only just gotten my license. And when we spun out of control, Cassia careened above me and her skull thudded against the window. She lay dying on me for so long. *Stevie, help me*, she said, her last breath fading, and I grappled my way out from underneath her, tight with panic, and lay alone beside the mangled car. On my pillow, I squeeze my eyes shut, the sounds of that night ringing fresh in my ears.

"Josh Hollander wasn't driving when we crashed, Jacob," I say. "It was me."

He glances back at the door, probably wondering if he should fetch someone. "I know," he says, his brow furrowing. "Why did you think—"

I peer up at him. "I think Nattie . . . I think she told me a different story, again and again, and I—" My head feels swirly and thick, but I remember Nattie's face when I confided in her the part I'd played in the accident. Her features had dropped so subtly—a sag of recognition, nonetheless, of the wild genetic blueprint in me she'd tried so hard to stamp out. But she wouldn't let it win, not again. So intent was she on squashing that demon—that one and all the others—that she buried the truth deep in me, changed it, until everyone believed the same lie.

"Nattie told me to put the whole thing away, so I did. It was easier than asking what it meant, what it said about me. Nattie didn't want to hear the real questions, and I was too scared to answer them on my own. I hid the most vulnerable parts of myself under that lid, along with the truth, just to absolve myself. But it was me! It was all my fault."

Jacob's shoulders droop. "Nattie said it would help you if I never referenced the crash. Josh and Cody had already gone away to college, then got jobs in the city. I went along with it because she knew you so well. And I wanted to help. The only thing you seemed to want to tell me about were the dreams, anyway, and the boys were never in them."

I take a long, shaky breath. "Nattie didn't know me. I'm not as straightforward as she thought. All she really buried was a time bomb."

Jacob studies me as if I'm slowly disappearing. "Stevie, the accident was just that—an accident. They didn't rule that you were driving too fast, just that Cassia wasn't wearing a seat belt. That was on her, not you."

I turn my head on the pillow, feel hot tears stream and blot the cotton pillowcase. "No, but I was in love with Cassia. With everything I had, I loved her. But she'd rejected me that night and I was furious."

"You're . . . This is . . . You're being—"

"I drove too fast on purpose. I wanted to hurt her, Jacob. Not kill her, but definitely cause pain. I'm no different from Tamsin, running at me on the beach—"

"That's . . . This is just nuts now. I'm getting a nurse." He turns, but I grab at his arm and he looks down at my hand as if he's never seen it before. When he glances up again, his eyes are afraid.

"I'm not who you think I am."

"Yes, you are!" His voice sounds stringy and desperate. "You're Stevie Erickson from Anchorite Bay and I've known you since eleventh grade. I don't care about any of these details—how fast you might have taken the corner, who hurt who—it was an accident! You're just in shock. Someone needs to sedate you."

"Jacob—"

"No!" He runs a tired hand over his face. Who is he trying to save now? Me or him? "I won't let you jump to crazy conclusions here. You're not Tamsin! You keep saying this got buried and that got buried, but it was eight years ago, and the truth is still true! You. Are. Not. A. Murderer."

I stare up at him, but he can't see me. He's still intent on the lid.

"Tamsin killed people on purpose." Jacob takes my hand, pressing it with both of his. "And when it came to you, she was just playing a—"

"Don't," I say. "Don't say it." Tamsin knew me. She saw me. She'd kissed me so tenderly as we'd sat on the dock. But on Dead Dog Beach, she ran at me with the dive knife over her head, a lover with a heart on fire, determined to inflict pain. She was both things at once, just like I'd been.

Jacob lets go of my hand. "She cut you, Stevie, and . . . and if you hadn't deked . . ." He trails off as both of us remember how she stumbled in the sand, plunged forward over the waist-high ledge of the well, clattered down into the echoing darkness. I tried to grab her leg, but she was gone, every lovely last part of her falling, falling, until she hit the hard ground and crunched. Everything went still. Everyone froze. And then it had all gotten frenzied.

"She wasn't straightforward, either," I say. "And neither was Leo."

Jacob looks up at me sharply.

"Where is he?" I ask.

"Upstairs. He had emergency surgery. But you should stay away from him, even if he asks for you. I'm serious. The police are still figuring out what part he played in all this." Jacob pats my knee, his expression moving back toward safety, to that resting state he has of reliable steadiness. "Are you all right?" *Everything's okay now*, he's saying. *On we go.*

But here is where our paths diverge. I can't go with him as easily as before. For years I've been haunted by Cassia's death, and on the day when everything finally splits open and the light floods in, there are so many truths to sort through. People to defuse, moments to better understand, wrongs to make right, first steps to take to forgiveness. Cassia was an innocent. Tamsin, Leo, and I were three unhappy members of a club none of us wanted to be in. All of us hiding things, all of us obsessive, and isn't that the truth about love? In its purest form, it *is* a drug. We consume the ones we want the most. We do it unknowingly at times, but always while we'd claim to be doing the opposite, and no matter how much damage we inflict.

Jacob waits for a reply. His hand hovers, unsure what else it can do.

"I'm not okay," I say. "But I'm getting there."

He nods gently. "I'll come back in a bit. I need to let them know you're awake." He reaches out for my face, his thumb hooked near my cheekbone, wiping the stream of my tears away. I don't return his gaze, concentrating instead on the starchiness of the blanket around my legs. When Jacob leaves the room, the door closing quietly behind him, I take a deep breath.

Upstairs in the hospital, there is another crate to unlock.

36

LEO

The walls of my hospital room are as blank as a projection screen. For hours, I lie staring at it, playing the movie reel in my head of when I last saw my mum, how my path crossed with Tamsin's and that moment in the Nairobi hostel when I saw Stevie for the very first time. All the stories blend into one as if they're acts in an overarching plot, a great fated swirling of scripts that led me here.

I met Tamsin at school. It was my first week at Ridings, the military academy to which I'd so clearly been banished, and I was standing in a Health Ed class among a dissident crowd of twelve, listening to the deputy head—a man with a comb-over who spent weekends in the Territorial Army—speak at length about CPR and the benefits of the recovery position.

"What is the first thing you do when you happen upon a person lying unconscious on the ground?" Mr. Berger asked, hands on his hips, whistle on a string around his neck.

"Nick his wallet?" suggested a girl to my left. She was beautiful. A snigger rippled through the class.

"You're not funny, you know." Mr. Berger tugged his nylon track-suit top lower. "Nobody's amused."

The girl shrugged. Her hair hung in long straight shards over each shoulder and was impossibly shiny. "I meant so that you can check for ID, sir. Why—what were you thinking?"

Mr. Berger exhaled as he spoke, his voice a measured line. "Do you have a partner, Tamsin?"

"That's a bit personal, sir. I'm only fifteen. Oh, you mean in *here*. For the recovery position. Yes. I'm with him." She pointed straight at me. I tilted my head and smiled.

At the end of the class, Mr. Berger made Tamsin and me pack up the resuscitation dummies. We carried one together to the storage cupboard, two conspirators dumping a body.

"You're trouble," I said to her, the hope in my voice poorly dis-guised.

"You're Leopold Cavendish. If anyone's trouble, it's you." She jammed the half torso on top of a mound of gym mats and turned to fetch another.

"Says who?" I asked, blocking the doorway. "And it's Leo."

"Everyone knows you set your parents' house on fire this summer."

"No, I—"

"And that's, like, such a massive triumph." She moved me aside with one hand. "God, I'd *love* to set fire to my parents' house. Or even just to my parents. I wish I'd thought of it."

"Why are you in here?" I trailed after her across the cement floor of the sports hall. "What did you do?"

"Cut off my sister's hair," she said lightly. "She was asking for it.

I can't stand her. My father sent me here because he 'knows me.'"
She inserted quotation marks around the words. "He's being 'preemp-
tive.' Preempt *this*, bitch." Her middle finger extended upward, and I
grinned, but only for a second.

"My father doesn't know me at all."

She picked up another rubbery body. "Well, it's give-and-take,
Leopold. Haven't you figured that out yet?"

"Oh, God," I groaned. "That's just what he would say."

"No." Tamsin pushed the dummy into my midriff, making me
carry it. "You're not listening. It's give them what they want. While
you take everything. You'll get it. You'll see."

I shift under the scratchy cotton of the hospital sheet. When did
it all go wrong? At the start, Tamsin seemed a fierce ally, outraged
at the fact of my abandonment, but when I look at it now, she might
just have been fueling conflict. Mum wrote me one letter at Ridings,
sneaking it past my father's security systems, even though it was
after she'd left him, so he'd have had less control over her by then.
She sent me reams and reams of paper with florid, soft-pressed
handwriting in watery ink, and I read the pages with Tamsin on
the roof of the geography building in the dark while we shared a
cigarette.

"She's living in Scotland on an island," Tamsin said, scanning
the pages as she blew smoke out of her mouth sideways in a flume.
"Sounds shit, though. Nothing but sheep and wind."

"Good," I said, even though my throat felt peeled on the inside.

"*My darling boy*," Tamsin read out loud, "*I feel so awful about it all.*
Does she, though? They have cars in Scotland, don't they? She could
always come and get you."

I took the offered cigarette, ignoring or perhaps liking the mushed,
sucked filter. I inhaled deeply. "Yeah. She knows where I am."

"*There are two little girls here, darling, stepdaughters. I haven't
mentioned you to them yet, but shall I?*" Tamsin snorted. "Fucking

blackmail. *Shall I?* Write back to her or she won't mention you to the replacement offspring. That's amazing." She read on.

"Who's the guy she's with?" I asked.

"Some earl with lineage. Owns most of the island." She glanced up. "How'd she meet him, then?"

"Fuck knows. Aqua aerobics, probably."

Tamsin laughed and grabbed the cigarette back from me, driving the tip of it through the top of the letter, right through the heart of the return address.

"Wait," I said. "Don't—"

"You don't need her." The pages of my mother's letter caught fire then, curling as the flames licked blue. "She's just another set of limitations. She doesn't deserve you."

"Right," I said, watching the letter vanish. "No, I know."

She tossed the remains of the pages off the roof. The next day when I was alone, I crept back to the geography building to search for them, but the rain overnight had destroyed what little had been left.

I try to sit up in my bed, but every movement hurts. My heart feels bruised, as if it's been stamped on, and there are bandages swaddling the whole of my left shoulder. It's exhausting to sift memories this way, when they all seem to have changed shape while they were in storage. I thought we'd left England to escape the aftermath of my father's death. I was the one on the run, not Tamsin. What a fantastic shield I made, hounded by the media and shamed by the courts, what a great distraction. Meanwhile, Minta Sloane choked on her own vomit in her Notting Hill home, apparently left for dead. Money and jewelry were stolen from the scene, and police were seeking a "second party, currently at large, who was thought to have been in the property with her." The morning after Minta died—literally before the body had even been found—Tamsin suggested we get out of the country.

"You've forgotten what fun's like, Leo," she said, chugging orange juice straight from the carton like someone who'd been up all night. "I think it's time we reminded you."

And when we got to Africa, the game she devised for us to play was purely for that reason. Just a bit of fun on the tourist trail. A laugh. She called it Double Date and said we could choose any couple we pleased and simply interject ourselves into their lives.

"Look at those two," she'd say, watching a young couple arriving in an Arrivals hall, or having coffee on their first day on a new continent. "Who do you think they are? What are their names and nationalities? Let's go and shake them up a little bit."

She chose only beautiful couples. Happy-looking ones. The closer they seemed, the harder she'd mess with them, as if their love was a personal affront. I went along with it at the start because I was angry and in exile, licking my wounds, unsure if I was the monster everyone thought I was. I'd lost my moral compass; I don't think Tamsin ever had one. But then I saw Stevie in Nairobi with her damage and her wolf-pale, Scandinavian eyes. She woke me up out of my stupor, reminded me of home, I suppose, a home I once had that felt intimate and only for me. In the quickest of heartbeats, I knew I'd walk that line for her—do anything, be anyone—and that we were irrevocably connected. Stevie gave me a purpose again. A quest. Everything about the game changed.

I'm watching the sky outside my window turn pink when the door opens and a thick-set policeman walks into my hospital room. He's followed by Titus, who stops beside the bed, standing like a bouncer with his arms crossed.

"Leo," Titus says, "this man is my brother-in-law, Kgosi. We've brought Tamsin's things . . ." His voice trails off and he swallows. "For you to keep." Beside him, Kgosi sets a white plastic bag onto my bedside table. "He needs you to tell us what you saw when Mr. Duran . . . when you were on the beach."

"Of course," I say. "Whatever you need." Within limits. I wait until Kgosi has set up the recorder on his phone.

"When I got to the beach," I begin, "Tamsin was sitting by the water. On boat watch. I was going to break up with her—I'd had enough—and I thought she was alone." I pause, while Kgosi and Titus nod. "But as I got closer, I saw that Duran was also with her. In the darkness, their outlines had blurred. I heard Duran say he knew what Tamsin had done, that Greta had already spoken with him, that Sloane had been in touch. But all the time he was talking, Tamsin was quietly reaching for Ted's dive belt—she must have found it astray on the beach. *You're right*, she said. *It's time I told the truth now. Gosh, it's almost a relief: it's been such an exhausting time.* She stood, the dive belt hanging invisibly by one thigh as she wiped sand from her shorts, and Duran must have felt she was surrendering. But instead, she swung the belt high in an arc against the back of his skull, and the sound it made was . . ." Now it's me who can't finish a sentence. Titus grimaces and Kgosi pauses the recording.

"Can you go on?" he asks.

Titus passes me a glass of water. I chase the straw with my mouth and then sip.

"I was stupefied," I say. "I couldn't believe what she'd done. But then I sprang forward, pushing Tamsin into the sand. I checked on Duran, but she'd hit him too many times. His whole body was . . . slumped. He was quiet."

"Why did you not report it? Why did you stay and bury Mr. Duran?" Kgosi asks.

"I couldn't tell anyone," I say. *Careful now, Leo. Carefully.* "She threatened me, and I was afraid of her. That's the honest truth, guys. I needed help getting away from her." And it is the honest truth. It's just not all of it.

I'd shouted at Tamsin, screamed at her as I tried to put pressure on Duran's head, even though I knew it was pointless, my hands sinking into the wet batter of his skull.

Tamsin licked her lips, wiped her chin with a bright-red forearm. There were specks of blood all over the side of her neck and face. "Fix it. Clean it up. Do it properly."

"Are you fucking out of your mind? You've killed him, Tamsin! He's dead."

She rinsed her hands and face in the water. "You'll help me get rid of the body, because if you don't, I'll tell everyone that you murdered your dad. I'll show the police the photo of the letter you wrote him. The little vials of drugs you told me to throw away at my bar, where they wouldn't possibly be traced."

She'd been so supportive of the assisted suicide. *It's not wrong, Leo, it doesn't make you despicable. You're doing it out of love, aren't you? So it's a pointless question.* Had she been hiding a shimmer of something other than empathy? Even back then her response had been unusual—she spoke so rarely of love. But on the beach, I realized something I'd always known: people can do a lot of things lovingly, and so many of them are despicable. My stomach knotted where I stood. Was she bluffing about the letter and the drugs?

"Always have a backup plan," she said, still picking sand from under her fingernails. "I learned that much from my father."

"You're lying—"

"Am I? You can't be tried twice for assisted suicide, but murder's a whole new bag. And from what I hear, it's a much longer jail term."

She'd known just how to skewer me. Because it was true. I hadn't helped Dad, I'd killed him, and—if I'm totally honest with myself—I'd wanted him to die slowly enough to know the difference.

By the bed, Kgosi pulls out a crumpled sheet of white paper. "One more thing, and then we will go." With a lurch, I realize it's the letter I wrote Stevie. She gave it to the police? "Why did you write this note for Miss Erickson?" He raises his voice for the recorder. "What does it mean?"

"Nothing. It's private." I shift in the bed and wince. "Is Stevie in the hospital right now?"

"You were tried for assisted suicide in your homeland," Kgosi persists, the rhythm in his sentence steady. "You were innocent."

"Yes. Thank you. I was."

"So what are the 'things that you have done'?" The paper wafts in his hand as we lock eyes. If Tamsin had proof like she claimed—photos of Dad's letter and those vials—they would have been on her phone, in her possession. Kgosi would be arresting me right now.

"I was trying to warn Stevie," I say. "About Tamsin. She was toying with her, playing a game, and I was apologizing for not stepping in earlier." All truth. Just not in its entirety.

By the bed, Kgosi switches off the recording device on his phone. "Thank you, Mr. Cavendish. You can rest now. We will be in touch."

He nods once at Titus, who hangs back.

"She was stealing gear from our camp and selling it in the village," he says, staring hard at my face, trying to see all the way into where the secrets are stored. *Eyes are the window to the soul*, my mother used to say. *Make sure you shutter and shield them*. "Greta tried to tell us, so Tamsin emptied her tank as a warning. All this time we thought it was you."

I reassure him that it's okay. Everyone gets me wrong. Even Stevie, although surely she'll have come to her senses by now. I saved her. I did it. It was the quest. Titus leaves my room and I'm alone again, the sky outside baby pink and fresh, just like it was in Nairobi that first day Stevie and I lay in the hostel together. That fated day we first met. When we were both for each other and everything was new.

37

STEVIE

We sit in a line along the beachfront wall, eight of us facing the ocean, none of us saying a word. Seven of us have bags packed, waiting by our feet. The boat's due at two-ish. It matters today that it shows up on time. I need to see through the decisions I've made.

"Should we stock up on some snacks? A few sodas for the road?" Ted asks, his face ruddy as he looks left and right along the row. Nobody replies. Not even Greta. Children run past in a gaggle of sound, but nobody really watches them. Instead, Manu stands and picks up a pebble, tosses it into the water so that a ripple widens. We consider it quietly. To the left of us under the palm trees, Crusoe lifts his head but doesn't give chase to the stone. It isn't a chasing day.

It's taken more than two weeks to get off the island. First, we had to wait for the Tanzanian police department to relinquish all of our paperwork, clear our names, allow those of us who wanted to leave to do so. There were organizational pieces and, once I was out of the hospital, there was the ceremony we held for Duran.

We built a huge bonfire on Dead Dog Beach and sat around it while Manu strummed his guitar and then we released papery lanterns into the midnight sky. Pretty much everyone on the island showed up. There was only one person on the whole of Rafiki who'd wished Duran any harm, and her violence had so little to do with him.

"You should stay on the camp." Apollonia sat next to me under the stars, almost the female version of Duran: strong in her outline, war-torn in her eyes. "My husband didn't speak much of his job, or the camp. But he did say he liked you and Jacob. And what he said, he meant."

"I know," I said. "I liked him very much, too." Had I, though? For so much of the time, I'd treated him like a barrier, a dim-witted teacher, a slow-moving parent. I'd been mesmerized by Tamsin, steered by her, to the extent that I'd absorbed whatever she suggested. As I sat beside Apollonia, I felt bedraggled with tears, wrung out and half-drowned, an unwanted cat only now just finding its way home.

"Stay," Apollonia said, putting her hand on my shoulder. "Run the camp with Jacob. It's what Duran would've liked."

I smiled, nodded, but didn't say anything more.

Next to me, Greta exhales in frustration. "The boat's late."

"D-I-A," I murmur, and Jacob smothers a grin. Greta's a hard woman to like. Everything she's said on the subject of Tamsin has been a variation of *I told you so*, but she didn't tell us. Sure, she mentioned to Duran that Tamsin was stealing gear, playing games, up to no good, but all of it was unfounded at the time, and Duran wasn't a guy who'd listen to idle gossip.

We sat around the fire at camp last night, Greta suddenly the most talkative one in the group, a torrent of information now that we were all beyond needing it. "I even told Duran about the canoe safari in

Zim. How she tipped the boat, sending my brother into the water with actual live crocodiles."

"She what?" Jacob asked.

"That's just what Greta thinks." Ted picked at the scab of a scratched mosquito bite near his elbow. "They had gotten into an argument that morning in the hostel—"

"It wasn't an argument, Ted. I caught her going through your pack, taking things. She literally had your wallet in her hand."

"But we don't *know* that she tipped the boat," Ted muttered. "I mean, that's a leap. I always said it was a crazy leap."

I stayed quiet, watching the lick of the fire. Tamsin tipped the canoe. I didn't have a doubt in my mind.

"Did she fall in, Ted?" Greta said. "No, she did not. And did it escalate from there? Jesus—not everyone's nice! I've been telling you this since you were twelve. Nobody listens to me, not even *you*." She turned on me again with her stubby forefinger.

"Me?"

"I told you she emptied my tank. That she'd done dangerous things before."

"But you weren't clear!" I stood up. "Sometimes you have to say things out loud, Greta, regardless of who's standing nearby at the time. Say them loudly and without equivocation. Stop putting lids on things. Stop hiding."

Jacob's lower lip protruded as I walked away toward the sleeping hut, but he let me be. For the first time since I'd been in Africa, I wanted to be alone.

Ted comes back clutching three tall glass bottles of Coke. "Anyone want one?" Greta, Jacob, and I shake our heads. He sets two in the sand by his feet. "I bought this postcard, too. Look—" He fumbles it out of his shorts pocket. "Palm trees and a beach. I thought we could write Leo a note, you know, before we all leave."

The three of us stare at him.

"We kind of sold him down the river, guys," Ted says. "And I feel bad he's being left here on his own to recover. I'd hate that. Wouldn't you? I'd want my couch, and Netflix, and Mom."

Greta rolls her eyes and goes to join Manu throwing rocks.

"You should send him the postcard," I say to Ted. "It's nice of you. Although Leo's leaving Rafiki soon, too. They're flying him home to England for knee surgery."

Ted throws an awkward glance at Jacob, as if to say, *Dude, how does she have such insider knowledge?* But the truth is I went to see Leo when I was still in the hospital, whether or not Jacob forbade it. The aide to the British High Commissioner had arrived from Dar es Salaam, and was just leaving his room as I hovered in the doorway, listening to the itinerary of Leo's return to the UK. There were all kinds of wires still attached to him and he was gaunt, his eyes too big for his face.

As soon as the commissioner guy had gone and Leo saw me, he immediately wrenched himself upward in bed. "Stevie, I was hoping you'd come. I've been asking and asking."

"I read your letter." I hung back by the door, tying and untying a knot in the cord of my bathrobe.

"Good," he said. "Why did you give it to the police?"

I shrugged. "To get rid of the last of the secrets."

There was a second where he just gazed at me as if I were an epiphany he might have in church. "Come in," he said eventually. "There's something you should see. In the spirit of transparency."

I edged inward and the door closed behind me. He patted the sheet, but I stayed standing beyond the reach of him.

"You're afraid of me," he said, crestfallen. "It's understandable. But, Stevie, our meeting was destiny, more than a happy accident. I couldn't possibly have rescued you if our paths hadn't—"

"I don't need to be rescued," I said.

"You did, though!" His jaw muscle tensed against the pillow.

"Look, I know there's a fine line between feeling connected to some-one and, and—"

"Stalking them," I said.

"I was going to say wanting to keep them close." He paused, bit his lip. "Tamsin targeted you. She could spot vulnerability a mile off—she was onto you even in Nairobi, when she followed you to the hostel toilets. You didn't deserve any of that. But the more I tried to block her, the less you trusted me. The more I told you, the less you heard."

For days I'd tried to reconcile the two versions of Tamsin I'd known, the one that loved me and the one that wanted to slice me open with a knife. As much as I understood the duality, I still ex-plained it away. She was cornered on the beach, frantic, and it was a mistake. Heat of the moment. She couldn't have meant it. But where fingertips had tapped in my head earlier, they wouldn't stop knocking now. And the truth was, Tamsin might have been similar to me, but she wasn't the same. She was more vicious. More calculated. More capable of a whole string of awfulness. And perhaps that was the first step in starting to forgive myself for what I did to Cassia. Realizing the depths to which I wouldn't continue to go.

"Did you know about the things she'd done?" I asked Leo.

"No. Not even the crocodiles."

"Did you know she was going to hurt Duran?"

"Not at all. It happened in the moment as I stood there." He reached across for a white plastic bag on his bedside table.

"Why didn't you go to the police?"

"She was blackmailing me." His eyes were a plaintive blue, like those of lost children in movies. "Please don't ask me how."

The court case, I thought, *Tamsin knew everything*. But was it murder? I'd read twenty articles from my hospital bed, and all I could think now was that Leo's past was a grayer area than I'd first realized. Everything seemed to be.

"Here." Leo handed me the bag. "Look inside. There are two things you need to see."

My breathing stopped as I pulled the photo album out into the light. "She told me this was yours. A tally of conquests."

"Not mine," Leo said.

I put the bag down, and opened the front cover of the album slowly, a fresh wave of dread washing over me. Of course the art book had always been hers. There was one word written in block capitals inside the first sleeve. DOUBLE DATE. A phrase I'd heard her use. It was as if she had been tossing out clues, enjoying the fact that I kept missing them. The pages crinkled as I flipped through, my brain rattling at photo upon photo of young men and women, peaceful and pure, the skin of their faces smooth in the flash of the camera. There were ten faces at least, every single one of them asleep. And then I arrived at the last image of the collection and the saliva in my mouth turned sour. There in the sleeve, wearing a T-shirt I recognized, was a photo of me asleep in bed in the Diani Beach bungalow. I could even see the edge of the broken wicker chair pulled right up along the bed.

I dropped the album on Leo's bed in disgust. He reached for it and, opening the back cover, he pulled out a loose photo and passed it to me.

"Why do you think she had this one?" he asked. "Were they really the next target?" The photo was the one Tamsin stole from Duran's office, of him and Apollonia in front of the Red Sea dive boat.

"Or she was arming herself. Knowing her enemy. Apollonia was a link to Sloane."

Leo wasn't done; he was pulling the next item from the grocery bag. A tin. One that rattled as he transferred it to my hands so that for a new repulsive second, I wondered if it was going to be full of teeth. I pried off the lid and inside were friendship bands—a whole cluster of them—each of them tied to a room key. On the one that matched mine was the key ring to Bungalow 8, dangling like a gold medal.

I felt like I might sway, but I steadied myself by grabbing the railing of the bed. My bracelet tickled my wrist and I immediately began pulling on it, tearing at it with my fingers and my teeth until it came off. I dropped it in the tin.

"Did you know she was in my room in Diani Beach?" I asked.

He shook his head. "We found your journal on the train by accident, except now I don't think that it was. When she put it back in your bag, she must have swiped your room key at the same time. I didn't know, I promise. I honestly thought the monkey took it."

I stared down at my feet in slippers.

"For what it's worth," Leo said, "I think the game fell apart for her, too."

I shook my head. Whatever magic he was getting at, I was no longer watching the trick. I gathered myself and turned for the door.

"I'm saying you were special," he said, the tendons in his neck straining as he tried to sit up. "You've always been special. Wait, can I see you again? You and me, Stevie, we've been burned in the same—"

"No," I cut in, whirling around. "We are not the same." I had to hold to that, if nothing else. It was the only thing that would save me.

Leo's face caved as I let the door close behind me.

Out of sight, I watched him through the crosshatch of glass as he pulled out the photo of me from the art book and slipped it under his pillow. I waited a couple of seconds before going back in. He looked expectant as I moved to the side of his bed as if I'd returned to kiss him goodbye. I slid the photo out, ripping it into three ragged strips while he watched me, his jaw muscle tweaking. Then I took the torn pieces with me when I left.

On the wall, Jacob bumps me with his knee. "Will you call me when you get to the mainland? Text me? Send me a note?"

I nod and he looks away at the horizon, knocks his thumb against the knuckles of his other hand. The waiting is difficult. It's impossible to leave and not have it be a snub.

In the past few days he's read my journal cover to cover, word for word, because I asked him to, and I no longer wanted the past and present to be separate. I'd even written a new entry so he'd know that for me, loving someone isn't ever a label to be stickered on; it can't ever be fixed. *It's chemistry*, I wrote, *it does whatever it wants*. And I know those are Tamsin's words, but I hold them dear. I'm allowed to. Because somehow she's not even *in* the opinions she had. She talked a big game, but I don't think she really knew how any of it felt. To her and to Leo, love's just a manic, grabby, fast-paced hunt of desperately needing to control something. I wouldn't describe it that way, but I also can't align with Nattie and Jacob, who believe that love can be portioned, a measurement as controllable as sound. Turn it up, turn it down. Neither of them have ever acknowledged the obsessiveness, the addiction, the all-out yearn—even though Jacob drew a hundred pictures of my face in high school. They won't admit it, but when love hits anyone it's a din. There is no dial. And the fact that my feelings for Jacob are so containable is the surest signal I have that I must leave. Because for me, love is an opportunity to accept that we're simply at the mercy of forces much bigger than us. We're never really at the wheel. That's what I'm learning.

It's two thirty by the time Louie spots the boat, a speck on the horizon, and yet certain enough of its own progress that we all exhale. Axel gets up, stretches his skinny arms, dusts off his shorts.

"Now is the time. A half an hour and then we go," he says, walking down with Greta and Ted to join the French boys by the water.

Jacob turns to me. "Are you sure you won't stay?"

"I can't." I need to travel alone, navigate by myself, be my own team. I won't go back to Anchorite Bay, not straightaway, perhaps not ever. All the hurt I arrived with—the grief over Nattie, the muddle of her having no will, the loss of the pub—it feels somehow smaller now. I don't even think I want to live above the pub again. And it's not that

I miss my grandmother less, it's just that some things you can carry with you wherever you go. In a good way, not only a bad. And life *is* bigger than the town in which I lived. Nattie was wrong to deny that. I see why she did it, but she ruled out too many things. I can choose my own definitions now.

"I'll come back when I can, Jacob. And I do love you."

"Yup. You said." He looks down at his thumbs. "You had feelings for those girls, though, that you never had for me."

Those girls. I look at him, at his shorn hair, the scar on his earlobe from where Leo raked at him during that terrible fight on the beach. "What if I had feelings for you, though, that I never had for them?"

"Okay," he exhales. "Okay."

We sit quietly beside each other for a while, trying to enjoy the simplicity of water, sand, palm trees. We should do that, I think, at least once before I go. The boat is pulling into the bay when he puts his hand over mine. "I hope you sleep well from now on. *Lala salama.* No more bad dreams."

"They're already losing color, they're less vivid," I say quietly. "My memory's washing itself in its sleep."

"Good. That's good." His face is so open.

The hug I give him feels real but neither of us lets it linger. He hands me my backpack, kisses me on the top of my head. As I file down the gangplank with the others, I glance back. Crusoe is standing beside Jacob's thigh, his soft head looking up at him. Jacob's ruffling his ears.

On the dhow, Hugues, Louie, and Manu sit by the stern, Axel with them. They get out cards and cigarettes. Greta settles beside Ted at the bow, yawning, leaning her head on her brother's shoulder while he stolidly eats chips. I sit separately, my journal in my lap. To other travelers, we could be strangers, the only thing linking us this journey, the happenstance of the same boat. But I know these people. I've watched them out here, day in and day out, studied all of their mannerisms and habits. We were thrown together in the most arbitrary of ways and here we all are in our fragmented lives. I feel a smile form, hug my journal to my chest at the realization. Beaten up and knocked about, there are parts of myself that have fallen away in the scuffle. And yet I'm not leaving the island a different person than the one who arrived. I'm just leaving as more of me.

acknowledgments

I feel like I'm best friends with this book, but there are a lot of people who helped me along through the journey of it—and it's *always* a journey—and set me straight if I veered off in the wrong direction. Thanks to Sarah St. Pierre and Nita Pronovost, razor-sharp editors at Simon & Schuster Canada, to whom I owe so much. The whole team there has been so great to work with—Felicia Quon, Kevin Hanson, Adria Iwasutiak, Rita Sheridan, Morgan Hart, and all the crew who put everything together.

Thanks to Joe Veltre, my agent, and Tori Eskue—my new team at Gersh.

Every writer needs a trusted inner circle of first readers, and my circle is kind of unbelievable to me. Thanks to Chevy Stevens, who whipped this early manuscript into shape as if it were a televised boot camp, her edits so hilarious in the margins that it was always fun to get shouted at. I adore you, Chevy, and always will, even though you pretend it isn't reciprocal. Thanks, also, to Robyn Harding, another fake adversary on social media platforms whom I adore wholeheartedly. Thank you for everything you've done and continue to do for me, including calling me every writing day and being supportive while I'm trying to light the wood stove. A big thank-you to Sioux Browning, brilliant woman, who has taught this little Pantser how to plot. And thanks to the lovely, generous Samantha Bailey and Hannah Mary

ACKNOWLEDGMENTS

McKinnon for their early reads and support, and to Jo Histed, Bertrand Pirel, and Carolyn Forde, all of whose input I needed and value.

I'm so grateful to the community of writers, booksellers, readers, librarians, social media gurus, and bloggers who promote and cheer and read the books, and send messages or post stories that are so fueling on days when we can feel a little bit lost. It's been a strange time to try and come up with something creative, when a lot of everyone's headspace is filled with worry. In some ways, this book has been the greatest of refuges, but it's a perturbing thing when a story of murder on an isolated island is preferable to what's actually happening in real life. The book community continues to rally, however, and I'm so grateful for that. Here's to happier times, freer people, and the possibility of moving on and being better.

To my family in the UK, who I miss terribly, thank you for continuing to ask about the books through all our chaotic video chats. Mum and Dad, this one's for you. Thanks for reading everything I write, even if some scenes are eye-openers (Fiction! It's fiction!). You raised me with a spirit of adventure that saw me live out this dive camp (minus the violence) for real, while building such a lovely home for me that I'll always hurry back. To my sisters, Jo and Sal, thanks for always cheering me on, and get the team jumpers ready.

And finally, as always, thank you to my little family here in the mountains of Nelson, BC, living with me through a pandemic in our house in the woods, cooped up and having to find all-new sanctuaries. Clint, Cash, and Rue, thanks for allowing me to escape into mine, for weighing in on plot points, and for letting me have all the Wi-Fi when it's Zoom time. Here's another book with all my love.

about the author

© Kathryn Gardner

Roz Nay is the bestselling author of *Hurry Home* and *Our Little Secret*, which won the Douglas Kennedy Prize for best foreign thriller in France and was nominated for the Kobo Emerging Writer Prize for mystery and the Arthur Ellis Best First Crime Novel Award. Roz has lived and worked in Africa, Australia, the US, and the UK. She now lives in British Columbia, Canada, with her husband and two children.

RozNay.com
🅕 🅧 @RozNay1
🅞 @RozNay

Also by Roz Nay
NATIONAL BESTSELLERS

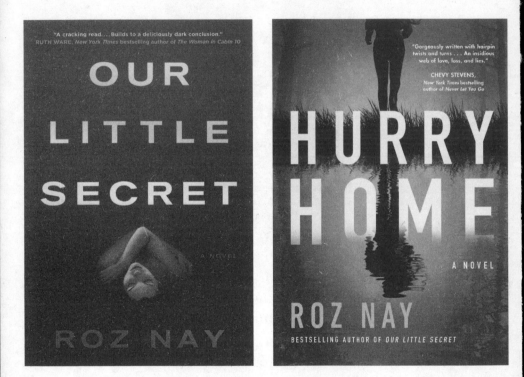

"Roz Nay just gets better with each book."

CHEVY STEVENS, *New York Times* bestselling
author of *Never Let Me Go*